Sometimes the past refuses to stay buried, and sometimes it comes back to bite you in the ass.

Eli is an ancient vampire with an ego the size of a planet and a sex drive to match, but his tumultuous past left him broken, so he hides from humanity and cowers from love, left to endure the crushing guilt that haunts his every waking moment. Even his best friend Malachi, a ghost who is hopelessly in love with Eli, remains unaware of all that transpired in London. Malachi can never know the truth.

When the Angel Daniyyel pays an unwelcome visit, Eli must face his secrets, secrets that he has tried so long to hide. To make matters worse, a chance encounter with the most beautiful man he has ever seen shatters his beloved isolation, pushing him into the world of the living once more. Something about this strange man seems so familiar, but Eli can't even remember who he was before he became a vampire, never mind explain the unwanted emotions the enigmatic stranger ignites in his dead heart. So Eli has a choice — return to the world that ruined him, or continue his self-imposed exile with no hope of salvation.

The unauthorized reproduction or distribution of this copyrighted work is illegal. Criminal copyright infringement, including infringement without monetary gain, is investigated by the FBI and is punishable by up to 5 years in federal prison and a fine of $250,000.

This book is a work of fiction. Names, characters, places, and incidents either are products of the author's imagination or are used fictitiously. Any resemblance to actual events or locales or persons, living or dead, is entirely coincidental.

Dead Camp One
Copyright © 2016 Sean Kerr
Cover art by Latrisha Waters

ISBN: 978-1-5207-0071-7

All rights reserved. Except for use in any review, the reproduction or utilization of this work in whole or in part in any form by any electronic, mechanical or other means, now known or hereafter invented, is forbidden without the written permission of the publisher.

Published by eXtasy Books Inc or
Devine Destinies, an imprint of eXtasy Books Inc
Look for us online at:
www.eXtasybooks.com or www.devinedestinies.com

Dead Camp Book One

By

Sean Kerr

Dedication

To my friends Krys and Jayne who read Dead Camp and encouraged me to carry on and tell my story. Thank you for believing in my book and for giving me the inspiration and encouragement to see it through.

To my husband Derek, for his patience while I had this torrid affair with my laptop.

To Craig, well, just for being my friend, and for being well... Craig.

To my Mother and Father for their constant love and support.

But most of all to Laura, no longer with us but always in my heart. She loved Vampires too.

Prologue: The Burning Dream

The sensation of all-consuming dread lay heavy in the pit of my stomach, nibbling away at the lining of my spasming organ with sharp, relentless teeth. I felt disorientated, dizzy, my head spinning, on the verge of disgorging my innards in a never-ending pile of steaming lungs and bloodied intestines, all my anxieties laid bare for the world to see in a rush of vomit-inducing trepidation that left me exposed and perilously vulnerable.

The floor of my stomach detached and fell away into the folds of my asshole, while my head took off in a dizzying flight of surreal *what the fuck?* There wasn't a drug in the world that could hold a candle to that sensation. My hole began to blow kisses like a Gourami, and to make matters worse, sweat erupted across every pore of my body to stab at my gorgeous flesh in waves of shivering pinpricks.

And that was how the burning dreams always started, with sick, fuck and stabbing.

What had I forgotten? What had I done? What could be so bad that it made me feel so... persecuted? London was not my fault. No bloody way could that pile of steaming crap lie solely at my feet. I saved a shit load of people — I killed the real monsters.

Guilt, wave upon wave of nauseating guilt — I felt like I'd been caught doing something wrong, like my mother had just walked in on me having a wank. Except that I was damn sure I didn't have a mother. There was no evidence to suggest I had ever crawled out of any female's vagina. There was no evidence I was ever human at all.

But that was not the point. My mother had just walked in on me as I was about to ejaculate into a sock and I was deeply ashamed. That was how it felt. I was humiliated, weighed down by the guilt of a deed unknown, the repercussions spilling out before me in a never-ending sea of screams and blood, imbuing me with an overriding sense of apprehension—apprehension that was rapidly turning into fear, no, terror.

I wanted to scream out loud and ask what I had done, I wanted to pray on my knees and beg for someone to help me, but my voice could not rise through my swollen neck or penetrate through my lips that had sealed themselves closed beneath layers of trembling wet flesh.

I wanted to beg my accusers to see the contrition in my eyes, to absolve me of all my sins, but I knew they could not see the penitence burning within them, because my eyes were nothing but milky white orbs, blinded by panic, blinded by ignorance.

I cupped my hands around my ears so I could better hear the screams and accusations hurled in my direction, but all I felt was soggy macerated flesh where my ears once sat.

See no evil. Hear no evil. Speak no evil.

It was a terror so profound, so deeply felt, the piss ran freely down my leg, warm and excruciating. I threw up, but the vomit stayed in my mouth, the acidic cocktail burning my throat, exploding from my nose in steaming chunks of filth. So I ran—I ran for my life.

Something was behind me, something immensely powerful and mightily pissed off. I could feel its emotions— the trembling sensation of anger, the crushing weight of disappointment, the bitter taste of utter disgust, all crashing over me in tidal waves of familial disapproval that threatened to reduce my existence into a cloud of nebulous, insignificant molecules.

There was nothing more lamentable than to have disappointed, or angered, that which you have loved so very much. I felt that knowledge like a knife in my heart, cutting through the muscle with deadly intent. As I fled through the endless, grabbing, accusatory masses, it was all I could think about, bitter disappointment and unending pain.

But whatever I had done, I meant it. I felt the conviction and the passion of my beliefs coursing through my veins just as much as I felt the excrement running down my legs. The passion of that belief burned, even though I did not know what I believed in — I just felt it, I was it, all of me. So how fucking dare they tell me any different? How fucking dare they try to take my belief away?

So I stopped running.

With trembling fingers, I ripped open the drying slits at the side of my head, teasing open the wounds so I could hear the torment that threatened to shatter my world. Cries of outrage and incrimination mixed with the clashing ring of steel as the monstrous song of war sang its discordant tune into a burning sky. Why were they fighting? They shouldn't be fighting.

I had to say something. I had to make them understand. It was not my fault. I pulled at the strands of flesh that sealed my lips and ripped them away in bloodied strips that slapped at my feet. I began to scream through clenched teeth, pulling my lips further and further apart, ignoring the blood, ignoring the searing pain as my flesh tore open. I screamed at them to stop. Can you hear me screaming? I was screaming. Listen to me screaming.

Something warm and metallic splashed across my face. The sky was bleeding, filling my mouth with suffocating crimson. Then that thing was upon me, that terrible being that oozed disappointment and disgust, and my body flew backward with a fury that nearly split my soul from my flesh.

Flying, falling, endlessly falling, swallowed by blackness, consumed by infinity. Nothing mattered anymore as my dazzling beauty burned. Skin crisped and skin split. My blood boiled and burst through ruptured veins like a series of volcanic eruptions across my devastated flesh. Hair and nails disintegrated, scattered to an ashen trail behind my fiery body. Intense heat split my teeth and jaw and I would have closed my eyes against the pain had my eyes not already exploded from my blackened skull. My head, my shoulders, my arms, melted into one amorphous blob. I was a burning star, a supernova.

And that was my dream. It was the dream that haunted my every thought and tormented my every waking moment, every day. Every fucking day. Nothing but sick, fuck, stabbing, shit, wanking, piss and burning.

Chapter One: The Turning of My Door

He was opening the door. I knew the little fucker was keeping something from me, sly little bastard. How dare he keep that away from me? How dare he hide such a massive thing from me? He was opening the door right in front of my disbelieving eyes, and yet again I felt the betrayal of a man stinging my heart.

Men are twats. It was the only word I could find in the English language to adequately describe the male of the species. I should know, I was one, both male and a twat. Who was it riding the Prince of England while my ex recovered from a huge gash to his throat? Fuck me — that cut was so deep I could see his spine, a great big gapping slit, as if someone had carved him a second mouth, and to think his one mouth was bad enough. He was not the man I thought he was, too many secrets and lies, the core of any good relationship.

It was a desperate time and I was a desperate man. London. Those were dark, black, terrifyingly painful days. I did not handle it well. I could not deal with the horror of it. I could not cope with the agonising reality of having everything I cherished stripped away from me, layer after excruciating layer. So I lashed out and got off my tits and parted my legs for the first bit of cock that came along, and if that made me a twat, then tough shit. Anything to staunch the agonising pain of treachery and the overwhelming knowledge that he was gone from me, that I had lost him, that he did not want me anymore. I could find no better comfort than sex and drugs, or sex for drugs.

Sex had always been my greatest pleasure, but in that God forsaken city, it became my greatest escape. What man didn't like having his dick sucked? And most men would shove it into any willing hole, be it an ass or vagina, as long as they were satisfied. I had to tame the beast at least once a day, and if I couldn't find an appropriate receptacle then there was always my hand, or Malachi.

And there lay the crux of my anger, the fucking bedroom-door-opening twat that was Malachi.

The British had a word to describe men like Malachi, those screaming queens with their limp wrists and effeminate ways, *camp*. Fuck me, Malachi was camp, not a manly bone in his ethereal body, and a voice so high pitched it could shatter glass. I loved him really, even though his constant wittering and outrageous mincing set my nerves on edge, but by opening my bedroom door, he had betrayed my trust, and that was a road I had no intention of revisiting.

I needed to calm down. I needed to control my temper before I did something I would regret. London taught me that much at least. And who was I angry with really, Malachi or myself? He just wanted me to love him, and who could blame him for that? I was divine, after all. But I would not and could not love him, not in the way that he wanted, no way. Love was not an option. That would be so wrong on so many levels.

I would never love again, not after London.

My ex—he had crushed my love and he stole it from me. I would never allow myself to feel that again, to feel the humiliating, agonising pain that accompanied the loss of love. I was nothing but a black ball of pain when Mal found me, a walking talking mass of impenetrable darkness, and it took me a long time to put that pain to the back of my mind and cover it with a smile. But the pain was there, at the corners of my eyes, ready and waiting, to show me how bleak my existence could be, and nobody would make me feel that again, nobody.

Perhaps, then, I should not have shagged Mal. But I was horny and I was lonely. Surely I was not the only person on the planet to have a shag pal.

I was a twat, a slut, a hypocrite, an asshole. See how my attributes grow.

I was lying in my bath thinking about my ex, and my cock was sticking out of the water winking at me. I knew Mal was watching, he always watched, but that particular time I encouraged him, and he seemed so solid in very many ways, so I called him in. When you got past Malachi's innate campness, he really was a very good-looking chap, just a bit transparent. And that was the point. Mal was a ghost, an ectoplasmic fart of the human he once was. We couldn't fuck each other, we couldn't suck each other off and we couldn't touch each other. So he watched as I pleasured myself, his own hands moving to cover my own even though I could not feel them moving in time to my rhythm. I shot, my load passing through his body, and it was as though he ejaculated too, his whole body shuddering in time to my own, pleasure rippling through his insubstantial form. And that was the extent of our shagging activities, the occasional voyeuristic wank, heavy petting, but without being able to feel the petting.

I didn't like Mal at first. If circumstances had been different, we would not have been friends. His endless fawning over me, his incessant cow eyes that never left my being, his unremitting ability to be in the same space as I—it was irksome, to say the least. But he caught me off balance during a particularly dark period of my life, and I ended up with him more as an after effect than intent. One of the huge disadvantages of being immortal is that past hurts combined with every new hurt experienced and each new pain just added to the last so that every agony compounded the rest. We felt it very deeply with no way of turning it off. Who would have guessed vampires could be such emotional twats? But Mal worked tirelessly, he forced me to live again, to want to live again, and with each new baby step, he made me better. Stupid love-blind ghost, how could he have known? He didn't have a clue.

And Malachi could never know.

But sometimes I needed real sex, real hard-core filthy bend me over sex, and I would leave the sanctuary of my home in search of something long and pointy. I never told Mal where I was going, but he knew, he always knew, I saw the pain lurking behind his eyes, silent and invisible.

There was a German base a few miles away at the other end of the valley, and it was amazing how pliable a sex starved Nazi could be, coupled with my considerable vampiric charms and dazzling good looks, with dinner afterward, a marvellous bonus. I did not kill them. I had learned from that particular mistake. I just messed about with their memories a bit. I made certain they remembered the gay sex, but not the feeding, or the memory of my face. The bite marks were of no concern to me—I didn't bite their necks.

Mal followed me one night. I caught him gawping at us through the trees just as some random Nazi was pounding my ass. I was furious, and the row that ensued went on for weeks. I was a gnat's foreskin away from throwing him out. Poor Mal, he just wanted me to love him, so perhaps I was a bit harsh. He apologised eventually and we air kissed and made up. From that day on, he would never question my little excursions, but there would always be silence between us when I returned, not deliberate, not malicious, just someone dealing with their pain as best they could.

But I should have known Mal would have a plan B up his insubstantial sleeve. How ironic—I could see right through him, but his mind and his thoughts remained an enigma to me. The fact that he was opening the door, physically turning the knob and opening the door, changed everything. I could not get my head around what he had done in order to achieve such a feat. It blew my mind, the sight of it freezing me to the spot, my eyes unable to tear themselves away from the door as it swung open on its creaky hinges.

The morning had started so beautifully. Pale fingers of yellow sun climbed through my window, caressing my perfectly smooth, naked flesh to arouse me from my sleep. Not sleep as a human would know it, more like a semi-conscious coma, where my senses remained acutely alert, always aware of all that took place around me. Useful if I needed to spring into action when some twat tried to ram a piece of sharpened wood into my chest. That little cliché may work against my siblings, but not against me. Hurt like a fucker though—I would rather avoid pulling splinters from my lungs for days on end.

I could spend days in such a state, my flesh as immutable as the mountains that surrounded me. Unlike my brethren, sunlight posed no threat to me. I was one of a very rare breed of vampire able to walk by day, and for that, I was immeasurably grateful. To be able to walk in the light of the sun, free from the bonds of darkness, was a gift and it made me feel that much more human. And I so wanted to be human. But the point was that I loved the sun and the sun woke me up and it felt good.

I heard the sound of the old ceramic doorknob rattle as it turned. My skin prickled. I heard the sound of the iron hinges groan ever so softly as the heavy oak door primed to open. The oak itself gave a weary sigh as the wood prepared to offer its considerable weight up to those same ancient hinges and my flesh felt that slight change of air pressure brush across its surface as the door swung open.

Mal walked in, but it was not the fact Mal was in the room that shocked me—it was the fact that he had opened the door. Mal actually opened the fucking door. I could see his hand upon the doorknob. I could see his physicality interacting with the doorknob. And then he walked, he didn't float, he didn't mince, he walked, swaggered into my bedroom with the biggest grin I had ever seen plastered across his face.

Despite my considerable age, I had not had that much experience with ghosts. In fact, I had always made a concerted effort to avoid them. No good could ever come of it. All that torment and unfinished business crap did my bloody head in. But the one thing that I did know was that they could not touch things, they were wisps of disembodied souls, nothing but wind and piss. I had let rip with more substantial farts than most ghosts I had ever come across. Maybe some of the older spirits could develop telekinetic abilities, over time, but it took one hell of a lot of energy to influence a physical object beyond the parameters of the odd plate flying across a room or a door slamming. Malachi had only been dead for fifty odd years, fifty-six years to be precise, so no way was he old enough.

And he floated everywhere. He even minced as he floated. And he always floated through the doors, never the walls, and that little quirk never failed to make me smile. I often wondered to myself if the door thing was his concession to having once been human, a last memory of his lost humanity. Not that I would ever ask him about it—it would have opened up too many... doors.

Mal was looking very pleased with himself as he stood framed within the doorway, smug even.

My mouth was so far open I could not bring my lips

together to form words. He walked toward my four-poster bed, bold as brass, and my fabulous vampire eyes could see the dust motes swirl around his booted feet. Real, solid footsteps assaulted my ears as his heavy steel-toe-capped boots scuffed across the ancient flagstones.

Fuck me pink if he didn't sit on the edge of my bed, making the mattress move beneath his weight. I recoiled backward in shock and I hate to admit it, but a little girly squeal escaped my lips as I nearly tumbled ass over tit to the floor. But a hand grabbed my wrist and pulled me back onto the mattress, a strong hand, a solid hand that was warm, that felt human, smelled human.

I looked down at the fingers gripping my fabulously muscular arm and I could see it was real. I could feel it was real. I could see my own hard skin denting around his tremendously strong fingers and my head reeled at the strength needed to accomplish such a thing.

I risked a look at his face. I would dearly have loved to see the expression plastered across my own shocked features, because it made Mal laugh. God, his eyes were so blue and his laugh was so gruff, so butch. He began to pull me toward him, our faces so close I could feel his skin radiating heat, and the expression on his manly face declared I had absolutely no choice in what was about to happen.

Warm human lips touched my own cold mouth. My eyes widened in shock and his closed slowly, his lashes brushing against my cheeks with a whisper as he pulled my naked body close to his broad chest in a stunning show of effortless power. My magnificently chiselled torso touched his soldier's uniform, the fabric itchy and coarse against my skin, and I could feel his human heart beating within his chest, pounding away at his rib cage with insatiable urgency. The pounding of his heart, the throb of his pulse and the sound of his blood pumping through his veins pushed me over the edge of caring. Pain danced across my lower lip as his teeth sliced into my flesh, and it pushed me over the edge of desire. It aroused me. Blood always did. My cock stiffened, instantly.

Malachi's tongue forced its way into my mouth, pushing past my lips to explore the wetness within. Then I could contain myself no longer and began to push back with my own. By then we were falling back onto the mattress and he was on top of me, his dick hard inside his trousers, grinding mercilessly against my nakedness. My hands moved down between his legs to explore his pointy goodness, but in one astonishingly swift movement, he grabbed both my hands in his and slammed them against the mattress above my head. My vampiric strength meant nothing to him. Somehow, he spun me around, his actions rough and calculated as he pushed my head into the mattress, his full weight upon my back. I dissolved into horny heaven.

With one impossibly strong hand holding both of mine above my head, his other hand began to fumble with his belt, the fabric ripping and tearing with his eagerness. The roughness of his grip, the animalistic grunts that exploded from between his pursed lips made my skin crawl with excitement. It was fucking fantastic.

The agony and the ecstasy of his exquisite penetration made me groan with pleasure. He was a big boy. I thought my tight ass would rip away the foreskin from his pulsing head, but it did not seem to bother him as he pounded mercilessly at my flesh, a deep guttural groan howling from between his clenched teeth, propelling my desires skyward. With my hands free, I pushed myself up onto my elbows so he could penetrate deeper, and deeper he went, until I thought his whole body lay inside me. His strong masculine hands grabbed my waist and pulled me down, harder and harder, impaling me until I thought my bones would crack.

The momentum was uncompromising. Some tremendous power seemed to be pushing him to the limit of human endurance as he invaded me, faster and faster, with inhuman ferocity and speed, slamming my ass onto his dick so that my bedroom filled with the sound of flesh slapping against flesh. And his voice, so butch, so rough, so bloody manly, made me scream.

Big hands lifted me off the bed until only my knees rested against the mattress. One arm held me tightly around the chest while the other hand stroked my cock, pulling at my dick with as much fury as he pounded my ass. I was close by then, so very close, and I wrapped my hands around his back, pulling him into me as hard as I could. A sharp pain as teeth sliced through the skin of my neck made me cry out in ecstasy as my ejaculate pumped hard and fast from the tip of my penis in a never-ending flood of rapture. And for a moment, my room turned black as the exquisite sensation knocked me senseless. It was the best orgasm I had had since London.

London. Malachi was English, so why could I smell German blood? Malachi had brown eyes, not blue. And why was Malachi wearing a Nazi uniform? And in no way did the word butch belong in the same sentence as Malachi.

Every single nerve ending of my vampire body screamed. What was that thing with its cock firmly implanted in my asshole? Because it was not Mal, the dead Mal, the Mal that looked at me with puppy dog eyes, the loyal Mal, the Mal who really should be running away from me, running away from me screaming.

And he would if he knew.

My Mal could barely influence a speck of dust, never mind bring me to such a ball-splitting orgasm. My Mal was the quintessential Englishman. He smelled English, his blood oozed Englishness as only English blood could, all old books, smog, fine tobacco and tweed. That was how English blood should smell. That was how Malachi used to smell, when he was alive.

It took mere seconds for all that information to zing through my brain. It took even less for me to spin around, rip the man out of my ass and throw him across the room, where the Mal thing slammed into the wall and slid to the ground.

"Who the fuck are you? What are you?" I could barely conceal the frightened tremor in my voice.

My body was on fire and my teeth unsheathed painfully, slicing into my bottom lip as my fury manifested. I crouched on the edge of my bed ready to attack, my eyes boring into the entity before me, but I held my vampire back.

The Mal thing struggled to his feet, pulling up his trousers before straightening his uniform. It was a very gentlemanly gesture, very English of him. All camp elegance and finger flourishes. The outline of his body blurred, distorted so that two sets of features superimposed themselves over the same skull then he shuddered. Blue Germanic eyes sought out my own, but it was Mal's pain burning within them.

"I thought you would like it." His voice contained so much pain I winced. "I have done this for you, for us, so we may be together, properly." It was difficult not to hear the underlying hope that laced each word, the desperation that underlined each letter.

But I was having none of it.

"What have you done? What have you done?" As soon as I saw his features curdle, I regretted my angry tone. I needed to remain calm or risk releasing his drama queen.

"Listen to me, Mal, just tell me how you have done this, I need to understand what this is, what this means." That was the sound of me being reasonable. It was a new experience for me. My body relaxed and uncoiled in one perfectly smooth silky movement, less aggressive. Fuck, I loved my body.

"It means that I can give you what you want, that I can be what you need me to be, a real man. You do not have to look elsewhere anymore—I can make you happy." If I had a heart, it would have broken. So much sincerity in those words, so much conviction that we could be together—that I could love him, and I pitied him for that.

How I hated myself at that very moment.

Feelings could not stand in the way of what he had done. I had to pull him back, before it was too late. The path Mal had started down could only lead to Hell.

"Explain to me, Mal, I need you to explain to me what you have done." Calm, measured, reasonable words, and they worked, because I glimpsed those puppy eyes beneath the German.

"I have been practising for months, maybe longer. I had to start with small animals at first—there is a distinct lack of fit young men around here for me to practise on. It's so much harder than it looks, you know, I really have to concentrate, and you know how I am with that. And the trick at first was to get the animal to stay still long enough for..."

Of course, I knew what he had done and it terrified me, but I needed him to spell it out so I could drag him back from the precipice upon which he teetered. Damn his clipped Englishness, it was all I could do to stop myself from screaming in his face, but no, it was the new me, Mr. Calm, Mr. Composed, Mr. Patience.

"I know that, Mal, but what exactly have you been practising? I need you to explain, to help me understand."

"Possession."

I leaped off the bed, my hands flying into the air. "Are you out of your fucking mind?" I screamed at the top of my voice. The new Eli flew out of the window.

"Yes! Maybe I am out of my mind for thinking you would understand, that you would welcome this! Do you not see what this means for us?"

I was beside myself with disbelief and anger. Possession, I had seen it before, I had seen what it could do to a spirit, how the soul would slowly change, twisting until there was nothing left but a raging demon, and from that, there was no turning back. I would not witness Mal become a monster — there was room for only one of those under my roof.

"Do you know how dangerous that is, Mal? Not to mention how perverse it is! There are certain laws in the world that cannot be broken, not without consequences, it's not natural!"

In a sudden flash of speed that took me by surprise, Mal rushed forward, snarling and spitting into my face. "You fucking hypocrite. You're a fucking homosexual vampire, how perverse is that? Tell me how natural that is."

"And you're a dead man sitting inside the body of a living human being."

Mal's body began to shudder. His outline blurred as the two souls fought for control of the one body and with a loud sucking, popping sound, the spirit of Mal ripped itself from its host. With a scream of utter fury, he flung the still living man at me with all his newfound supernatural strength and I crumpled onto the bed with the soldier's limp body strewn across my lap.

"There! Don't say I never bring you breakfast in bed!" And he flounced out of my bedroom, floating through the door.

Possession fit. Mal never broke from his beloved English, all clipped and proper. And Mal never swore. His rage, his intense anger and the vehemence by which he spoke to me, were all clear signs of a possession fit.

My teeth slid onto my bottom lip, the temptation of a quick snack almost too tempting. I had not eaten for days. Reluctantly I threw the unconscious lump into the corner and rushed after Mal.

With effortless speed, I reached my magnificent stone balustrade and looked down into my spectacular entrance. Like me, there was nothing modest about my home. Mal was spinning around the marble floor like a tornado.

"Mal, you stupid fucking twat, possession is dangerous, it will consume you, destroy you. Is that what you want?" Mal stopped pirouetting and glared up at me, giving me the finger. He actually gave me the finger.

In one elegant explosion of my fabulously muscled body, I leaped over the balustrade and plummeted to the hall below to land gracefully at his feet. The beauty of my movements would have taken my breath away, if I had any to take.

"Possession leads to damnation, Mal—you will no longer be you. There will be nothing left of you but a monster, a demon and this world will be lost to you. I will be lost to you."

"Not if I am careful. I can control it, it need not change me."

"You are a fool if you believe that. This sort of thing *never* goes unnoticed. They will see you. They will hunt you down."

That stopped him. His face darkened with worry. He drifted closer to the ground, his bottom lip trembling as moisture threatened to spill from his wide, frightened eyes.

The laughter was unexpected and it erupted from between my pursed lips with violence. The thought hit my brain so fast I could not control my reaction and the look of alarm that blossomed across Mal's face made me laugh even more as tears of uncontrollable hysteria poured down my cheeks.

"And what, may I ask, has tickled your fanny?" demanded Mal indignantly.

"Animals!" I squealed, barely able to control my voice. "You possessed animals?"

That did not amuse Mal, and the harder I laughed, the darker he became. Not for the first time that day, I thought my sides were going to split.

"What of it? I do not see what you could possibly find so funny in that!" he squealed.

By now, I was on my knees, slapping the floor with the palms of my hands. "You possessed a fucking bunny! Ha!"

As I fell onto my back screeching, Mal placed his hands on his hips, his scowl turning into a grin.

"Well," he declared, suddenly very camp and very giggly, "let's just say that my ears were the only floppy thing about me."

The sound of our laughter filled Alte. My best friend, the ghost, flittered around my head guffawing like a mule and I had never been so relieved to hear such a welcome sound in all my long days. Malachi was back in the room.

Suddenly, a loud German scream interrupted our amusement. The handsome Nazi soldier leaned over the stone balustrade above, his face blood red with terror and anger.

"Who are you? Where am I?"

"Better lock him up," I tried to squeeze out between coughing fits.

"Save him for later!" howled Mal and we started to laugh again.

A loud knock at the front door stopped the hilarity dead and I flashed Malachi an accusatory look. Had he led others to my sanctuary? The little shit flashed me his sweetest, most innocent look, and yet again, I could not help but laugh, so I staggered toward the two huge doors, pausing for just the briefest of seconds as I remembered my nakedness. Tough shit, it would be a treat for whoever stood there.

My hands twined around the large brass handles and I pulled the doors inward.

There was an angel standing on my doorstep.

Chapter Two: Alte

So I lived in a castle. I liked to think of her as my castle, even though she was just a grand fake, the ostentatious creation of a mad, lovesick genius. But to me she was glorious, my very own little Folly, hidden deep within the remote reaches of Paderborn forest. We called her Alte, Hebrew for old one, even though she was much younger than her Saxon façade implied.

My ex and I had travelled the world during our long lives together — we had witnessed such wonders of incredible beauty as to move us to tears. The Grand Canyon, glowing with the deepest orange as the sun kissed its sedimentary layers, the Pyramids of Giza rising so majestically out of the undulating sands of the dessert. And I would never forget the sights of Rome and the magnificence of the Coliseum where I imagined all those sweat glazed Gladiators going at it. But my heart would always belong to the Alma Valley. The place held a particular fascination for me, and there was something akin to a masterpiece about it, as though the hands of some grand master had reached down from the clouds to fashion the perfect aspect of each stone edifice. Seldom had I seen snow-capped mountains of such glittering brilliance reach so majestically into the sky, as if to touch the blue of Heaven itself. Slopes of white gave way to lush green vistas that melted into a shimmering crystal river, flanked by the verdant emerald nobility that was Paderborn forest. It was magical.

We found Alte in 1879, and it was love at first sight. It was a glorious late September afternoon, and the sun lay dappled across the leaf strewn ground, its fingers gently pushing their way through the thick green canopy of bright green leaves that rustled so softly above our heads. He loved the sunshine. It was a blessing to be able to walk in its glory and it should have been romantic, the two of us, walking hand-in-hand through miles of lush green forest, our voices joined in easy laughter instead of bitter argument.

But like Alte, it was all a façade.

He was my reason to exist, so many centuries together, so many experiences, so much love and laughter. One moment he was my life, the next he was gone. How could they not be with you, after all that time, centuries of love? But he had changed before that. Our relationship lay withered and broken by the wayside and I could not help but look over my shoulder at its desiccated remains with bitter longing stinging my eyes.

Sex that once was mind-blowing became a chore to him, perfunctory. Personally, I considered myself versatile, I liked to give and take. But in my experience, get a vampire into bed and he always cried *fuck me* because there was not a bloody man amongst them. He was the same, all muscle and fabulous big arms, but a turnover. I sucked him off, I fucked him, and if I was lucky, I got a hand job for my trouble. Or he refused me, telling me to come back later, but later never came. It began to hurt. It began to fester. It began to infect every aspect of a once loving relationship, that and all the secrets.

So I began to look elsewhere for affection, just that little acknowledgement that others still found me attractive, that someone still wanted me.

When a human was in me, the feeling was unlike anything else. Humans were warm, hot living blood pumped through their dicks, and I felt every pulse, every throb as it entered my cold, tight opening. Oh my god and when they ejaculated, when that hot semen pumped into my body, it was like an explosion of lava inside me, it made me feel so... alive. I couldn't get enough of it. It consumed my every waking moment, dictated my every decision and distracted me from my very existence. I would travel for miles to find one living breathing man willing to stick his big thick cock up my ass. Maybe willing was too strong a word, perhaps *persuaded* would be more appropriate.

That all added up to another layer of pain, new pain, the pain of my betrayal and guilt. I tried to curb my need, my almost insatiable nymphomaniac tendencies, but I was no nearer to succeeding in that than I was to becoming human.

Alte rose above the canopy of trees like a huge magnificent erection, and when I stood before her, I was breathless. I would say speechless, but that just wasn't me. Nestled within an acre of land, she sat in her throne of land like a regal queen — proud, beautiful, and very well-dressed. Four superlative towers flanked each corner of the main square building, their crenulated fingers reaching defiantly skyward some seventeen metres. Each tower contained three arched windows with a final, smaller, circular window set into the uppermost section, while the main square block enclosed a magnificent set of oak doors and a large double arched window complete with a balcony and gothic stone balustrade. She was immaculately proportioned and a joy to behold.

I felt an instant connection to the building. It was a building created with care, with love, with attention to detail that oozed from every stone. I could see it blazing from its surface like a heartbeat. And she was just waiting there, waiting for someone like me to open her doors and love her back. The thrill of it almost made a little pee escape down my leg.

Better still, she lay abandoned, with nobody around for miles. I knew Welwelsburg Castle, a true bastion of the Renaissance era, lay in ruins at the opposite end of the valley, but it was too far away to be of any concern to me. She, my new castle, was remote and secluded and she belonged to me.

Over the years that followed, I discovered a great deal about my new home. James Wyatt, an English architect of some renown, had designed the Saxon styled tower. A German Master Builder with a mouth full of a name, Georg Wenzeslaus von Knobelsdorff, pilfered the plans and built in 1746 as a beacon to look out across the forest. Rumour had it that good old Georg built the Folly for his lover, a certain Frederick II of Prussia. But Frederick was under too much scrutiny, what with him being a royal, so instead of fucking Georg senseless in their new shag pad, he opted to invade Austria. Frederick severed the already strained relationship with Georg—his right Royal Highness never even set foot in the castle. Georg was devastated and abandoned the Folly. He moved to Belgium to build a church for his jilted king, where he later died of liver disease. Tragic.

The doors moaned loudly as I pushed the heavy wood inward, and I made a mental note that the hinges needed lubricating—but then, didn't we all. They opened into a magnificent hall with a black and white marble floor and a central staircase that splayed out to the first floor landing, all adorned by a wonderfully ostentatious stone balustrade. Access to the towers was via doors cleverly concealed to look like the hand painted walls around them, a glorious Jacobean damask motif in wonderful hues of faded green, faded but still so vibrant. The floor lay soiled with dirt and leaves, and neglect hung heavily upon the atmosphere, but with a bit of love and affection the place would come alive again. Just like me.

I skipped up the grand staircase to explore the rooms above, all two of them. She was all frock and no knickers. But I didn't care. They were two glorious rooms, one painted in a beautiful shade of royal blue in wispy floral motifs and the other a soft baby pink with block prints of pineapples in tarnished gold.

As I stood in the blue room, my room, gazing out of the circular window at the breath-taking vista before me, I laughed. It was a castle with only two rooms, two bedrooms at that. The rooms in the turrets were tiny and of no consequence, old servants quarters, a bathroom, a kitchen of sorts, but otherwise the entire construction seemed to be centred on the two bedrooms. It was a shag pad indeed.

Maybe it was the excitement, or maybe I just needed it, but we fucked in that Folly there and then. It was not something that he meant to happen. God forbid that he should ever instigate sex, but I felt his hand touch my shoulder, the huge muscles of his enormous arms rippling beneath the tight cloth of his shirt, and it was all I could do not to rip his head off with my tongue, so fierce was my kiss. He was shocked and more than a little reticent, but I really did not give a shit at that point. He was going to get it whether he liked it or not. I slammed his huge muscular body into the wall and thrust myself against his groin, feeling with some satisfaction the growing hardness within his trousers. So I ripped them off. He made to complain, but I took his stiffening cock deep in my mouth, my tongue flicking around his throbbing head until he groaned with pleasure.

With shocking ferocity, I threw him toward the opposite wall, but even before he crashed into the plasterwork, I was there to catch him. I turned him around and I flung him against the blue surface of the wall, where I parted his legs. He had a butt of steel, tight and round, and I parted it, drilling his ass with my tongue, eliciting a gasp of astonishment. When he was moist, I replaced my tongue with fingers, inserting two at first, exploring the glistening cavity while my tongue licked his taut testicles. My fingers found that magic spot that only men possess and I manoeuvred myself between his legs so I could take his cock into my mouth, being careful not to send him over the edge too quickly. I wasn't finished yet. Three fingers, then four, pushing deeper and deeper, and I could feel his body begin to sag so I knew he could not last much longer. I pulled my hand out, and I was not gentle.

The lust was upon me so fierce that it almost blinded me. I had no control. My head spiralled away into ecstasy as I forced his head down onto my own swollen member. I gripped his lustrous hair in my fist and I rammed my cock deep into his throat, thrusting until there was nothing left, my balls slapping against his chin. Exquisite pain shot through my loins as his teeth pierced my shaft and I could feel my blood pumping down his throat, his whole body convulsing as he drank and there was nothing left for him but me, he saw only me, he felt only me.

My own teeth extended and I bent over with every intention of plunging them into his bared shoulder, but he flicked me away. I nearly lost it. There and then, with my cock in his mouth, I nearly exploded as anger and rejection began to overwhelm my sexual desires. But then his fingers were in me, searching with surprising urgency that made me gasp. I groaned as the orgasm pumped long and hard, dribbling from the corners of his mouth, mixing with my own blood, and I felt his own ejaculate explode across my legs as he finished himself off.

It was a fantastic blowjob and one of our last good ones.

It took just over a year to restore Alte. Over our long lifetimes, we had accrued great wealth. Money always helped. We spared no expense, employing the talents of a pioneering inventor Friedrich Winzer to install great tanks of natural gas to power lighting. Cities all over the world benefited from his pioneering techniques, and what was good enough for Paris was good enough for Alte. I embraced new technology and I revelled in the creative mind of man, their inventions fascinating me. Later it would be the miracle of electricity blazing through the circular windows of Alte, but until then, the raw flames of Hell itself would bathe my castle in its flickering light.

Most of the restoration we undertook ourselves. Our vampiric nature allowed us to work ceaselessly, and the work progressed at tremendous speed. Love and obsession restored the castle with a sympathetic hand. We cleaned walls with delicate strokes to restore their colour and scrubbed the stonework to within an inch of its life. The marble floor shone with a lustre that was deep and rich. Furniture from our various homes across the globe arrived by the cartload, filling the space with our own ostentatious taste, and I revelled in it. Alte was truly a home befitting kings, but now it was a grand residence for two queens.

He never loved it, not the way I did. Philistine.

And then there was the dungeon. Who knew what naughty old Georg had in store for his king, but I could only surmise he was a man after my own heart. Lurking beneath the main hall and accessed through a secret door hidden behind the main staircase, the dungeon came complete with a long wooden table for those late night torture sessions and a large iron cell with its own set of chains and handcuffs bolted to the wall. Kinky. We never used it, surprisingly.

I never thought for one moment that I would get to use my dungeon for its original, rather repugnant purpose. And yet, there I was, locking up a Nazi soldier. Fair play, he had a strong pair of lungs and an amazing vocabulary. I found myself wanting to plant my fist down his gob as I locked the cell door, but fisting would come later, so I settled for reaching through the bars and giving him a good sharp slap across the face. The man positively withered before my eyes.

"Don't worry," I whispered, pushing my lips through the bars toward him. "I'm not going to hurt you... not yet anyway." For some reason he did not find my words very comforting and he spat at me, his fluid running thickly down my cheek.

"I know what you are," he hissed.

I felt the smile creep across my face. That bit always entertained me, the realisation, the horror, the dawning knowledge that monsters really did exist, the terror in their eyes as they realised what they faced. I also found it quite horny.

"And tell me, little Nazi man," I crooned, pushing my face deeper into the cell, "what am I?"

Suddenly he was at the bars, a small silver crucifix on a thin silver chain clenched between his fingers thrust toward me, and it was my turn to fall away in fear.

The burning dream was upon me. My veins pulsed with fire. Terror paralysed me as I felt those accusing hands upon me, tearing at my unearthly flesh, demanding to know why. That cross, that humble shape, all pain and agony, rejection, disappointment, loneliness and utter damnation.

"I can't help it! It's not my fault!" My voice, it was my voice screaming in the darkness, pleading, desperate and I burned.

"Close your eyes. Close your eyes. Look away." Another voice cut through the pain, the angel's voice.

Even through my tightly closed eyes, I could see the light, white, blinding, searing my retinas through my immortal flesh. The silence came and I was no more.

Chapter Three: The Question

It was all I could do to lift my head off my fabulously expensive, hand painted French Louis XV dining table, imported from Paris at great expense. I sat sprawled across one of the hand carved, hand gilded, Acanthus carver chairs in an exhausted heap. My legs throbbed. My arms throbbed. Even my eyes throbbed. But my dining set was gorgeous. And I looked good draped across it.

I was not shallow — I just loved nice things. Maybe I was a little shallow.

My body was as limp as one of Mal's wrists. That Nazi bastard had taken me by surprise, and the sight of that crucifix sickened me. German twat.

Searing pain flashed through my eyes, fire, terror, echoes of something terrible. I clutched my head to block out the images still so fresh in my mind. I needed to feed, and my stomach was screaming with hunger. I needed to regain my composure, especially with an angel staring straight at me.

"What are you doing here?" My tone was sharper than I intended — not a very clever thing to do with an angel — but I was in no mood for social niceties. It had been one hell of a day.

"Is that any way to speak to an old friend who has just pulled you out of purgatory?" Fuck me sideways — that voice, that soft, resonant, incredibly sexy, almost melodious voice, like silk against my flesh. It sent shivers down my spine and made me twitch in places that really should know better. "It's good to see you too!" he quipped teasingly.

I could not help but smirk. That indomitable sense of humour was still present, each word laden with a wicked twinkle and knowing smile. If I hadn't felt like shit, I would have been hard. I scraped my face off my expensive table and dared to point my gaze in his direction.

Well, hello.

How did one describe an angel? With great difficulty is the answer to that, because the moment he was out of sight, the moment your gaze left him, the memory of his face faded. It was almost as if your mind could not perceive him. The memory of the encounter quickly evaporated until it felt like nothing but a distant dream, an echo of something lovely that you thought you may have experienced, but you would not like to say for definite. It was a neat trick.

To most, he appeared just the once, usually at the point of death or just after, and therefore memory of the meeting was unimportant, an inconsequential side effect. But I had seen him on a number of occasions, and with each meeting, my mind held onto his memory that much more. I was a supernatural being, a creature that walked the fine line between life and death, so normal rules did not apply to me.

As if any rule could ever apply to me.

I could remember his eyes. Such a pale blue as to be almost transparent, flecked with shards of pure gold that glittered as though powered by some internal force. I could drown in those eyes.

I could remember that his face was smooth, that those perfect eyes were unsullied by lines or creases and that his perfect voluptuous mouth sat within a faultless complexion that could rival my own immaculate pale skin. Even his hair was perfect, a golden mop of tight curls that framed his radiant face, pretty yet manly. To think of an angel was to conjure up every cliché described or painted by man, but when you looked as good as he did, who gave a fuck.

His clothes really pissed me off. How dare he wear them so perfectly? Sackcloth. I wore the most exquisitely tailored outfits shipped in from Italy. He, however, wore sackcloth, a simple white cotton seersucker shirt that clung to his body in all the right places, straining over his tight sinewy body that rippled and undulated perfectly. Not muscular, not Gladiatorial like my ex, but tight, perfectly proportioned... did I say it was tight? And that stomach, so hard, so rippled, so... tight.

I could only imagine what it would be like to run my tongue over that rippled surface. Nice, now.

I loved big arms, big fuck off lift me up and lower me onto it arms, and while the angel's arms were not big, they were muscular and well-defined, with prominent veins threading through the surface of the skin, so very, very tight.

As for those snug brown britches, well, I always tried not to look down there, at the thing bursting to break free from the seams. Like a dwarf's arm.

Was it wrong to lust after an angel? Did angels even fuck?

And that was not even his real form. The true angel lay just beneath the surface, beneath the vision of manly loveliness that he allowed us to see. I had never seen his true appearance, and neither would he show me. He called it his battle armour. The Nazi in my dungeon had seen just the briefest glimpse of the true angel, and that was enough to render him a jabbering idiot curled up on the cold damp flagstones like a child.

Daniyyel always said that he only brought out his true angel on special occasions. Was I not special enough?

I almost laughed aloud at the sight of Mal staring at him, mouth agape, overwhelmed by Daniyyel's presence, transfixed by his beauty, spellbound by the charisma that positively radiated from his fit body.

"Close your mouth, Mal, you're drooling."

Daniyyel chuckled gently at my words, and my flesh goose pimpled, so I turned to face him. Wow. "And you, angel man, have not answered my question. Please tell me you *have* just come to say hello and dazzle us with your good looks."

Daniyyel threw back his head and laughed loudly, a husky, horny laugh. "Do you ever change, my friend? Always with the wisecracks and the innuendoes, you are always so funny!"

"I'm so happy that I amuse you. And no, I never change. And *you* only ever turn up when there's something going on, so spit it out."

"May I?" He gestured toward a throne-like dining chair opposite me. He even made sitting down look good, the bastard.

We sat at my dining table looking across its expanse, two immortal beings gazing into each other's eyes. I was looking at an angel. It had been a long time since I had last done so, and I did not care to remember it.

"I haven't seen you since..." I was trembling, my lips unable to form the words. It hurt too much.

"London, yes, my friend," he said gently, "and that is partly why I am here."

I sat back heavily into my chair. I had always known that it was coming. I had always known that London would catch up with me one day and bite me in the ass. And I deserved it.

See no evil. Hear no evil. Speak no evil.

Daniyyel's soft voice drifted across the table toward me. "It is not what you think, Eli. It is not my job, or my wish, to judge or exact punishment. Not on you." He leaned over and stroked the back of my hand with one immaculate finger, sending ripples of pleasure through my body. "Never on you." I crossed my legs. Thank god, I had put on some clothes.

"Then why?"

"I need you to tell me what happened to Vicky."

The whole world fell out of my ass. "Oh."

"Do you think I would not know?" So gentle, so kind, always so kind. "As I have said, I am not here to judge or exact punishment, but I do need to know what happened to Vicky."

"Well, obviously you already know what happened to her!" I was being rude again. My day was rapidly turning into one great big pile of steaming shit and I was losing the will to live. And I was embarrassed. He knew about Vicky, amongst other things, and I did not wear humiliation well.

"From the beginning please, Eli, in your own inimitable way." Daniyyel assumed the position of the attentive listener, his gaze boring into mine while Malachi slid into a chair, placing himself a respectful distance from the angel, who did not tear his focus away from me. "Hello, Malachi."

Those simple words of warm greeting sent Mal into a blushing frenzy. He brought his hands up to cover his semi-transparent face and I laughed despite myself.

"You know my name," Mal whispered with all the wonder of a child discovering Christmas for the first time, all wide eyes and wonderment.

"Yes, Malachi, I know your name, I know all about you."

"Why do you want to know about Vicky?" I asked quickly, desperate to change the subject.

"Because it is time to ask her the question." He turned his full beatific gaze upon Malachi, his eyes blazing with heartfelt sincerity and love. "As I have come to ask you the question, Malachi."

"Now wait a fucking moment!" I was on my feet, my teeth extended in anger, bearing down upon the angel without a second thought. "You've never even asked *me* the question! In all these years, you have never asked me the question. How come he gets to be asked?"

Malachi was looking from me to the angel in utter bewilderment. Poor bastard, he had absolutely no idea what was going on. But I did, and I was not amused.

"The question is not for you, Eli, but for Malachi it is time." He was so fucking calm in the face of my anger. Lesser beings would have trembled at my wrath, but not Daniyyel, not the angel.

"And why shouldn't I be asked? Has it ever occurred to you that I don't want to live like this?" My anger flowed down my arms and into my hands as I slammed them onto the surface of my very expensive table and I could only watch in total helplessness as a fissure ripped its way along the length of its surface. "Look what you made me do! Do you know how expensive that was?"

"Eli, the question is not for you." He was insufferably patient and so sickeningly sympathetic.

"You know how I hate this. You know how I hate being a monster. And you won't make me human. The constant need to feed, the constant horror, I don't want to be like this. I deserve to be asked the question!"

"Is that why you turned Vicky?"

Well, that took the wind out of my sails. I slumped back into my chair, wounded, utterly humiliated. There was not a lot I could say to that.

"Go to Hell, you winged freak." It was a preposterous comeback but it was all I could manage. Daniyyel smiled at me gently, but his insufferable compassion was beginning to grate on me.

"Will somebody please tell me who Vicky is and what the heck is this question you want to ask?" Malachi's outburst was so sudden and so unexpected that I jumped in my seat. I stared at him in astonishment. Even his tantrum was camp, and I could not help the burp of laughter that burst from my lips. "Pray, tell me what is so funny?"

"Forgive me, Malachi," said Daniyyel, so calm, so unfazed. "I understand that this must be... unusual for you." The angel shot me a withering look and I made a concerted effort to control myself. I think I was a little hysterical, swinging from anger to laughter in a heartbeat. My emotions were all over the place.

"Ask him the question. Go on." There was no more laughter, just deadly seriousness. I was not encouraging Daniyyel, I just wanted to get the agony of it over with, because depending on the answer that Malachi gave to the angel, I was on the verge of losing him, of losing my best friend, my only friend, and I was terrified. I damned my eyes for burning.

I wanted to tell Mal to ignore the angel. I wanted to tell him that I loved him and that I could not bear an existence without him in it, that he made my life better, that he made my life bearable. Selfish, very selfish, but I could not help my feelings or the tears that were threatening to spill down my cheeks.

"I have come to ask you if you are ready to go home, Malachi." The kindness in his words was unbearable to me. His words were unbearable to me, that he should be saying them to Mal, that I could lose Mal because of those words and because those words were not spoken to me.

"My goodness, you had me worried then," cried Mal, relief rippling through his body and accentuating his high-pitched voice. "But you have to understand, I am home, I know no other."

Oh Mal, my poor uncomprehending Mal—he really did not have a clue.

"You misunderstand me, my friend, what I am asking goes far deeper than your ties to this castle. I am asking you if you want to come home, with me, to Heaven."

Bang! There it was, as if someone had just hit him full in the face with a wet fish, realisation.

"Heaven? Are you asking me if I want to go to Heaven?" His voice was nothing more than a squeak. A giggle welled up inside me and I swallowed it, hard.

"Yes, if you are ready."

Every part of my being wanted to say something to Mal, to make him consider carefully the choice that lay before him, but the angel held up his hand to silence me, anticipating the words threatening to spill from my lips, and I found that I could not speak.

I could almost hear the cogs whirring in Malachi's head. That single devastating question had thrown Mal into a state of utter confusion, and for once, I wished that I could read his mind. Or send him a telepathic message begging him not to go. Stay with me, I wanted to say, please don't leave me alone, help me to find my motivation to continue, help me to find my own humanity beneath this monstrous façade, help to become something better. Help me to deserve my own question.

Help me to be less selfish.

"What is it like?" asked Mal as he drifted closer to the angel, his face glowing with wonder. "What is Heaven like?"

"He won't tell you." I should not have said that. It sounded very churlish, spiteful even. I regretted it almost instantly, especially as it earned another look from Daniyyel, and I checked myself over for salt crystals.

"It is not for me to say," continued Daniyyel patiently. "Heaven is something that you have to discover for yourself. I can only invite you in."

"But how may I be expected to make a decision when I do not know what is waiting for me? I may not like it." I never realised Mal had such big brass balls. Daniyyel threw back his head and chuckled.

"Well I did not think it that funny." Mal pouted.

"I can't say," gasped Daniyyel between guffaws, "that I have ever," more laughter, "in two thousand years, had anyone worry that they would not like Heaven. That is so funny!"

"Well, I am so happy for you. I am so glad that I do not disappoint."

"No, my friend," gasped the angel, trying to recover. "You do not disappoint. You have never disappointed. That is why I am here, that is why I am asking you the question."

An uncomfortable silence fell over the hall. I looked at my friend, trying to work out what he might say, but he was in obvious pain, the turmoil written all over his face.

I was in pain too.

"I... I do not know. I do not know what I am meant to say."

If my heart had been beating, it would have stopped. He was obviously considering it, seriously considering it. Malachi was actually thinking of leaving me. Damn, my eyes were burning.

Only that morning, I had rebuked him. Only that morning, I had told him I did not love him. I told him he was not my type, that I could never love him and that I did not want to have sex with him. I told him the truth, for once.

But he was my best friend and I needed him. There would be only darkness without him by my side. If he stayed, things would have to change. I would have to change. No shag pal, just best friends, I owed him that much, and much more besides.

"You are meant to say what is in your heart, Malachi. What is in your heart? Do you want to come with me?"

"What is in my heart?" Mal looked directly at me, and I would never hate myself more than I did at that moment. I was a cowardly selfish inconsiderate bastard. "I know in my heart that I am not ready to leave. I still do not know who I was, or how I died, for a start."

"So there is nothing that is familiar to you? No memory that may reunite you with your past?"

"To be honest, no, and if I am going to be completely honest, I cannot say that I have really, truly looked. Eli has given me such a wonderful home, such a wonderful life. I have loved every moment of every day that I have spent with him, and I am not ready to give that up yet."

"So you will stay here because of Eli?" He did not say it in an accusatory fashion, but I could not help but take it as such.

"Because of Eli, but also *for* Eli—he needs me. We are the same, he and I, both strangers to ourselves, both looking for answers."

"And yet I do not see either of you actively looking for those answers." He said that *with* an edge of accusation, a very hard edge that cut me to the core. And it alarmed me. To be under the scrutiny of an angel is not something one may take lightly, and of course, he was right.

I was feeling flippant and desperate. "I am Menarche, what more is there to know?"

Daniyyel looked at me with eyes full of sadness. I resented his eyes. "Yes, my friend, you are Menarche, the first occurrence, but every beginning has an origin, is that not so?"

"If you say so."

"But you come from somewhere. Does that not matter to you?"

"No one else seems to give a shit, so why should I?"

"Oh, my friend, that is not true. You do care, I know you do, as do I."

"But you don't care enough to ask me the question, do

you?" How I hated the vampire condition. How I detested being Menarche, different even from my own kind. Outcast, as far from human as was physically or spiritually possible and therefore too far from the reach of Heaven's embrace. The question would always elude me—I was not human enough.

Daniyyel's voice cut through my sarcasm with a kindness that stung. "I know you care and I know you have searched, but I also know that you have lost your way. You have suffered more than most, perhaps, and it is my hope that that yearning will return to you. It must return to you Eli." He shifted his gaze to Malachi, much to my relief. "But you, Malachi, you I am surprised with. You are so very young, a spirit for such a short time, and yet you seem to have no curiosity regarding your past and your identity. Do not misunderstand me, I am not here to judge, and it bears no relevance to the offer I give, but for the sake of my own curiosity, can you not tell me why?" He spoke with such eloquence, such passion. I was dribbling again.

"I found Eli on the floor in a pool of blood on the banks of the River Thames. He was soaking wet and hysterical, as wretched a creature as I had ever seen. I cannot begin to describe the pain that I saw in his eyes, the desperation and the need to die that nestled within those eyes and the agony that shook his entire body. He was so broken, so alone. His heartbreak was so palpable that I could not turn away from it. How could I turn away from it?"

I had to turn away from him. I did not want to hear it. I did not want to remember it, and I certainly did not want to relive it through the eyes of Malachi. He spoke with such anguish, with such compassion and love, and it crushed me, his every word slicing through me worse than any crucifix. If I could have died on the spot, I would have chosen death rather than listen to his wretched words, words that crippled me, words that crucified me. But I had to hear it, no matter where it led. Let the truth bleed out.

"If you had seen him there, you would not have been able to leave him either. I defy anyone to say otherwise. I tried to comfort him, and I talked him through his tears until the sun came up. I was worried that he would burn... what with him being a vampire." It was like a light bulb above his head, that sudden flash of inspiration. "I never thought of that before. How strange, I knew he was a vampire, I knew it instinctively, how weird."

I was on the edge of my seat, my palms sweaty, dread dripping down my chiselled chest, I was so nervous. To my relief he tossed the revelation aside and continued with his story. I exhaled loudly, my hands wringing the flesh from their bones beneath the table.

"Anyway, it took a lot of persuasion, but I eventually coaxed him to his feet and took him home. I never gave myself another thought after that, not really. You see, it took a long time to get Eli even to feed, and every day, for so many years, I filled the hours with the task of making him want to exist, to make him feel like part of the world again. He hated me at first." I spun around to complain but Malachi silenced me with a flick of his wrist. "It is okay, I knew, I always knew, but you did hate me at first, almost as much as you hated yourself, I think."

"I'm so sorry, Mal." My inadequacies blossomed. Pain stabbed at the empty space where my heart should have been and tears spilled over my eyes and down my cheeks. I was not prone to crying — crying was a luxury I had denied myself since London. But my face was wet and I could not stop the tears.

"I like to think that it was all part of your grief," he continued, smiling at me so kindly, and I knew I didn't deserve him, his kindness, or his friendship. "I wanted to be there, I wanted to be the one you could take it out on. I chose to be there, for you." He turned to Daniyyel, his face so earnest. "And that is where I still want to be, by his side."

"I understand. And that is why I am asking you the question, because of your selfless desire to look after Eli. You are a being that cares so very much, a being so full of love for others, that it eclipses your own needs and desires. You are deserving of the question, my friend, and it humbles me to ask it of you."

My tears were cold, like ice running down my face. I wiped them with the back of a trembling hand, but they continued to flow, falling onto my lap in big wet splashes. I bowed my head, unable to look at him, not wanting them to see me weak, to see me break.

To see the relief that the truth remained buried.

"But may I be permitted to ask you a question, if such a thing is allowed of me to an angel." His perfect English cupped each word so beautifully and I felt as though I was seeing him, hearing him properly, for the first time.

"Please do."

"Why now? Why ask me the question now? Why not when I died?"

"Some of that I cannot tell you. It is up to you to discover your past and perhaps the answer to the latter half of your question. As to the now? You have proved your worthiness with an act of selflessness, and therefore you deserve the question. But consider this, Malachi, and consider it well. I can ask the question only twice. Refusal in the first instance on the grounds of unfinished business is understandable and acceptable. To ask a second time and still receive a refusal will result in the withdrawal of the offer, permanently. For you to refuse a second time is to reject the hand of God."

"And then what? If I refuse a second time, what happens

to me?"

"You will be taken by somebody else and you will become something else, something ungodly and permanent, which is all I can say."

A cold shiver flowed down my spine like an army of icy fingers and I could see that Daniyyel's words had greatly disturbed Malachi.

"When will I be asked again?"

"At a time of my choosing."

"Oh."

"Do not fret, my ghostly friend," said Daniyyel softly. "You will not be asked again unless I am absolutely sure you are ready. The first time I ask is more out of courtesy, a gentle warning if you like, that you need to wrap up any loose ends. It gives you time to finish this existence properly, if you wish it. I believe the Americans call it closure. Yes, closure, I like that. And a surprising amount of spirits say yes the first time. But those who say yes the second time around are more contented souls, and Heaven becomes all the richer for it."

"Do many say no the second time?"

"Yes, a few. But I can usually tell those who are going to do that. Their souls have a darker edge to them, a malady that cannot be lifted. While it saddens me to lose a soul, I realise that you cannot have light without the dark, and in that I take solace. Balance, it all comes down to balance." Suddenly he turned to me with the full weight of his gaze, and I withered under its might. "And now you are going to tell me about Vicky."

I squirmed uncomfortably in my chair. Oh, it was going to be painful.

"Oh yes. The girl you turned," chimed Malachi acerbically. "That must have been a novelty for sure. So go on, who was Vicky?"

I bowed my head in shame. "I turned Queen Victoria."

Chapter Four: Vicky

As related by Eli

London. 1889. This was the story of how I fucked up. I should have been in recovery. I should have been pulling myself together, which meant no drugs and no sex with only enough blood to keep me going—oh, and no turning humans.

Yeah, right.

On a positive note, this was the story of how I saved a country, again. The story of how I saved a Monarchy from collapsing under its own dissolute weight.

This was the story of my descent into madness.

Situated on the northern bank of the river Thames opposite Rotherhithe, between Ratcliff and Millwall, the Limehouse area of London was as rough as a sheet of sandpaper against your bare ass. Home to a community of rambunctious sailors and a thriving Chinese population, the area had gained such notoriety that in 1878 the government deemed it necessary to build Limehouse its very own court house. Rival gangs fought with police for supremacy on a daily basis, and violent domestic fights played out like theatre on the cobbled, shit-strewn streets.

The sight of a horse would forever remind me of shit and the smell of shit would forever transport me back to Limehouse. My god how intoxicating the smell of any city was to a vampire, and oh did London smell. No matter where I went, it was impossible to escape the tang of human and animal excrement mixed with the erotic scent of semen and blood. The air was thick with it. And always that invigorating cacophony of aromas lay intermingled with the rancid stench of the Thames that wound its lifeblood through that daunting city, metallic, salty, putrescent. Of course, humans were none the wiser to the most prodigious vapours, but I inhaled deeply. It was so alive.

Mixed liberally with the exhaust fumes of everyday life, Limehouse had the greatest smell of all—opium, sweet mind-fucking opium that was both my saviour and my downfall. Its smell permeated everything. My vampire nose could pick out its perfume with almost pinpoint accuracy, even on those wet days when sewage overflowed from the Thames and made a thick stinking carpet underfoot.

There were days when I wandered those busy streets like a stricken waif, one foot aimlessly stumbling before the other, a slave to the scent of the poppy. I tried to resist it. I tried to block out the fragrance from my senses, but such was the power it held over me, such was the distraction from reality that it offered. Such was the power of its smoky, comforting embrace that it rendered me powerless. My trance, my hypnotic amble always ended in the same place, always in the middle of Limehouse.

Now that was addiction.

Industrialisation had already tainted the tall buildings of London with a dusting of black detritus. Thick black smoke pumped out of myriad chimneys and factories, forming a dense layer of cloud that clung to London like an umbrella, trapping the moisture beneath its canopy. It created an atmosphere both dank and oppressive. As a result, London always felt dark and somehow very intimate because of it.

The streets were full of the desperate and the dissolute. Seldom had I witnessed such disparity between the wealthy and the poor. Hope and ambition were the remit of the rich and the powerful, the rest discarded into the shit-strewn streets, unwanted and uncared for. Most of the city crawled aimlessly across the land to create one big slum, overcrowded and riddled with disease. Too much humanity crammed into one space. But no one told London that.

Limehouse was the perfect example of pessimism, where the population went through their daily routine with the sole aim of surviving it, murderers, thieves, prostitutes, the sick and the homeless, all shoehorned into one tiny area. And the buildings were just the same, tall black monoliths jutting into the smog-filled sky, narrow and crammed together, compacted into rows that refused to look orderly.

Squeezed between two such buildings sat Ah Sing's Launderette.

On any given day, a forest of billowing sheets, hanging on a web of lines strung taught between tall wooden poles would afford only a tantalising glimpse of the Launderette beyond. On a good day, those lines would be six or seven deep. Disembodied voices floated between the sheets from the long table positioned at the front of the Launderette, where oriental women of various ages had their hands immersed in great metal basins scrubbing the latest intake of washing. Their hands were red raw and sore from the caustic soap. So fast was their chatter and so high pitched were their voices that they sounded like a flock of excited seagulls engaged in some elaborate mating call. It never failed to make me smile.

As I made my way through the forest of cotton trees, the women spotted me, their voices rising in excitement. I never understood a word of it, but they knew *why* I was there. Out of courtesy, I nodded toward the interior of the Launderette and the ladies squawked with excited, animated agreement. There was always lots of bowing.

The inside stank of perspiration and soap. It was very

dark and claustrophobic, a sensation made even more tangible because of the washing that hung from every conceivable surface, a sea of knickers, corsets and bloomers and all those intimate items unbefitting a public hanging.

A discreet trap door set into the floor at the back of the shop lured me into the dank interior. Positioned over the opening, perched on a large oak barrel, sat a wizened old Chinese man smoking a beautifully carved dragon pipe, and his eyes lit up at the sight of me. The sight of me always made him smile, the thought of the bulging wallet in my pocket an effective aphrodisiac.

"Come, come," he would mutter enthusiastically. It was the only intelligible word I ever heard him speak. His gestures, however, left nothing to the imagination as he thrust his hand out to me. There was no language barrier there.

We always performed that same routine. I would fill his hand with a wad of notes and he would sniff them, giggling before stuffing them into his pockets. He liked my packet. Then he would shuffle to one side and point toward the barrel.

That barrel weighed a ton. But the trap door beneath weighed more. I moved both obstacles easily, and as I flexed my perfect muscles, I felt his eyes upon me, marvelling at my strength, his eyes glinting mischievously. And then he muttered a phrase, as he always did, an unintelligible mishmash of sounds that bugged me. For some reason it always made me feel like he had the upper hand, as though he were toying with me, but that day I was particularly lucid and it occurred to me to have him write the phrase down on a piece of paper. And surprisingly he was all too pleased to accommodate.

The intricate, incomprehensible scrawl defeated me and he knew it. That really pissed me off.

I imagined myself sinking my teeth into his filthy throat. His flesh was probably as tough as old leather and his blood as rancid as piss, but it would have been most satisfying to wipe the smile off his face. I did not do it of course—I could not risk giving myself away, not if I wanted to continue using the facilities. Plus, I was on a fasting day.

The darkness below beckoned, calling me into its warm comforting womb and I descended into the murky depths below with giddy anticipation.

Compared to the hovel above, the basement felt positively luxurious. Only the wealthy could afford such a pastime, so an effort to provide a certain degree of comfort was evident. Chinese lanterns festooned the low ceiling, casting a flickering glow that did nothing to dispel the gloom, but they created an otherworldly atmosphere I found enchanting. Silk hung from the ceiling to the floor creating individual booths, private areas in which lay mattresses and multi-coloured cushions promising a warm, reassuring environment. A thick layer of straw coated the flagstone floor that helped to muffle the sound of any careless footsteps.

There was nothing worse than the annoying clip clopping of feet when one was mounted.

I noted my favourite cubicle in the corner lay unoccupied. It had the added benefit of only one fabric partition and two solid brick walls that I found most beneficial when off my tits. During a particularly violent trip, I had once torn down the fabric walls surrounding me, causing a small fire that nearly burned the place down, so brick was good.

I was Menarche. Fire would not destroy me. But I had no wish to experience the lick of flame again, not on my stunning face.

No sooner had I crawled onto the remarkably comfortable mattress, plumping up my nest of cushions, than Ah Sing appeared. Now he was a sight to behold.

When I thought back to that time, to Ah Sing, it always conjured the novels of Sax Rohmer, for surely he had met Ah Sing.

The sight of such a creature was exciting and exotic in 1889. He stood there tall and fabulously elegant in his Manchu hat and full Mandarin blouse of cobalt blue with gold embroidered dragons and his incredible moustache that hung down below his pointed chin was a thing to marvel. But Fu Manchu he was not, for while undoubtedly a criminal, Ah Sing did not have an evil bone in his lanky body. Courteous and efficient, with a towering intellect, Ah Sing was someone I liked very much.

Mr. Ah Sing died by very mysterious circumstances in 1890. He knew too many people, too many important people.

He bowed, low and deep, and I felt the excitement begin to well up inside me like a tremendous fart bursting to let rip, because at any moment he would offer me the long pipe, the long pipe of utter happiness. Then I suddenly remembered the piece of paper with the old man's scrawl upon it. I thrust it without explanation into Mr. Sing's clasped hands, and he very politely and very slowly, unfolded the scrap of yellowed paper. His eyes were so sharp, sparkling green, emerald green and they flashed across the paper taking in every detail, until suddenly his face lit up, flesh wrinkling into the most glorious smile followed by the gentle shrugging of his elegantly dressed shoulders as he chuckled. I had never seen him laugh before—it suited him.

"You wish to know meaning?"

Fuck me sideways, the oriental bastard could speak English. How many times had I visited that joint, using wild hand gesticulations while speaking to him in a slow moronic fashion to make myself understood? I felt like a right twat.

"Yes, please, if you would be so kind." My voice sounded meek, humble, a sound unfamiliar to me. And he knew it. His mouth twitched as he tried not to laugh.

"The meaning of the characters is *you are capable,* but the meaning of the phrase goes much deeper, if you have ears to hear and eyes to see."

I thought as much. The old wrinkled cumquat knew. Mr. Ah Sing knew.

"Then why? Why do you..."

"Let you in, Mr. Eli?" Long, immaculately manicured, fearless fingers brushed my cold marble cheek ever so gently. "It is known, Mr. Eli, that you saved us — that you saved all of London — from the true monsters that lurk in the dark. To our way of thinking, that makes you less of a monster and more of an angel. As long as I draw breath, you will be welcome at Ah Sing's."

I kissed his hand gently, touched by his kind words. I had heard precious few of them in London. "Your understanding is much appreciated, Mr. Sing, and much needed by one who has known little kindness of late."

He ruffled my hair — actually ruffled my hair. Did he not know how old I was? That really tickled me, and I would hold that moment, that kindness, in my heart for many years after he died. A slight flicker of alarm flashed across his face as he realised what he was doing and he quickly assumed the persona of the ever so efficient Chinaman again, all clasped hands and bowing.

"Ah-pen-yen?" He offered me the little black pill of intoxicating goodness and I nodded eagerly. His left hand swept out to the side in a graceful ark, the silky movement continuing right to the tips of his fingers. In another life, Mr. Sing would have made a fantastic ballet dancer. He had lovely arm extension.

Two miniature Chinese men in identical clothing scuttled from somewhere behind Mr. Sing, children almost certainly, but I had seen much in my time, angels and demons and all the things in between, and in that culture one could never be certain. Something about their faces betrayed an understanding beyond their outward youth, and they made me shiver. One handed me a long black pipe as tall as Ah Sing, and I lay back onto my nest of cushions and placed the delicate end of the pipe between my willing lips. As I settled into position, the other child thing placed a small black shiny pill into the pipe's bowl, and in one fluid, magical movement, Mr. Sing produced a flame out of thin air and bent over to ignite the pipe.

I closed my eyes and inhaled deeply.

There was nothing quite like being off your tits, and no two experiences were ever the same. Once I became an orange dot — all that I was, all my gorgeousness, my towering intelligence, reduced to an incandescent orange dot. Another time I sat in a battered old wing chair as the world around me began to break up, to disintegrate because it was not real. That was a bad trip. That one actually made me cry. It made me think my life with *him* was not real, and the pain of that was more than I could endure. My tears had flowed fast and my cries had been painful to hear. Or so they told me.

Most men could not manage an erection while under the influence. But I could. I was always at my horniest just as I was starting to come up and away from the deepest edge of the trip. I could fuck a man to death, I would be so hard. More often than not, I would visit Ah Sing's with a lover, and I would let him finish me off just as I started to come around. Half mounted themselves — they didn't give a shit. I would ram their heads onto my cock and fill their mouths with my spunk, the orgasm prolonged by the poppy. It would be such a powerful shot, as though I had ejaculated my entire body contents through the head of my dick. It would pump ceaselessly, filling whatever receptacle happened to be in the way. And after the orgasm, I would be perfectly lucid, as though the experience represented some tremendous cleansing ceremony that culminated in spunk.

I allowed the smoke to take me on its mystery tour. My body began to fall into the depths of the trip, weightless, sliding down that tremendous u-bend toward the pits of ecstasy. But it would take at least one more pipe to get me into that hole. I gestured blindly, expecting the attentive child things to place another pipe to my lips, but when nothing happened, I struggled against the u-bend of oblivion and opened my eyes.

Eddy stood over me, looking rather dashing in his tailored tweed suit and high-collared white shirt. He had his rather magnificent cock in his hand, stroking its veined shaft with that horny, naughty smirk I had grown to love creeping across his unconventionally handsome face.

Thank god he'd had the common sense to close the curtains behind him.

Not one to stare a gift horse in the face and more horny than high, I scooted forward and took his cock in my mouth, my tongue flicking around his pulsing round head. It tasted delicious with a slight, just washed soapy aftertaste.

"You like that cock in your mouth don't you?" Eddie just loved dirty talk, and I enjoyed hearing the filth pour from his royal lips. "Bend over and take it like a fucking dog, you dirty bastard!"

That did it for me.

I buried my face in the soft cushions beneath me as rough, eager hands practically tore my trousers off. I closed my eyes, moaning loudly as he parted the cheeks of my ass, the warm deliciousness of his tongue flicking around my hole.

He pulled my ass further apart, forcing his wet tongue deeper into me, pushing into me with all his might, his teeth biting into my skin as he sought out my sensitive inner flesh.

Eddie sat up and gripped my waist with one hand while his other began to guide his thick member into my moist receptacle. My knuckles turned white as I gripped the cushions in expectation of the pain and I could feel my entire body trembling in anticipation of the ecstasy to follow. But despite all that tongue play, his cock would not go in.

I was tight. What could I say?

Suddenly his hand was pulling at my hair, wrenching my head around violently to force his cock deep into my mouth. Both hands pushed at the back of my head, pushing his shaft down my throat until barely his balls remained. I had no gag reflex so I took it whole.

I was a greedy bitch.

Cock suitably lubricated he pushed my head aside and threw me back on my knees. I heard him expectorate and felt the wetness of his spit hit my twitching hole, and then his cock entered me.

Eddie ground my ass as though his life depended on it. I moved my hand between my legs and dug my fingernails into his balls, gently at first, then harder until I felt him flinch. His scrotum tightened at my touch, his testicles hard as cannon balls. I curled in on myself so that my eager fingers could reach his ass, and I inserted two digits into his wetness with brutal force. He moaned loudly as my fingers moved around inside him, and he began to pound harder and with such urgency that I knew he could not last much longer. With the opium still heavy upon me, I used my one free hand to manipulate my own throbbing cock, pulling with quick desperate strokes, and as Eddie threw his head back, grunting at the power of his ejaculation, I shot my own copious load all over the mattress beneath me. Satisfied and exhausted, we collapsed into each other's arms with a contented sigh.

I loved a good quickie.

History has said enough about Eddie, and most of it unfair. He was neither stupid nor dim-witted. He just wanted everyone to think he was thick so no one would bother him. But I liked him. Eddie was my friend, and I saved him once, from so many things, but he saved me as well. He saved me from falling completely into despair. He was part of that life in London that I had tried so hard to forget, but to remember Vicky was to remember Eddie, no matter how much pain it recalled.

I only wanted to remember that bit, no more, not the rest — I didn't want to remember the rest.

Eddie was born Prince Albert Victor and was the grandson of Queen Victoria. He was very tall with a long neck like a swan and he always wore extra high, crisp white collars to disguise his perceived deformity. That earned him the nickname of *collars and cuffs* in the media of the time, but I always called him Eddie.

I found Eddie's unconventional looks rather attractive. Not a muscle in sight, he was certainly no Adonis, and unlike his rotund relatives, Eddie maintained the stature of a lanky streak of piss. But by god, he was a dirty fucker, and he knew what he liked. There was no preamble with Eddie, he just got straight down to it, and I liked that.

Eddie was an addict, *was* being the operative word. For him to enter that poppy den took a lot of real courage and guts on his behalf. He had kicked the habit. So had I, or so he thought.

"Don't get me wrong my dead friend, I really needed that, but can you explain to me why you are here when you led me to believe that you are otherwise cured of this addiction?"

He talked like Mal, just a bit dirtier.

"My underpants needed a good scrub."

"You are not wearing any."

"Exactly."

"Liar."

"They were really dirty, skid marks and everything."

"I am no fool, Eli."

"And your point is?"

"You thought I was a pipe bearer. You have had at least one pill that I can discern."

"Who are you, fucking pill police? Well, you would know all about that now wouldn't you, Mr. Collars and Cuffs." I threw those words at him with as much vitriol as I could muster. How dare he ruin my high? "Two puffs and you used to be fucked!"

"I think you will find, dearie, that it was you who were just fucked," he said calmly, as though my acid was like water off a duck's back.

Touché.

"This is the first time I have been here in weeks."

"This is your second visit this week, and you came here once last week."

"How the fuck do you know that? Have you been spying on me?"

His inquisition really pissed me off. I liked Eddie, but I did not belong to him. I belonged to no one anymore.

"Oh please, I am a prince. I know everything."

"More like a fucking queen, you mean." It was a retort unbefitting my intellect, but it was gratifying none the less. I needed to lash out at somebody—I wanted to *hurt* anybody. Eddie was just handy like that.

"I presume this unwarranted attack is to disguise the fact you are embarrassed and ashamed you lied to me? Why are you using again, Eli? You were doing so well." That was the thing about Eddie, no judgement, not even a hint of pity, just straight talk and a slight undercurrent of concern, of friendship.

"I can't forget. I *need* to forget." I stared into his beautiful round eyes and saw my own desperation reflected back at me. That hurt. "After all I have done, after all we went through, I am still alone, and I am still here. Nobody knows who I am, and nobody knows what I did. Did you tell Mr. Sing?" I demanded with a sudden flash of insight.

Eddie nodded.

"I thought so. Just for one moment... just one stolen blissful moment... that little bit of acknowledgement made me feel so..." I couldn't quite get my words out because my lips were trembling so much.

"Human?"

"Appreciated. I felt appreciated." A single tear spilled down my cheek and he wiped it away with a slender finger.

"I appreciate you, Eli. You will never know my true appreciation for what you have done for this country and me. You are even more heroic for having to bear that knowledge by yourself, to carry such a burden that no one else can know or understand. I will hold you and the memory of what you have done in my heart until the day I die."

Until the day he died. That turned out to be a joke.

"But who am I, Eddie? Who am I? I need to know, who am I, where am I from, where am I going, why am I here? See? I can see by your face there is no answer. There is no answer, is there—not for me, not for the vampire, just loneliness and never-ending existence."

His gentle hand wound its fingers through my hair and I kissed his palm, grateful for the intimacy, grateful for the connection.

"This place does not help, Eli. Your addiction will only

exacerbate your sense of loneliness, of disconnection."

I pulled away from his touch, furious.

"Disconnection? Are you telling me that if I give this up I will be welcomed into the arms of society? Will you welcome me into your circle? Will I be one of you, even though I am vampire?" The opium had almost worn off by that point and the downer had started to kick in, hard. I felt the blackness of despair begin to creep in at the corners of my eyes once more, and the grief that masqueraded as my life pressed down upon me like the weight of a mountain on my shoulders. I was Atlas, carrying the agonies of the world.

I had to control my anger. I had to take control of my acerbic words. It was not Eddie's fault. I was not his responsibility.

"Dear friend, I meant the disconnection from yourself. You have envied humanity for so long that you have forgotten the marvel that is you. I cannot help but feel the sting of jealousy when I think about all the things you have seen, all the places you have been and experienced, the wonders your eyes have beheld and the people that have enriched your being throughout history. Yours is a God-given existence, my friend, and one that I covet as you would covet my humanity. You will get over this. It will take time, and time, my dead friend, is something that, unlike the rest of us, you have in abundance."

No way was that prince an imbecile.

"Am I to do this on my own, then?" The question had more of a pleading edge to it than I would have liked, and I knew instantly from his face and the silence that filled the void between us the end of our brief time together was nigh. He had just fucked me for the last time.

"Grandmamma wishes to see you."

That bloody well woke me up.

"Fuck. What the hell does she want to see me for?"

"I'm sorry, Eli, but it is not for me to say. I am merely the errand boy. Grandmamma will explain."

"Hard as fucking nails, that's what she is, with a face that could curdle milk. And she called her children ugly? Fuck me."

My ex always accused me of being ostentatious — I made no bones about that, so Buckingham Palace suited me down to the ground. I loved it. I owned a castle, but she owned a palace and nothing could beat its grandness. But I swear if I stood still long enough in its sacred halls, someone would gild me. Doors, ornate cornices, tables, chairs, hardly a surface remained untouched by the master gilders hands. Oh, and the colours. Walls covered not with crude wallpaper, but with fine damask fabrics and silks in the most bewitching jewel colours. Emerald green, turquoise, ruby red assaulted my eyes in a cacophony of weaves and embroidery that overpowered the senses in a stunning vomit of colour.

Eddie opened a pair of huge doors that should have crumbled under the weight of the gilt carving that embellished their surface. They led to a blood red anti-chamber and a set of gilt chairs. And *he* was sitting on one of those chairs.

Gideon, the muscly man-thing that was my ex.

"What the fuck are you doing here?" His piercing blue eyes paralysed me, every sinew of my body unable to move under their devouring gaze. How dare he sit in front of me after what he did, all blond hair and bulging muscle, and damn him for looking so good.

"I don't want to be here anymore than you do," he spat out. Even his voice thrilled me, so very manly and butch, so gruff and gravely, making my skin goose-pimple.

"Then fuck off then!" My fingers elongated, my sharp

vampiric claws cutting into the flesh of my palms. The horror was still too fresh, his betrayal still too raw, the pain still too recent. The sight of him made me want to curl up into a tight ball and scream. "Eddie?" I glared at my prince but he simply shrugged.

"She wants to see you both, and you know Grandmamma, what she wants she gets. Now you two children play nicely and I will call you in when she is ready." With a wink in my direction, Eddie disappeared through a set of inter-connecting doors.

"Sit down, sweet-cheeks, you're making me nervous."

"Don't call me that!"

"Sorry."

"Now there's a word I never thought I'd hear pass between your lips."

"Nice to see you haven't lost any of that sharp wit of yours."

"It's all I have left," I grumbled as I slumped into the furthest chair from him. "You didn't leave me with anything else."

Gideon buried his head in his hands with a deep sigh. "Don't do this again, Eli, not now, not here."

"When, then, Gideon? You took yourself away from me, without explanation, without any regard for what we went through. I thought we meant something to each other, all those years together…"

"Enough!" Those eyes were so cold, and I could see it, crawling inside him, the secret that ate my being little by little, day by day, I saw it, the killer within him, the murderer pounding at the glass of his soul trying to get out once more, staring back at me defiantly from those pools of blue. It frightened me.

I tore myself away from his angry gaze and stared at the plush carpet beneath my shoes. A single tear fell onto the woollen surface and glistened for a moment before the pile absorbed the moisture into itself. I found myself wishing I was that tear.

"They did mean something, those years, all of them." Such gentle words from such a huge man, but the sound of them did nothing to ease my aching heart.

"Then why? Why won't you tell me? If it is forgiveness you want then I can give you that, we could start again, do things..."

"No." The finality of that single word sat in my stomach like a lead weight.

"I can forgive you anything, even..." I could not bring myself to think about it never mind speak it aloud—that would make it real. "If you will just tell me, just tell me why you did it."

"I don't want your forgiveness. It is not yours to give."

"Do you still love me?"

"Yes."

"Then tell me." I was on my feet again, my entire body trembling with rage. He just looked at me with those wonderful eyes, and I felt the last of my hope drain from my body as I saw he was gone from me forever. I had lost him. "But you love me."

"And it is not enough, Eli. I'm sorry."

The doors opened and Eddie stood there looking at us both.

"Do I detect an atmosphere?"

"Oh shut up, Eddie." The prince amused me no more.

"She will see you now."

I pulled myself up to my full impressive height and straightened my dinner jacket. "You look fine," smirked Eddie.

"I look fucking amazing!" I countered. I plastered a great big cheesy grin across my face and marched forward to meet the Queen of the British Empire.

She was standing directly ahead of me in front of a stunning Ormolu fireplace that blazed like the infernos of Hell. The heat didn't seem to bother her.

I said she was a witch.

She looked like a short black Christmas pudding, both in colour and in shape. Round and draped in black with a plump head and a white frilly cap thing plonked on top for good measure. Silly bitch was still in mourning for her dear departed husband and refused to wear anything but black.

To her left sat an ornately carved sofa, French, I thought, and heavily gilded, of course. Everything was pink, sickening really, like walking around inside a vagina. I was vaguely aware that a man sat on the sofa, I could just make out the back of his head, but I paid no attention as I rushed toward the Christmas pudding and wrapped my arms around her in a loving embrace.

I could be a false bastard when I needed to be, and I knew how to play the game. "Vicky, darling, you look lovely as always."

She remained as stiff and unyielding as a statue and her face told me she was not amused.

I turned around, intending to give Eddie a sly wink, but then I saw who was sitting on the sofa—Inspector Abberline.

"What is this?" I demanded, looking between Eddie and the thickly moustached Inspector. It felt like some bad joke, Eddie, Gideon, Queenie, and Frederick Abberline. It felt like my past was conspiring against me and I was the only one not in on the joke.

"Calm yourself, Sir," warned Abberline, flashing me a look at the gun strapped to his waist. I laughed despite myself.

"Don't be such a dick." Then, like a jigsaw puzzle, pieces that I did not realise existed began to slot into place. How did Eddie know I was at Ah Sing's? How did Eddie know I had started using again?

And there it was, smothering me, suffocating me, letting me know it was never far away from me, that they would always be my companions, those bitter waves of disappointment and betrayal that crashed upon my wretched soul. My furious eyes flashed upon Eddie and he flinched under their accusation.

"You had him follow me didn't you?"

"No, Mr. Eli, it was we who commanded Mr. Abberline to follow you, both of you." Victoria had spoken—she used a full sentence. Her majesty did not speak to anyone she did not think worthy of her attention. She spent her entire life suffering everyone else, including her own children whom she loathed and found inadequate in every conceivable way.

"Her Majesty knows, Eli," continued Abberline, his hand resting gently over the hilt of his gun. "Her Majesty knows everything." He held up a thick notebook in his other hand and I felt myself stiffen. Abberline knew what I was. Abberline knew the entire sorry story.

Victoria shot him a look more deadly than any bullet and he withered back into the soft embrace of the sofa like a scolded child. Then her steely gaze fell upon me, without fear, without hesitation, just determination and a resolve that I had rarely seen in a human. There stood the Commander of many nations, the supreme ruler of half the planet, and my god, standing before her penetrating gaze, I believed it. I had learned that the human spirit was an indomitable force, but Queen Victoria epitomised the very meaning of the word.

"This is our country, Mr. Eli. We are its queen and protector and it is our business to know when monsters walk amongst our subjects."

"And I have just saved your subjects and your land from

the real monsters," I said boldly, refusing to flinch beneath her stare, "and this is the thanks I get? To be followed? To have my every move scrutinised, like some criminal?" Eddie looked horrified. No one spoke back to Queen Victoria, ever. "And may I add," I continued, emboldened, "that by saving your land and your people from the *real* monsters, I also cleared your family name and prevented the scandal of the century."

I glared at Eddie, my words ringing their painful truth in his ears. If it were not for me, the history books would brand the Prince Royal a murderer for all eternity. And if it were not for me, Abberline would still be looking for a ruthless killer with the press demanding his resignation and his head on a silver platter.

Both of them looked horrified. Even Gideon looked uncomfortable.

As well he might.

"If you have quite finished, Mr. Eli?"

I was about to answer her back again, but she raised a hand and made a gesture as if to snatch the very words from my lips. To my utter amazement, she stepped forward until I could feel her breath against my cold flesh, and she met my eyes with her own unyielding gaze, not a flicker of fear in sight.

Now that was a woman filled with spunk. I liked her.

"Do not make the mistake of thinking us a fool, Mr. Eli, or that we do not know all that transpires in our jurisdiction. Outside of this room is an army of God-fearing men armed to the gills with the most modern up-to-date weapons. We do not know what it would take to destroy such a creature as you, but mark my words, and mark them well, when I say that one word from us and they will do all in their power to hunt you down. We will command the dissemination of your body throughout our great empire, buried so deep into the bowels of this great earth that even the hand of God could not reach them. Do we make ourselves quite clear?"

"Indeed you do, ma'am." What the fuck was I supposed to say to that? Bravo, queenie, bravo.

With dignity, grace, and perhaps a bit less like a Christmas pudding, Victoria resumed her stance in front of the fire.

"Yes, we are aware of what has transpired. We are also aware of the false claims erroneously made against one's grandchildren regarding the Ripper murders and the role you *both* played in reversing such slander." I risked a quick glance at Gideon, who looked as though he would throw up at any moment and I noted that Abberline was observing him closely as well. A shiver of fear flickered in my stomach. How much did the moustached detective know?

"It was my honour, Ma'am," I said meekly.

"Yes, Mr. Eli, it was. That is why you are standing before us now, for there is one more service that we would have you do for us."

Wow, Queenie wanted a favour from me. I was intrigued, and she had my full attention, but Abberline was flicking through his notes with manic purpose, and the sound of the rustling paper irritated me. I wanted to rip the pages from their binder and wipe his ass with them.

What did he know? What was in that bloody notebook?

"We wish to be made like you. We believe the correct term is to be..."

"Sired, Ma'am, the correct term is to be sired."

"Thank you, Inspector. We wish you to sire us."

Well fuck me seven ways to Sunday, I did not see that coming. I was numb, speechless, horrified, and outraged, all at the same time, a vortex of a mind fuck. Had the Queen of England just asked me to make her a vampire?

"Did you just ask me to make you a vampire?"

Victoria looked exasperated and scowled at Abberline. "Is this creature simple? Did we not just demand, in the plainest of English, our desire? Does he require the instruction in the written word?"

Eddie quickly interjected in an attempt to defuse her sudden mood swing.

"Eli, please, listen to her, there is a very good reason that she asks this of you, that *we* ask this of you."

"This I would like to hear!" I didn't mean my words to sound so scathing, but there it was. Eddie looked toward his grandmother pleadingly, and she gave him the slightest nod of encouragement.

"You see, Grandmamma is dying."

I had to sit down—information overload. I needed Ah Sing and three fat pills to send me on my merry little way into blissful oblivion. I didn't want to hear any more, I didn't want any part of that madness and I didn't want to understand or listen to the excuses laid out before me. I just wanted to run, away from her, away from Eddie, away from Gideon, away from London.

And away from that fucking book, which Abberline was flicking through again.

"Haven't I done enough?" That was the sound of the meek vampire again. But I felt the strands of inevitability pulling at me, dragging me toward my own helpless end.

Victoria looked at Abberline and he nodded. Her lips formed a tight line and I could tell her next words were difficult for her to articulate.

"It is our understanding that you and my grandson have done more than enough."

Eddie blanched under the barely concealed threat.

"Grandmamma..." She silenced him with a flick of her wrist.

"It is also our understanding Gideon has done more than

enough."

I turned around, my fears there for all to see, dripping from my cheeks unchecked. Gideon was gripping the back of a chair, his head bowed. When he looked at me it was with such sorrow, and that last little bit of me, that last little bit I was trying so hard to keep hold of, shattered.

"Now do you understand, Eli?" Gideon moaned, his eyes two circles of utter desperation. "This will never end, this will never go away, I cannot be with you anymore."

"Do I need to go on?" asked Abberline. I thought I detected a degree of sadness in his voice, that his queen should reduce him to blackmail, to spying. But I felt no pity for him. I had no pity left.

"No," I spat from between gritted teeth.

"It is because of this that we expect this service of you now." Victoria the resolute, Victoria the great protector, Victoria the vampire.

I felt nothing but disgust for all of them. At Abberline for being the coward that now lay revealed before me, at Eddie for having no balls to stand up to his grandmother and for betraying my trust, and at Gideon for putting me in that situation to begin with. But I was also angry with her, for demanding the impossible of me.

"And yet you would have me make you vampire."

Something about her changed. Her whole body seemed to sink, become smaller, as though she could no longer endure the burden resting upon her shoulders. Victoria's face softened and for the first time I saw a woman, a helpless, desperate woman, and more than that, I saw her pain.

"I have worked very hard all my life, Eli, to make this country the great nation that it now is." That was the first and only time I had ever heard her refer to herself in the first person. For some reason it touched me, the sincerity in her voice melting the anger from my tense body and I found myself hanging on her every word. "It was my dream and that of my dearly departed husband, that this country reach a peak of excellence that has never before been witnessed and that we build a Monarchy, a constitutional Monarchy built on strong moral values the people could be proud of and perhaps even love."

Abberline sat forward eagerly, his face a mask of undisguised adoration. "And you have, ma'am. This great nation—this Great Britain—is a power beyond all expectation. You are our industrious queen, our great benefactor, the mother of our nation."

Queen Victoria was made of steel and not a woman easily affected, but his little outburst, his little show of adulation must have stirred something deep in Victoria's soul, and for a moment, there was a smile, a small genuine kind little smile offered with gratitude and affection. It quickly disappeared, but I felt I had just witnessed a rare glimpse of the real woman that lay buried beneath the burden of duty.

"I am dying, Eli. The cancer that has so cruelly scythed through my family tree has ordained to taint me while there is still much work to achieve. While my doctors tell me I have barely a year left to me, I find this wholly unacceptable."

As I considered my measured reply, my gaze did not leave the book still clasped in the Inspectors fingers. Would he know if I lied? It was a risk, but I had to take it, to save myself from the horror laid before me.

"What you ask of me I cannot do. You cannot possibly understand the consequences of such action, what it would do to your royal personage."

She paused, and any mistaken kindness in her eyes blinked out. That great indomitable lady seemed to grow in stature before my very eyes, her face a blazing beacon of passion.

"We are Queen of Great Britain and half the known world, Mr. Eli. Do you think we would not have done our research? Do you really think us such a fool? You will allow us this gift, the gift of everlasting life, so that one may continue to serve."

And then I said the lie, with one eye on Abberline and his damn book.

"Everlasting life, is that what you think? You will be a monster, a mindless creature obsessed with nothing but drinking the lifeblood of those subjects you wish to serve. Do you think you will be like me? Like Gideon? No. You will never again see the light. You will never again be able to see your family. You ask me to take away your humanity — to turn you into some uncontrollable demon because that is what you will be... nothing but an animal."

Victoria glanced at Abberline and he squirmed nervously in his seat. The pudding gave him a commanding gesture, a flick of the hand that said a dozen commanding words, a flick of the hand that only royalty seem to master. With trembling fingers, he searched his notes and reluctantly began to speak.

"These are your words, Eli. *We are Menarche, Inspector, original beings.*" My eyes bore into him, my rage ripping into his brain, but he continued regardless. Not so much of a coward after all, I realised. He was simply more afraid of his queen than he was of me. I closed my eyes because I knew what was coming and I felt sick with the sheer horror of it. *"The sun does not know my mortal form any more than I do and so I am given the freedom of the day. But to sire another condemns them to everlasting darkness, for the sun recognises the mortal within and will burn away the demon to release the soul. But if my children were to sire, so far from my bloodline would they be as to be nothing but shadows, consumed by blood lust, feral beasts twisted out of all recognition. So you see, Ma'am, he could sire you and you would remain much as you are now."*

"What else have you got in there you little prick?" Without realising it, I was bearing down on his cowering form, my vampire partially revealed, and I could barely hold back my blinding outrage. I could smell the fear bursting out of Abberline's pores in great fat globules of terror. But again, he showed his mettle.

"Everything I have done, my duty for queen and country."

"Who gave you the right to document my every move?"

"We did, Mr. Eli." Victoria stepped forward and placed a surprisingly firm hand on my shoulder, and I realised with shock that my hands were around Abberline's neck.

I could so easily have snapped that fragile bone, one swift twist of my hands and his spine would have crumbled beneath my fingers. I looked into his wide terrified eyes, my teeth scraping against my chin. Anger always brought out the monster in me. But I had had my fill of death, of wasted lives and worse. So I backed off, removed my trembling hands from around his neck and squeezed myself into a ball on the floor, making myself as small as possible, terrified by what I had just done, fearful of what I might yet do.

Gideon watched the entire thing in silence—he didn't lift a finger to pull me away from Abberline. He just watched as I cowered on the floor. And I hated him for it.

"Why?" I looked at Gideon as I said it, but he just shook his head in a mixture of sadness and resignation. But Victoria answered.

"It is the price one pays for mixing with royalty, Mr. Eli. We all have files on us somewhere, files that contain useful information. Knowledge is power and power breeds control and we wish to have control, Mr. Eli, which brings me back to our command that you sire us."

"And you are prepared to feed off others to sustain yourself are you, to kill?" I heard the anger in my voice but I did not feel it. I did not feel anything.

"We are Gloriana! We already have a great deal of blood on our hands! We are born into this world of imbeciles and fools who would undo the great work we have started." She began to pace the floor, her voice becoming more and more impassioned. "Even our children disappoint, ugly ungrateful toads that suckled at our breast and failed even to be born with one ounce of decency, each one a depraved and dim-witted being unsuited to the life they were born into. My eldest grandson, Kaiser Wilhelm II, is of greatest concern to me, and I cannot find rest while such a threat raises its ugly head above this great country. Even our own government plots against us at every turn, and we will not scupper this ship and drown our people. No! We will not let this great and beautiful country fall because we have been tainted and marked for death, Mr. Eli. The vampire condition is not a luxury one desires to continue life, but a tool to build and maintain an empire."

Eddie looked embarrassed. A favourite of his Grandmamma, he was well aware of his parent's shortcomings and the distaste she held for her own children. But I had to admit the woman astounded me. It was a wonder to me she did not simply command the cancer to leave her body.

I unwound from the floor and perched on the edge of a chair, exhausted. I was fighting a losing battle and could see no way out of it.

"Okay, okay, I get it, you have unfinished business, believe me I do understand. But then what, when those around you start to grow old yet you remain on the throne, unchanging, ageless, how do you explain that one?"

She looked toward her favourite grandchild and Eddie stepped forward eagerly.

"Well you see, Grandmamma has already thought of that,

too. All she need do is stay *alive* long enough to see me ascend to the throne."

Jesus Christ. Was that constitutionally possible? More to the point, had that been Eddie's intention all along? Had everything I had been through in that god forsaken city been a ploy to get me to that point?

Betrayal, all around me, duplicity, by all those I knew, by all those I loved. I no longer knew what to believe, who to believe, who to trust, what was real and what was manipulation. Had all my long life on earth taught me nothing? Obviously, it had not.

More pain, yet more bitter disappointment, piling up and piling up, threatening to annihilate me under its crippling weight, anger crashing down and around me in huge crushing, unrelenting, tumultuous waves of agony. I could not see — there was nothing but darkness, the blinding blackness of total despair. I needed... no, I wanted... I wanted to kill somebody, anybody. Someone had to die.

"Sorry, old boy," chirped Eddie cheerfully. "Don't take it personally, you know how it is."

I wanted to smash his fucking face and suck his veins dry until he was nothing more than a wrinkled bag of putrefying shit.

"Yes, I do." I stood up, but fell straight back down, my legs trembling so much I could not control them. I clutched the armrests, partly to steady myself and partly so I had something to burrow my fingers into that did not consist of human flesh. "And what if I was to rip you all apart here and now, where will your fucking Monarchy be then?"

One word, which was all it took, one word to change everything, one word spoken by the queen of half the known world.

"Mary."

I looked up just in time to see Gideon pick up a golden

chair and slam it against the wall, shattering its gilded spindles into so much tinder. His face rippled with his vampire as he struggled to contain his anger. His huge beefy fists pounded into the wall, piercing the fabric, cracking the plaster beneath it into dust. Abberline was on his feet, his pistol outstretched in his trembling hands while Eddie screamed.

He was always such a man.

"I assume those are not... the only records," I whispered between gritted teeth.

"You assume correctly, Sir," stuttered Abberline, the gun shaking so much in his hands that it was a wonder it did not fall apart in his grasp.

It was not my fault. Mary was not my fault. The Whitechapel murders were not my fault. I had to keep telling myself that, I had to keep believing that. I had to believe my insane obsession with becoming part of the human race had not led me to that terrible inevitability, that my desire to be accepted, to become involved in some meaningful way had not led me to that treachery. Surely that was not the meaning of being human.

"Enough!" Gideon stopped and glared at Victoria, his eyes black as the night sky, his teeth long and dangerous, ravaging his lower lips so that blood flowed freely down his chin. But the vampire could not disguise his sadness, or mask the dreadful loneliness that had long since claimed his heart. My Gideon was gone, forever, nothing left but a shell. He was a shell crushed by the overbearing weight of his own secrets and lies.

And I could do nothing to help him. How could I, when he would not let me into his life? How could I when he kept so much from me? How could I when I did not even know him?

The room spun around me. I was hungry and I was

frightened. Just when I thought my life could not get any worse, just when I thought I had nothing left to take away, that day happened. I lay ragged, decimated in a pool of deception.

"Leave us," commanded Victoria. I felt Eddie's hands brush my shoulders, the gentlest of touches, but I did not look at him, I could not bear to see his lying cunt of a face. I would never see him again. Three years later, on 14 January 1892, Prince Albert Victor — Eddie — died of influenza.

The smell of blood hit my nostrils in unrelenting waves of lust. To most, the smell of blood was like iron, a sickly, sticky metallic tang that instantly screamed blood. To me, I smelled life. I could almost see each individual cell, wrapped in insubstantial memory, a glimpse, a hint of all that the donor experienced, a liquid emotion, a living sea of flimsy experience and uncontrolled thoughts. Blood, for the shortest of moments, filled me with life. It invaded every molecule of my being. It made me a warm living thing. It made me human. And then instantly it was gone and I was vampire again. It was the best of feelings and the worst of feelings, a torture of passions.

Queen Victoria sat on the edge of the sofa holding up a bloodied wrist. She clutched a small golden letter opener in her one hand, while the other dripped blood wastefully onto the Persian carpet.

"We do not know how this is done, Mr. Eli, but we presume it starts with blood?" The lady's mettle was bleeding out.

"Why don't you consult your notes, Abberline?" I might have reached the lowest ebb of my existence, but I was still a smartass.

"Ah... well actually..." he stammered. "You never talked about that bit."

I shot him my best fuck-off look. My teeth sliced into my

lips as I spoke. "I want him out!" I was struggling to control my hunger—all I could see was the blood pouring from her wound, and it was driving me insane.

"Abberline stays. He will be of use to us if this plan is to succeed." So said the fucking queen.

I approached her wrist, my fingers creeping through the air before me toward her gash, my lips parting from my gums, my vampire fully aroused. Was that fear I saw beneath her eyes? Was that a flicker of doubt?

The blood filled my mouth and I drank deep. Blossoms of life bloomed behind my eyes, exploding into the next image before my mind could reconcile the experience. Her life, nothing but a jumble of duty and sadness, disappointment mixed with the bitter aftertaste of grief.

Welcome to my world.

Not many humans had experienced as much as she had in their lifetimes. All her life had been moving inexorably toward that throne, an unloved child, forbidden to experience the joy of being a child, a young woman who lived by the rule of duty and expectation, the adult who gave so much of herself and lost so much more when Albert died, her one true love. A life filled with so much pain and very little joy, a life of complete dedication.

It overwhelmed me.

With a scream, I pulled away, collapsing against a chair, blood spilling over my chin, her blood, Queen Victoria's blood. Abberline was shouting at me, shouting at me to complete the transformation, but all I could do was stare at her limp body lying across his lap, her life ebbing away, to be absorbed into the carpet like my tears.

Someone was crouching before me, slapping my face, calling my name.

"Eli, Eli! Wake up man, pull yourself together." My eyes began to focus and I saw him, my love, my reason to exist, my Gideon, my liar.

My lips trembled as tears spilled from my eyes. "Take me away from all this death."

"Finish it. You must finish it, now, before she dies." I felt his hand rip open my shirt then a sharp pain as his nail sliced into my chest. I moved without intention, his hands pushing me toward the dying Monarch.

"What... are you... doing?" I groaned as he guided her head toward the bleeding wound on my chest.

"Drink, drink deep," he shouted. "Let her drink, Eli. You must start it..." I thought he said something else then, something like *and I will finish it,* but I could not be certain, my world was spinning too much.

I had never had a woman suckle at my breast. And I never wanted to experience a woman sucking me off again. I knew I was making the wildest of faces, and to a fool like Abberline those expressions must have seemed like ecstasy. It sounded like I was shooting my load. God only knew that I was making enough noise. In truth, it was repulsive and deeply uncomfortable to have my life sucked out of my tit by an old woman whose idea of personal hygiene consisted of a quick fanny wipe of a morning. I had only ever experienced bloodletting during the throes of a fuck, culminating in the most fantastic orgasm, whereas this experience was seriously threatening to culminate in vomit.

"Enough!" I pulled her head away from me with as much force as I dared without breaking her neck. The dirty bitch had pissed herself so I knew the change was about to begin. Her body would purge all that was human and soon she would be filling her knickers with shit.

"Get out!" bellowed Gideon. I stared at him, confused. "Leave. Leave London and don't come back. Ever."

Gideon pulled something out of his inside jacket pocket, a beautifully engraved golden flask. He hastily uncapped it and pushed the open flask into Victoria's mouth.

"What the fuck are you doing?" I could not understand what I was seeing, what he was making her drink. But the explosion of rage that erupted from his lips was clear enough.

"Get out! Get the fuck out! Get out and don't come back!"

"But he can't leave, what about her?" pleaded Abberline, his face white as a sheet as he clung to the mantelpiece for dear life.

"That's your problem," I hollered, "and she will need feeding. Put that in your fucking book."

The last I saw of Queen Victoria, she was flapping like a stranded fish, strewn across a gilded sofa with shit and piss running down her legs.

The last I saw of Gideon, he was screaming at me to leave as he forced something down Victoria's throat.

The last I saw of Abberline, he was clutching the marble fireplace with shit and piss running down his legs.

That night I left Buckingham Palace and lost myself in the foggy streets of London. I was nothing, a mindless creature filled with rage, a lost soul in torture, a monster that knew no control, a monster lost to the cravings of death.

Chapter Five: The Body in the Woods

"Well, do not leave out a single detail now will you, no matter how superfluous," bemoaned Mal in astonishment. I thought I detected a little exasperation curling up at the sides of Daniyyel's plump lips, or it could have been gas, one could never tell with an angel. Daniyyel always kept his cards close to his wings.

"He asked me a question and I answered it, in my own inimitable way." That little remark made the angel smirk, though he quickly tried to conceal it.

"Remind me never to ask *you* a simple question!"

"There is nothing simple about the questions Daniyyel asks," I replied curtly, "when you are finally asked the question, that is." God how I loved my mouth, so sharp, so fucking kissable.

"Your time will come, old friend." Daniyyel chuckled playfully then my stomach exploded with an indignant gurgle of hunger.

"I need to eat, I'm bloody starving. That German twat knocked the shit out of me. Speaking of which, what do you intend to do with him?"

Mal threw up his hands in a queenie huff and began to float around our heads flapping.

"Questions, questions, questions. Why are you asking me so many questions? Really, is there any need? I cannot cope with any more questions."

"Get your fat ass down here and stop behaving like it's none of your concern. You brought him here, so you can bloody well deal with him."

"My bum is not fat," he pouted. "My cheeks are firm and bouncy, like a trampoline and tight, so tight my bum bangs shut when I go for a number two. And as for Mr. Stud Muffin downstairs, I do not know. What would you like me to do? He was your present, after all." He floated back into his chair, his lips tight and his arms folded. If he had been solid, I would have slapped him.

"Bum? Would it hurt you to say the word ass?" I was laughing. I couldn't help myself. Daniyyel covered his mouth with a fist and turned away quickly, unable to conceal his amusement.

"I do not swear—I use the English language as it was intended to be used, properly. And I have not the faintest idea what to do with him."

"Well we can't let him go—he'll come back with all his Gestapo buddies." The Germans stationed at the other end of the valley knew nothing of Alte or my presence, and I intended to keep it that way. Their steel-toed boots would play havoc with my marble floor.

"Oh, perish the thought," crooned Mal wistfully. I shot the dirty fucker a killer look, but he shrugged it off as though we should all have been thinking the same thing.

Perish the thought.

"Well he can't stay here indefinitely. You brought him here, you deal with him."

Mal's eyes narrowed and he brought his little pinkie finger up to the corner of his mouth.

"Well, you did say you were... hungry."

"No. Oh no. No, no, no and hell no. What if he dies while I'm drinking? You've already fucked him up with that possession trick of yours. I would rather chew off my own tit than he kick it under my roof. Not gonna happen."

"Why? Afraid he will haunt you?" Mal could be a right

twat at times.

Silence. Death by evil stare. Dismemberment by crushing eyebrow.

"Vampire mind trick, anybody?"

We both snapped our heads around to look at Daniyyel. He was clever as well as beautiful. How horny.

"I'm not going back down there to perform some mind fuck while he has that bloody thing around his neck. One torment by burning a day is enough, thank you very much."

"You will be strong enough, once you have fed. As for his faith, well, that is a fear you need to overcome. To have faith in oneself is almost as powerful as ones faith in God. You are the one with the problem, not God."

Angels, they were always working, never any down time.

"Will you still be here when I get back?" I wanted him to say no, but part of me also wanted him to stay. He looked so good at my table. But trouble followed that angel, something that came with the job description, but when he was around, I always seemed to lose something. And I had nothing left to give.

"Yes." That was that, then. "I would rather like to see how things transpire with this soldier, professional curiosity you understand."

Fucking fabulous, that was all I needed, an angel watching my every move.

"And you," I said pointing my finger at Mal, "behave. Play nicely with our German guest." Mal pointed at his own chest, his face agog with a look of shocked innocence and I shook my head in exasperation. How did you solve a problem like Malachi?

March was a stunning time of year in the valley. The first half so icy, bitterly cold, but the latter half always promised summer, all bright sparkling sunshine and momentary glimpses of warmth. A fluffy dusting of snow blanketed the valley in a sheet of picture perfect whiteness, but not deep enough that the struggling bulbs of a rapidly approaching spring could not push their welcome colour through its surface. Trees for miles around wore their winter coats with elegance, a sea of toilet brush pines dusted with icing, and nothing gave me more pleasure than to soar over their majestic spires.

It was an odd sensation, flying. It started with a kind of itch, a tingle up and down my spine that centred between my shoulder blades. It ended with a pull, an irresistible tug that lifted me skyward and gentle as you like, my feet would leave the ground and I would be soaring upward, my hands outstretched to clutch the heavens, unfettered by all that was mortal.

I had never met another who could fly. No other vampire, no other Menarche. It was mine and mine alone.

I moved so fast I become a blur, indistinguishable from the bitter wind that tried and failed to bite my skin. Past forests and lakes, past mountains and rivers, the world was a smear beneath my feet. Not even the falling snow had time to settle on my immortal brilliance. I rivalled the sun and the moon and even the stars bowed down.

At least they should have.

The smell of blood hit me so hard I came to a sudden stop, a sonic boom ricocheting off my marble hard body. Death filled my nostrils with its rancid stench, mingled with the sour stale reek of blood long spilled, intoxicating, delicious, so strong it nearly knocked me out of the sky. I closed my eyes to concentrate, turning slowly in the air, feeling the aroma, letting it fill me, letting it guide me. And then I had it. The scent was thrumming through my body like a musical note and I plummeted from the sky, a burning comet, pulled inexorably toward the source of my impending pleasure. Gripping the top of a spruce, I spun down its trunk in a helter-skelter of splintering branches and needles until I reached the frozen earth, landing gracefully on all fours.

God I was good.

So dense grew the trees that the snow had barely kissed the earth beneath their protective canopy, so the human detritus that surrounded me lay exposed and naked to the elements. Like a wound carved into the forest floor, a wound of human devastation, open and festering.

Sadness overwhelmed me and my eyes stung with frozen grief. I was a predator, I fed to survive, but I respected life, human life in all its diverse fragility, I aspired to it, I was even jealous of it. So the sight that assaulted my eyes hurt at a most profound level. It made me sick.

Crude, makeshift shelters woven from old clothes and branches created a frost encrusted web between the closely packed trees, underneath which lay shallow trenches, inadequately camouflaged with leaves and twigs, dark muddy spaces barely capable of concealing a man. Muddied, blood stained clothes and discarded belongings lay scattered in the mud, books, reading glasses, cutlery, plates, even items of jewellery, claimed by the hungry earth, lost and forgotten. It disturbed me.

Bodies, riddled with bullet wounds, lay scattered across the ground, left to rot where they fell. Some lay half concealed by the makeshift shelters, hands and arms outstretched, pleading in death, frozen into lifeless lumps of discarded meat. But the one corpse, the one broken soul that demanded my attention, tore at my sanity with merciless fingers, mocking my love for mankind. He was kneeling in the mud, arms hanging uselessly by his side, half his head missing and what that poor bastard must have gone through in that final moment of his death revolted me. Did he feel the metal of the gun against his skin? Did he feel the heat of the gun as it discharged its deadly payload? Did he feel that bullet rip into his flesh and tear his head in half? The desperation, the futility of knowing that death was at hand, the terror that must have gripped him in those last seconds overwhelmed me.

I had to turn away, and when I did, my eyes fell upon a completely new form of Hell. I froze. My body convulsed. My lips opened to give rise to the scream of horror that blossomed there. My fingers clamped around my face like a vice, shielding my eyes from the nauseating sight before me, forcing my agonised scream back down my throat, afraid to let the sound out for fear the world would hear my cry. I wanted to sink to my knees and pound the earth beneath my angry fists, but I dared not, I could not, for fear of accidentally touching them, desecrating them, the dead mutilated children that lay at my feet.

A circle of dead adults surrounded the broken, infantile bodies in a corona of death, like an obscene flower, opening its grotesque petals to a disbelieving world. The adults had tried to enclose the children, to protect them against the hail of bullets that tore their lives away, but they failed, cut in half by the cruelty of man.

Blood, intestines, indiscriminate body parts, frozen into ruby nuggets, glittered maliciously in the cruel light of day. The image burned itself into my brain and I wanted to tear my eyes from my skull, to spare myself the torture of their dead faces. But no one spared the children.

Then I saw it, the thing that made me rage against the world. An old woman holding the hand of a dead child, their fingers desperately intertwined in a last futile gesture of comfort, stomachs ripped open, faces staring blankly into a heaven that did nothing to prevent the travesty of their deaths.

I wept. My tears howled down my cheeks in rolling torrents of grief, I lifted my head toward the sky and I bellowed my fury toward God.

But God didn't answer. God never did.

Was that the humanity I aspired to? The same humanity I worked so hard to protect, losing everything in the process. Did I really want to be one of them, just another type of monster?

I heard a sound. A moan, a sigh so weak that at first I thought it was the wind grieving for the dead. Then it came again, stronger, desperate. How could anybody survive amid such devastation? I turned and listened, grateful to avert my eyes from the abomination behind me, scanning the carnage that littered the forest floor.

I picked my way through the debris, my keen eyes searching for the slightest movement, but all I saw was bits of lives trodden into the bloodied mud. My boot kicked something that glittered, a book. The beautifully embellished bindings showed signs of great age, the leather cracked and worn with use and startlingly blue gemstones pierced the intricate gold surface. It was a Tanakh, a Hebrew Bible. The dead that littered the floor were Jews. Then I saw a bundle of books strung together with cord, yellowed pages sticking out all over the stack. I reached toward it, curious.

Suddenly a hand gripped my ankle. My blood froze in my veins and it was all I could do to contain the scream that threatened to burst from my lips. I swallowed the offending sound with a resounding gulp and hunkered down, removing bits of wood and cloth from atop the ditch until I began to reveal a man and when I looked upon his face, something inside me snapped.

Centuries of men, in countless positions, I had had them all. And strapping examples of the species they were too, most of them. We were all entitled to the odd, drunken mistake. But the creature that lay before me, half buried in filth, was unlike anything I had seen before. Not even Daniyyel could rival his beauty. He was so beautiful it hurt my eyes.

I fell back, suddenly afraid, his huge emerald-green eyes burning with pain, beseeching me not to leave him in that shallow grave. The sight of him shocked me, my world was in a spin, that perfect muscular physique so familiar, yet there lay before me a total stranger. That face, the high cheekbones, the mouth voluptuous and plump beneath a perfectly judged nose, the chin with its deep chiselled cock rest and I knew if I ran my fingers through that closely cropped, black-brown hair, I would recognise it.

I was losing it. I had never seen him in all my long life and yet he was as familiar to me as the sight of my own trembling hands before my disbelieving eyes. Memories stirred and long withered emotions exploded across my reeling brain, I should have run, away from that forest, away from him, but I didn't, I couldn't.

I crawled toward him, my fingers reaching toward his body, and before I knew what I was doing, my fingernails were digging him out of the trench. As more and more hard flesh revealed itself, my digging became more frantic. My skin brushed against the bulging mass of his arms and a thrill of excitement shivered through my body, but then, as I ladled out great handfuls of muck from his torso, I gasped. Beneath my hands lay a beautifully defined chest, so very smooth, with plump pink nipples that stood out rock hard in the bitter cold. And his stomach was a thing of exquisite artistry, rock hard and rippled to perfection.

I was in a swoon. The world vanished around me and all I could see was beauty. I wanted to touch him. I wanted to run my fingers all over the hardness of his muscles. I wanted to taste his flesh against the tip of my tongue, lose myself in the massiveness of his arms. I belonged to him and he belonged to me. All my existence had led to that point, inexplicably toward him, to that Adonis in the mud.

"Please," he gasped, raising goose pimples on my flesh at the sound of his deep, rich voice. "Please... don't hurt me anymore."

Something stabbed at my chest. Was that sympathy I felt? Eww.

"Don't try to speak, save your energy, big boy. Can you show me where you're hurt?" I called him big boy. I was doomed.

I felt his pain as his hand moved downward, slowly and with great effort, beneath his incredible body, only to reappear smeared with blood. The smell of it filled my nostrils. I could taste the blood in the back of my throat and I pulled my hands into my chest, my elongated fingernails cutting into my flesh. I was so hungry. I backed up, terrified of the hunger burning my face, but all I could see was his bloodied hand reaching out, thick red thirst-quenching goodness dripping from his fingers, falling wasted to the ground.

"Shot," he whispered.

Trying desperately to ignore the smell of his blood, I began to dig him out with renewed zeal, pulling his torso and legs out of his own shit and filth. The smell was so malodorous as to make me wince, and although I had a strong constitution, the sight of the stuff squelching between my fingers and embedding itself beneath my fingernails nearly made me wretch.

With a sickening wet sound, his body finally broke free of the earth. A cry of agony burst from between his perfect lips and his head fell back against my shoulder. I felt his long eyelashes brush against my neck as his eyes flickered in defiance of the blackness trying to consume him.

"Stay with me fella, stay with me, we'll be home in a jiffy."

Home, back to my castle, what the fuck was I thinking? I was out of my little fucking mind. I didn't know the man. I owed him nothing. I had an angel in my dining room and a German soldier in my dungeon, and to top things off, I lived with a ghost. Yet I still wanted to take him home? No, I was intent on taking him home, I had decided that the moment I saw him.

But why? Why should I get involved? Why should I tread that path again, the path that could only lead to pain? It always did. And yet, as I held him in my arms I felt it, something inescapable, something I could not understand, a stirring, a feeling, like something found when all hope of ever finding it had been forgotten. Something complicated.

A tingle of warning trickled up and down my spine making my hair stand on end. I lowered the hunk to the ground, slowly, carefully and whispered into his perfectly shaped ear. "Remain quiet."

In a flash of lightning speed, I leaped into a tree, clinging with one hand to a thick branch while my legs wrapped around its thick girth. Someone was out there, and not just *Mr. Fuck Me He's Perfect*. The smell of human, living heart pumping human was unmistakable, that incomparable odour carried on the wind to entice my nostrils and excite my senses, and I was dutifully excited. But there was something else there too, a feint undercurrent, an elusive aftertaste that went beyond sweat and skid marks, an elusive scent that pricked at my memory, the smell of demon.

I saw him then, a German soldier winding his way through the field of corpses. His uniform, a grey-green *feldbluse* replete with bottle green collar and shoulder straps, made him almost invisible amongst the branches and the sludge. I could not see his face beneath his field cap but I could easily make out the eagle and swastika emblem embroidered on the bottle green cloth and I noted with disgust the Sturmgewehr semi-automatic rifle hanging loosely from his shoulder.

The Nazi stood barely six metres away from my injured future husband. *Do not move, lovely man,* I said to myself, *do not move, and don't make a sound and if you can, be still your beating heart,* because to me it sounded like a jackhammer pounding through the forest. He was frightened and in pain. His eyes darted everywhere looking for me, desperate for me, pleading for me to drag him out of that Hell.

I saw the agony flash across his face before the sound escaped his lips. My entire body tensed. Too late, the soldier heard his pain.

He was running then, running toward my Adonis in the pit. Without hesitation, I soared through the air and landed with feline grace before him. The soldier fell backward with a bloodcurdling scream. The rifle landed at my feet and I picked it up, rising to my full magnificent height, slowly and with purpose, relishing every moment of fear that blossomed across the soldier's white features. I snapped the weapon as easily as if it were a twig and threw the shattered weapon at his feet, watching with satisfied relish as he scrabbled backward in the mud, his mouth curling away from his face as his terror burst from his throat.

"Demon! You are not from the camp. What are you?"

My teeth extended and my eyes flashed black. My vampire was out. In one swift movement, barely visible to the human eye, I leaped at him, pulling him off the floor with effortless ease, lifting his flailing body high above my head. I threw him with all my might at the nearest tree. His spine snapped with an audible bang as his fragile body wrapped itself backward around the trunk of the trembling pine, his lifeless body sliding to the ground and my stomach rumbled. Dinner was served.

Blood flowed gently down his forehead from a ragged gash, but without a beating heart to quicken the flow, the blood would soon congeal. Bending low, I licked the rivulet, savouring its warm taste, its iron rich life coating my eager tongue.

Bang!

I heard the sound before I felt the pain. I saw my flesh rip open on my shoulder, a tulip of blood and skin and eject the bullet before I felt it enter my back. The shock and the impact made me fall forward over my dinner and his blood smeared thickly across my face.

I knew the wound would heal almost instantly and the pain was nothing but a momentary discomfort. But that was not the point. My shirt was ruined. I liked that shirt.

I turned around slowly, angry with myself for missing the second assailant. That would teach me for showing off. The uniformed lump of shit stood before me, his hands trembling uncontrollably, threatening to shake the smoking rifle from his unsteady grip. The rifle fired a second time but the bullet whizzed past my head, close enough for me to feel the heat of the projectile against my cheek.

I snarled at the Nazi, my true self revealed before his terrified eyes. I was a nightmare wrapped in flesh, long chin, high cheekbones, no hair, pointy ears, eyes black as pitch and teeth glistening like swords against my chin. I could feel my talons pushing their way out of my elongating fingers, vicious extensions of my hands, itching to rip human flesh to shreds.

That was the real me, the warrior me, my vampire.

Before he could turn and run, I was at his throat. My long spindly fingers held his head to one side and he was powerless to move, lest his neck crack like an eggshell. I ran one slender finger along a well-defined crease in the fold of his skin and watched, hypnotised as blood floated gently to the surface. My forked tongue, eager and hungry, slithered from between my lips and lapped it up, savouring the appetiser. The bastard needed to live while I fed—I wanted him to feel every drop of blood leave his system, I wanted him to feel his veins shrivel within his body and I wanted to hear his heartbeat wither and die in my ears. With a slight twist of his head, I lowered my mouth toward his exposed neck. The tips of my teeth touched goose-pimpled flesh and slowly they pierced the skin with a gentle pop. He sighed in exquisite ecstasy. My lips caressed the wound as blood pumped freely into my eager mouth and I closed my eyes as the orgasm of blood filled my body. My cock was hard against his back and I thrust it purposefully against his carcase, gyrating hard as his blood pumped fierce and hot into the back of my throat. He did not struggle—he had no fight left, just a breathless acquiescence to my hunger. As the life began to slip from his body, I closed my eyes, then his body shuddered with a last involuntary orgasm and a groan hissed between his blue lips. I let out my own moan as I reached my very own little pleasure.

I killed him. I broke my own rule. And I didn't care.

I let his empty body fall to the ground, licking the thick red blood from my lips and my teeth, savouring the final drops against my tongue. I opened my eyes.

The Adonis was staring up at me. He had witnessed everything.

Chapter Six: Ethan

The look on their faces as I walked through the door carrying my backpack of muscle was fucking priceless.

"Hi honey, I'm home."

"What? Do they provide takeout now? Who is that?"

"Lap it up, Mal—you're not the only one who gets to bring home a guy." Sarcasm, I loved it. "He's hurt. I need hot water, clean blankets, anything you can find to clean him up—oh, and we will be in your bedroom."

"My bed?" I knew he would like that bit.

"Yes, your bed. You don't bloody use it anyway, so put your newfound touchy feely thing to use and find something to clean him up." He just stood there, open mouthed, eyes popping out of his see-through skull. "Move, Mal. He is going to die unless we do something, and no one is dying in my house tonight."

I hurried up the marble staircase, vaguely aware of Daniyyel's gaze following my every move.

"What is that smell?" he said as I swept past him.

"Demon. Now be an angel and give me a hand." Something about his face disturbed me, and I knew instantly something was awry. I knew that look. But without a sound, the right hand of God slipped by me on the stairs to open the door leading to Malachi's room, and I felt the air surrounding me swirl and undulate as his invisible wings brushed against my cheek. It was a sharp reminder of what he was.

I could feel the man in my arms slipping away. I could

feel his life force draining from his veins. I could hear his heart falter as it struggled to beat. His flesh burned with fever. And all the time, Daniyyel could not tear his gaze away from him, and there was darkness in those eyes, a darkness that made the floor of my stomach churn with trepidation, for I had seen it before, in another time, in another place.

"I know that look, what are you keeping from me, angel?"

"Don't, Eli."

"There are demons in the valley! I smelled them. Those Nazi bastards stank of monster." My anger meant nothing to him, to the angel, but the shadow of death hung heavy in my heart and I could not stomach any more. "Bit of a coincidence that you should turn up and then him? Who is he, Daniyyel, why do I feel so... so drawn toward him? Why are there demons in the valley?"

"I don't know any more than you do, Eli." He was so calm, so pokerfaced, so fucking patronising.

"Liar, you know what's going on, you always do. You did in London and you do now. And I'm sick of it. Why won't you tell me the truth for once, Daniyyel, please?"

"I can't, Eli." His sadness fell upon deaf ears, for my bitterness had made me impervious to such emotion and I was so angry with him, so very angry.

"I have brought these," Mal declared cheerfully as he floated in carrying a pitcher of water and a stack of fresh sheets. He stopped instantly when he saw me glowering at Daniyyel. "Do I detect an atmosphere?"

"We need bandages and something to close up the wound," I snapped ungratefully. My gaze burrowed into Daniyyel with deadly intent, but he refused to meet my gaze. Gingerly, Malachi walked around and placed the items down at the side of the bed, then stood there looking at us, waiting for the next round. "Now, Malachi."

"Yes, yes, no need to shout for heaven's sakes... oops, sorry, Daniyyel. What did your last slave die of?"

"You're already dead!" I shouted after him as he drifted out.

"Again with the reminder, do I look like I need reminding? No. Do I know I am dead? Yes. And I am not the only one," he sang and I buried my face in my hands and rubbed my tired flesh, determined not to smirk. When I turned around, Daniyyel was leaning over the bed sniffing my unconscious man.

"What the fuck?"

Abruptly, Daniyyel spun around, his face alive and alert. "I have to go."

"What? Are you serious?" I was dumbfounded. "Help him. Use your angel mumbo jumbo. Do something."

"You know I will not, that I cannot do that. I am not here to interfere, merely to observe."

"But he could die!"

"If it is God's will that he die, then who am I to intervene?"

"You hypocritical bastard." I called an angel a bastard, not one of my best moments. My body trembled with rage, but to my dismay, my lips would not stop moving. "Then send me a fucking angel who will. What fucking good are you to me?"

"There will come a day, Eli, when you will regret those words."

I was regretting them already, but his apathy sickened me. What use was a Heaven that would not help those in need? I was beginning to think I was not ready for the question, not because I wasn't ready for Heaven, but because Heaven wasn't ready for me. That sort of bollocks would not fly with me.

"Do you even like humans?" And still my mouth flapped.

"I beg your pardon?"

I had struck a nerve—I saw it in the way his head snapped toward me.

"Because you don't seem to give a shit about them. How many lie dead in that forest, Daniyyel? How many did your God allow to die? Do you consider them less than yourselves, is that why? Is that why you let them die? Do you consider all of us lesser beings? That's it isn't it, that's why you won't ask me the question."

"Do not test me, vampire."

I shivered. His steely tone made the hairs stand up on the back of my neck, but I continued to push.

"Then put your fucking wings where your mouth is and do some bloody good in this world instead of letting us *lesser beings* clean up your shit for you!" I was on a roll.

"You cannot know what you say."

"No, because you won't tell me!" Silence filled the void between us and it was excruciating. Disappointment stung my eyes and fouled the back of my throat with its aftertaste. "If you won't help, then perhaps you should go." I turned my back on him, on the one being who could smite me on the spot, Menarche or no Menarche. I felt him touch me as he moved, a gentle brush of his hand across my arm, his glory radiating through my skin, making me shudder, but I refused to look at him.

"Do not forget who and what I am, Eli." His words were gentle, but not without an undercurrent of warning.

"Don't worry, you never let me forget." The sharpness in my voice made him pause, but I still couldn't look at him.

"We all have rules by which we are *expected* to live by, Eli and it is my hope that one day, you will see that and understand."

"And maybe one day, you will understand that..." I felt the tremble of each word upon my lips and my vision blurred with the pain of it. "... that rules are meant to be broken."

"But by a better man than me."

The tear tumbled down my cheek, icy cold against my skin. With a crump of wind that ruffled the back of my hair, Daniyyel departed.

"It occurred to me that the soldier in our dungeon may have a first aid kit on him, and bless my soul, I was right." Mal breezed triumphantly into the room but stopped abruptly when he saw me surreptitiously wiping my eyes. "What on earth is wrong with you? And where is the winged wonder?"

I snatched the little box out of Mal's hand. "He's gone, and I don't want to talk about it. How is your friend doing down there?" I was eager to move away from the subject of the angel.

To be fair, even Mal knew when not to push it, and he settled instead for one of his deeply concerned looks. "He is sleeping like a baby. Whatever Daniyyel did, it certainly tired him out."

"Good. Make sure you feed him when he wakes up."

"I will. So how is your new friend doing?" This he said with only the slightest hint of sarcasm, by way of consideration toward my bruised feelings. Bless him.

"He's alive, but barely. There were so many dead, Mal, so many butchered." I was exhausted, even my voice sounded knackered.

"Go and take a shower."

"He needs to be washed and his wound needs to be treated."

"I will see to that. Shower. Now. You stink. And throw that shirt away."

"I liked that shirt." I glanced down sadly at the bloodied tear in my shoulder.

"Darling. Purple. Really?"

"I like purple. What's wrong with purple?"

"You look like a beetroot. Go. Now. Clean oneself."

The shower certainly woke me up. Icy cold knives poured down onto my tortured flesh and I scrubbed my body hard to rid myself of the smell of death that permeated every pore. The soap felt good against my skin and I raised my eyes unto the heavens to let the purifying rain wash away the strain that tightened my hard muscles.

I had made the shower myself. It was quite simple really. A large sprinkler head salvaged from an old watering can suspended above my old dented copper bath connected to lengths of lead piping that snaked their way up through the ceiling into an insulated water tank on the roof made up my creation. The metal belly collected nothing but rainwater and it was bitterly cold, but I didn't care. The cold didn't bother me anyway.

Alte had no mirrors in her rooms—what was the point, when I could not see my own gorgeousness reflected back at me? Further evidence of God's revulsion toward the vampire was never more apparent than when one stood in front of a mirror. He was too ashamed of us to allow us a reflection. So I had to make do with the knowledge that whatever I wore, I would look good.

I had heard it said that clothes maketh the man, but I say I maketh the clothes.

With a little application of wax to my luscious hair and a generous slather of moisturiser to my face—a man should always moisturise—I was ready to face the world.

The stranger lying in the bed looked all the more delicious clean. The crisp white bed linen made him look healthier than I knew him to be, the flush of fever in his cheeks giving him a deceptively healthy glow. I stood in the doorway, quiet, watching, looking at Mal, who sat in an old leather

Chesterfield chair, perched on its edge, his eyes drinking in the muscles bulging beneath the sheets. I found that I was jealous of those eyes and it took me by surprise.

"How nice to see you looking half decent."

Mal's voice startled me, I had not realised he had seen me. "Only half? How's he doing?"

"The bullet went straight through, which is lucky for him. There was iodine in the medical kit and dressings, so I cleaned out the wound and closed it. I have given him one of these tablets, it should reduce his temperature." He tossed me a little bottle, which I caught deftly in one hand.

"Halazone... Halazone!" I laughed. I held my stomach and I laughed. Mal's heavy eyebrows knitted together as he scowled with indignation, so I laughed some more.

"Do share the joke before it kills you."

"Halazone, it's used as a purifying treatment for drinking water out in the field."

For a moment, Mal looked crestfallen, but then a wide glorious smirk split his face in two with a radiant grin.

"At least his urine will be clean." He laughed until tears streamed down his cheeks. Trust Mal to make a pissing joke.

"Here, give me that pouch." I emptied the small khaki packet onto the edge of the bed and marvelled at its contents. One packet of field dressing remained sealed tightly in a little cocoon of cellophane. There was a small bottle of Frazer's solution for the treatment of Athletes foot, a common and surprisingly debilitating infection when in the wet sodden trenches and Atabrine for treating Malaria and worms. Last, but most importantly, a bottle of Sulfadiazine tablets, a strong antibiotic to reduce the infection and temperature raging through his veins. I fed him two tablets, gently forcing them between his teeth followed by a few drops of water. As I laid his head back onto the pillow he whispered something, his cracked lips parting with great effort, a whispered thank you, then he sank once more into the welcoming arms of sleep.

"What was wrong with Daniyyel? Why did he leave?"

"You would have to ask him. See if he will give *you* a straight answer."

"He upset you."

"He... disappointed me. Daniyyel is not the man I thought he was." My voice could not have been more cutting if my tongue were made of glass.

Mal glided to my side and placed a wraithlike hand upon my weary shoulder. I could barely feel him, like a sigh against my flesh, but I felt the sentiment and the comfort it implied, and I was grateful for it.

"I sometimes think, my friend, you carry too much on those shoulders of yours. I wish you could let it go."

As I looked into his pale watery eyes, I wanted to tell him. I wanted to tell him everything. I wanted to let it go. But there had been enough pain that day.

"Go and see to your guest downstairs, he must be starving," I said gently, offering him my most reassuring smile and I hoped somewhere in my expression, he saw the thank you that lay unspoken within it.

I sat in that worn chair next to the bed and stared into the face of my mysterious stranger. No matter how much I looked at him the feeling persisted, the undeniable attraction, the inescapable feeling that he meant something to me—that he was going to be important. My stomach flipped with uncertainty and dread, a falling sensation in the pit of my bowels that was telling me I should run, run away before it was too late.

But his face, such a beautiful face. It captivated me, demanding my attention. His high chiselled cheekbones, the soft unblemished brow nestled beneath hair of black thread, the gentle curve of his lips, the perfect way his ears sat either side of his head. How could I run from that?

A yawn threatened to swallow my face as I slumped heavily into the comforting warmth of the faded chair. I felt drained, empty. So many memories disturbed from the darkest recesses of my mind, London, Gideon, Eddie, Victoria, the bloody angel. Memories exhumed from the darkest corners of my past to inflict new pain, memories that lay in splinters throughout the shattered pieces of my heart.

Why couldn't they leave me alone to hide from the world that destroyed me once? I could do hiding. It was living I had trouble with.

I wanted to close my eyes, just for a moment, a stolen second of time just for me. Was that too much to ask?

Running, fleeing from such rage, such anger, such crushing disappointment, hate stretching its ever-reaching arms toward me. It was not my fault, I couldn't help it, why was I to blame? Why were they fighting? Why was there so much blood? He was so close behind me, so close. I could feel him breathing down on me, the hairs on the back of my neck screaming in terror. I could taste his wrath and smell his displeasure. The horror was tearing me apart, ripping out the lining of my stomach with cruel talons, dread crashing over me in unrelenting waves of agony, pulling me down into the deepest darkest realms of despair. He was so angry with me, so very angry. The punishment would be more than my body could withstand. As I begged him for mercy, as I cried for his forgiveness, my flesh ignited and my eyes exploded. Skin seared and blistered as the flames consumed my very existence until there was nothing left but pain.

I exploded from the dream in a sheet of prickly sweat. My hands jumped to my face, feeling my lips, touching my nose, fingertips brushing across my eyes checking for ash, but my beauty endured.

"You were dreaming."

The voice startled me. He was awake and looking at me with his fascinating green eyes.

"You're awake. How're you feeling, are you in pain?"

"It hurts like a bitch, but I'm alive and I think I have you to thank for that." Pain flashed across his handsome face as he struggled into a sitting position. The sheet slid down from his perspiration-soaked torso. I couldn't help but look, it was right there in front of me, all rippled and hard, who could resist? And he saw me looking.

Without thinking, I was at his side with my arms wrapped around his frame, helping him to sit up. The hardness of his bare muscles against my skin, the slipperiness of his sweat against my arms, the heat of his body radiating into my cold limbs, all combined into a head rush of intoxication. He smelled of man, deep and musky. I had to force myself to take my arms away, and I dared not meet his gaze for fear he should see my desire burning within them. He tried to swallow more tablets, but his hands shook so severely I had to help him hold the glass to his lips, his great big kissable lips. If I licked those thick plump lips and placed them against the window, he would stick to the glass.

"My name is Ethan," he whispered, the green of his eyes penetrating me.

"Eli, my name is Eli. Someone shot you, but the bullet passed straight through. You ended up in a ditch and the wound was infected. But you are on the mend now."

For a fleeting moment, he looked confused and I could see his brain working frantically behind those magnificent eyes. "I think I remember — it's all a bit fuzzy."

"Can you tell me what happened?" His face darkened and his body tensed, muscle and sinew bulging beneath tight skin. Blood soared through my veins, pounding through my temples, bulging at the backs of my eyes. I had no pulse, no beating heart, but my chest was throbbing with the force of the blood raging against my ribcage, my blood pushing me inexorably toward him, but I fought to hold back, fought against my own rising lust. He was distressed. He was in pain, and I found that I wanted to take his suffering away. It must have been the first selfless thought I had had in years.

I surprised myself.

"You don't have to tell me, not now, not if you're not ready," I said anxiously.

"No," he said. "It's okay, I need to talk about it."

"What happened out there?" I prompted gently.

He held out his hand toward the glass, I filled it with water and he took it gratefully, swallowing the liquid with great heavy gulps. He gave me the glass and rubbed his hands over his face, as if to clear his head, arranging his thoughts into a coherent stream of information.

"I am trying to find my papa. I came down from Bremen—the city was bombed out of existence. They hit the factories, the dockyard, anything of significance, both military and civilian. I barely got out alive. Everything was on fire, the air itself burned. There was nothing left. Nothing."

A shadow washed over his face and he looked so haunted, so lost amongst the dead. A man haunted by so much pain.

"I had hoped to find Papa there, but all I found was death. I saw children dead amongst the rubble, ripped apart where they stood as the sky fell on them. It was Armageddon."

The world was at war while I sat safe and hidden in my Folly away from the suffering of humanity. And I had not given it a single thought, not one. Looking at his anxious features, I felt ashamed.

"Papa was taken from me by Himmler, and I have spent the last few years trying to find him. I heard Himmler had made Welwelsburg Castle his base of operations, so I came from Bremen to Welwelsburg village. Not much remains of the village anymore. Buildings and people have been cannibalised to rebuild the castle and the concentration camp that lies at its base. It was just by luck I stumbled upon an Inn. I was tired and hungry so I offered my help, anything to pay my way. The owner told me the village was dying, emptied of men, then women, and how even the buildings were torn down so their stone could be used to rebuild and expand the castle. He also told me the remaining villagers and children were going to leave, escape through the forest by night before any more disappeared into the concentration camp. He gave me a room, apologising that it was in such a mess, but just a few days before, SS guards had taken the previous occupant away and there was no one left to help him clean the rooms.

"He left me alone, promising to return with bread and cheese and I felt so very grateful for his generosity, his kindness. The room was tiny and smelled of damp, but I really didn't care. Against the wall was a small bed, a desk with a beaten old chair and a wardrobe that had seen better days. After what I had been through, it felt like luxury.

"Sitting on the desk was a bible and a pile of books tied with string. I recognised them immediately. They were Papa's. He had been in that room, slept in that room. I checked the wardrobe but it was empty. I ran to find the innkeeper, who told me that the man booked in under the name of Professor Silberman and that he had informed the innkeeper his stay would be short before he moved into the castle. A couple of nights later, SS troops escorted him away. That was over a week ago.

"I must have fallen asleep because I woke up to the sound

of gunfire as the innkeeper rushed into the room and beckoned toward the window.

"The SS had begun their final purge, emptying the village, rounding everyone up to be transported back to the concentration camp. The innkeeper whispered for me to flee, to climb out of the window into the surrounding forest. I grabbed Papa's books and thanked the innkeeper before leaping the short distance to the ground. I heard gunshots behind me but I didn't look back. I never saw the innkeeper again.

"I met up with others, some twenty survivors with a dozen or more children, running together through the undergrowth. We ran into the forest, as far from the village as possible, running until the sun began to filter through the canopy above. The young ones were frightened and exhausted, so we had no choice but to stop, sleeping in makeshift tents, huddled together to keep warm. What little food there was went to the children, but we knew it would not last us long.

"I sat with a little boy named Samuel and his father. Samuel was trembling with cold, so I gave him my shirt, and the three of us climbed beneath a blanket to stay warm. I feared for Samuel, as I did for all the children, feared that the cold and the lack of food would be too much for their little bodies to endure. Samuel's father offered the little boy his jumper, an old tattered blue thing that had seen better days, but Samuel was horrified and refused, saying that his mum would be cross because daddy *had* to wear it. I laughed, tried to encourage Samuel to tell me more, but suddenly everything exploded.

"The soldiers had found us. A few of the men tried to save the children, surrounding them with their own bodies, but the bullets that shattered their limbs did so without mercy, adult and child alike. Blood and fire rained down so hard we could barely see. One soldier put a gun to my head but someone dived at him, pushing me to the side. I watched as the soldier forced the young Jew to his knees and made him put the muzzle of the gun in his mouth. The back of his head sprayed all over me. The Nazi laughed as I stood there covered in brain and shards of skull then he shot me.

"I remember the ground reeling up to meet my face, my vision fading and the sounds of dying ringing in my ears. I remember crawling. I remember the sleet, hard and cold, the ground churned up beneath me. I remember thinking I had lost my books, Papa's precious books."

A wild coughing fit shook the water from his hand. I rushed to his side, took the glass from his rocking hand. He was soaking, his skin hot to the touch. Suddenly he became listless, his eyes fluttering and his body weak and limp. I eased him back beneath the sheets trying very hard not to think of the curve of his body against my skin.

"Sleep, get some rest, that's enough for now. There will be time for stories later."

He did not resist as I pulled the sheet around his broad shoulders, and as his head sank into the soft pillows, his eyes closed as sleep devoured him. I knew his dreams would be troubled, and I pitied him for that. I knew how he felt. I could only wonder at the horror stories yet to surface from his troubled mind, and I wanted to hear them. I needed to hear them. He was someone that had witnessed true horror much as I had done, and I felt a connection, I felt something deep in my soul blink into life in recognition of his suffering, of our shared misery, and I wanted to understand what that something was.

Mal had been gone a long time, so I decided to see what was keeping him. As I headed down the stairs toward the secret door that led to the dungeon, it suddenly struck me, if I were a human and a disembodied plate of food floated toward me, how would I react? I would be frightened out of my wits. I would scream my tits off, if I were human. And I already took his newfound touchy feely thing for granted. We had been alone in Alte for so long that to consider the sensibilities of humans was new to me, humans in all their horrendous, blowing up children and being racist cunts glory. After what I had just heard from Ethan's trembling lips, I would not piss on a human if they were on fire.

As I descended into semi-darkness, I could hear a strange noise, a sort of wet slapping sound accompanied by a low grunting moan. I hit my forehead with the palm of my hand. I couldn't leave Mal alone for two minutes.

The Nazi was sitting on the bench in his cell, naked. His superbly sculpted body glistened with sweat, and rivulets of water poured down his lovely six-pack of a stomach giving him a magnificent sheen. His blond Arian hair lay stuck to his forehead, his face a mask of concentration, and it almost seemed a shame to interrupt, so I leaned against the table in the centre of the room and watched, amazed as his hands moved in a blur around his impressive cock.

Okay, so it turned me on. I had a libido the size of a planet, and the sight of a beautiful man masturbating was almost more than my inner homosexual could cope with.

But I had a care of duty, to both of them.

"Get out of him, Malachi."

The possessed soldier looked up at me and smirked from within a sweat-encrusted face. "Just a minute, I'm nearly there. I've cum three times already."

Mal was abbreviating. That was not a good sign.

"Get out of him now, Mal."

The soldier's head jerked back as hot spunk shot upward like an erupting volcano splattering thickly across his chest. My pants twitched in sympathy.

"Better now?"

"Oh god, yes, I enjoyed that. This body is lovely and his cock is fantastic. It gets so hard, you know. It throbs so much it feels like it's gonna burst."

"I think you just did."

"I did, didn't I? Ha!"

"This has to stop, Malachi—you can't go hopping inside a body every time you feel like it. It's dangerous."

"Bullshit. You're only saying that coz you want a bit."

"Listen to yourself, Malachi, this isn't you. I'm telling you it's dangerous because it is. Possession only leads to bad things, Mal, very bad things. I know it's fun for you, to feel solid again, to feel flesh again."

"To have sex again."

"Yes, okay, to have sex again. But abilities like that come with a high price tag and believe me when I say you are not willing to pay it."

Suddenly the naked soldier rushed at the bars, his snarling face contorted with rage. Spittle flew from his mouth as he bellowed through the metal with such malevolent ferocity I nearly fell backward across the table.

"What do you fucking know about it, vampire, you who feed on the blood of the living. When were you ever alive? How do you know how this fucking feels? You know fuck all of being flesh and blood—you will never be flesh and blood. You are nothing but a walking corpse, without meaning, without purpose, without belonging. So tell me, who is the saddest of them all?"

The possession fit was stronger that time and it shocked me. I kept my voice low and gentle, as reassuring as possible as I approached the bars.

"Come back to me, Malachi, you are my friend, remember? You have helped me so much, in so many ways, we have been through so much together, please don't throw that away. This isn't you. You are the kindest, gentlest person I know. You couldn't hurt anyone. I know you wouldn't hurt me. Do you know why? Because we are best friends, Mal, the very best of friends. You and me against the world."

His face changed, became softer, almost contemplative.

"The vampire and the ghost, I say old chap, who would have guessed?"

The screaming from the bottom of the stairs took us both by surprise. My teeth shot out instinctively and my eyes burned black.

"Monster! Monster! You're a fucking monster!"

Ethan stood unsteadily at the bottom of the stairs trembling with anger, an accusatory finger pointing toward me.

Chapter Seven: A Short Conversation With the Devil Part One

As related by Daniyyel

I was an angel. I was beautiful and I was terrible, I was the light that calmed the trembling heart and I was the terror that set it fluttering. I walked where others feared to tread, and I did that because I was an angel and I had that right, given to me by my divine Father. Where fear darkened the shadows of the human heart, I brought enlightenment to guide it home.

Fear, the word held no meaning for me, it was a word that others used, nothing but a series of letters strung randomly together, an excuse for the horror mankind had inflicted upon itself, for more evil had been perpetrated in the name of that one word than any other in the human vocabulary. I had no tolerance for it.

So the uneasiness I felt, the uncertainty that coursed through my veins as I left Alte, quite perplexed me. I saw him in Eli's arms, a human, struggling to hold onto life, yet it still radiated from within him. I felt it, a shift, the turning point, the inevitability come at last.

I knew who he was.

It had come, the point of change, my time to choose. Heaven would either stand or fall because of it. Why should I doubt when I had waited for so long, why should uncertainty creep into my resolve when surely, my only course of action had long been laid out before me.

Things had to change. Father had to change.

The scent was easy to follow. Human and vampire, the conjuncture of two worlds colliding, as though a trail of breadcrumbs lay before me through the forest. All I had to do was close my eyes and let my wings unfold and I was there, there amongst the dead things.

Eli was right—the place smelled of demon, a faint bitter aftertaste that assaulted my nose, a lingering stench that would take an age to wash out of my feathers.

Eli was wrong. I loved humans. Of all Father's creations, they were the most beautiful, they showed the most promise, but they also displayed an unquenchable thirst for self-destruction. The evidence lay all around me. Shattered bodies and discarded lives in a wasteland of self-inflicted human tragedy.

There were children, mangled and broken. Precious lives discarded without thought and without mercy—without consideration. Children were always the worst. An adult had lived at least, a chance at life, but a child, a child was only at the beginning. Children, born to a higher purpose, the miracle of life given with a loving heart without condition or expectation, and fear had stolen that gift, fear mixed with ignorance. How my Father in Heaven would weep.

Except I knew he wasn't weeping. My Father in Heaven wasn't watching. My Father in Heaven no longer cared about his creations, for surely, if he did, such evil could not to proliferate. I wept for the humans and I wept for my Father.

I saw a flicker of light, a transparent movement amongst the shattered dead that sent my heart fluttering with sorrow. For a child to die before reaching its full potential was a crime against life, but to murder a child was a crime against creation, and the pain of their passing tore at my chest.

Even an angel's heart may break.

The flicker of light coalesced before my eyes, the spirit shimmering before me like an uncertain memory, its form barely discernible, an insubstantial recollection of a life that should have been. I knelt before the incandescent shape, the little boy's face floating in a miasma of mist before me, a tortured soul in an agony of confusion, eyes pleading for understanding.

"What is the matter, Samuel?" I asked the child before me, his name filling my mind, as did his whole life, his terribly short, agonisingly brief life. Such a lot of pain encased within such a short life. I let it fill me, I let it rip me apart, shatter my heart, tear at my eyes. But I did not let him see it.

When I heard his voice, the pleading, the confusion, the terrible loneliness that fashioned his speech, it caused me pain. Sometimes I hated my job.

"Where is everyone, mister? I can't find my papa. Have you seen my papa?"

"When was the last time you saw him, Samuel? Can you remember? Can you tell me?"

"Bad men came and there was a lot of noise. He told me to stay with the others, but they are all gone, mister, and I can't find them. Everyone was shouting and screaming, and there was so much noise. Where are they? Have you seen my papa?" His eyes flittered nervously, furtive glances at things he refused to see and refused to accept.

His bewilderment tore at my soul. I had seen it before. A spirit pulled so violently from its living body that it could no longer grasp reality, the trauma so severe it refused to accept the truth of its own death.

How did you tell a child they were dead?

"What does your papa look like, Samuel?"

"He has no hair, Papa said it fell out when Mama told him she was having me." Such was the joyful innocence that radiated from his glowing body as that beautiful boy described his father, as only a child could, that I laughed. "He has a big belly because my papa is a baker and he has to test all the bread and cakes he makes so he knows his customers will like them. He said it's called good practise."

"Your papa sounds like a very clever man, Samuel."

"My mama said that Papa is the best man in the world which is why she married him. But Mama always makes him wear a blue jumper that she made for his birthday, and Papa said it's a punishment for not behaving when he was little, so I must behave myself or I will have to wear the very same jumper when I grow up."

Behind the glowing boy, face down in a pool of bloodied mud, lay his father, the tattered blood-soaked remains of a blue jumper hanging from his bullet-ridden corpse. Samuel's father gave his life to protect the children, and it filled me with despondency.

I looked at the spirit flickering before me, his eyes avoiding the reality surrounding him, and I could not help but love him.

"Do you remember how your mama went to stay with God last summer? Do you remember what she said to you?"

Pain shattered his youthful features. Moisture filled his eyes and I watched helpless as his lips began to tremble at the memory of his mother, of her dying, of her holding him with her cancer-weakened hands.

"She said... she... she said..." A wild sob escaped his lips and I wanted to hold him, to pull him to my chest and comfort him, but I could not, I had to push him forward, I had to guide him to the end. That poor beautiful child, an innocence stolen from the world, and the world was a sadder place for his passing.

"Go on, Samuel, it's okay, it's okay if you cry."

"She said... that I was her brave little baker, that she was proud of me, that, that..." A bubble of spittle burst from between his lips as grief overwhelmed him, his heart shattering before my eyes. "She said that she could be at peace because I was there to look after Papa."

"And you did such a good job, Samuel, and your mama is so very proud of you. But you see, sometimes things happen, bad things, things that you cannot prevent, no matter how brave you are. So your mama came for your papa, she took him with her so he could be safe with her and God in Heaven and they are together again. And they are so happy, Samuel, they are so happy to be together again. But they miss you, Samuel, they miss you so much, and they want you to go with them."

"Will I see Mama again?" he whispered through floods of heart-breaking tears.

"Yes, Samuel, you will see your mama again and your papa."

"And she won't be sick this time, will she? I didn't like it when she was sick, it made Papa cry."

"No, Samuel, Mama will never be sick again, and the only tears your father will shed are tears of joy to have you back by their side."

The smile that graced his innocent face was one of the most beautiful things to behold, a precious gift that I took into my soul with welcoming arms, grateful for the warmth and joy of it. It was a gift of incredible beauty, wrapped in wretchedness.

"Do you know what it means to go to Heaven, Samuel?" I asked gently.

He hesitated. Slowly, painfully, he looked around, allowing his eyes to see, understanding what it was that lay crumpled in the mud behind him. He made a sound, a small strangled cry that died in his throat, and I knew it was time, I knew he was ready.

"Yes... yes, I understand," he stammered, trying to sound brave.

"Good boy, Samuel, so are you ready, are you ready to go home?" He nodded and looked into my eyes as sad realisation trickled down his cheek. I took his spirit into my arms, feeling him tingle against my flesh, a tickle of energy that burned with such love that my own body glowed in empathy. I pressed my face against his, my lips brushing his insubstantial flesh, and I whispered to him, so softly, so gently, my own emotions tumbling from my lips. "I love you, Samuel. I love you."

My wings unfurled in a blaze of silver, their softness surrounding him, wrapping his soul in all my glory, and I felt his joy, the elation that flooded through him at the thought of going home to those who loved him so much. He sobbed in my arms, tears of happiness that shook his insubstantial body as he pushed his head into the crook of my neck, his arms tightening around my neck.

"Thank you," he whispered. Beautiful white wings sprouted from between his shoulder blades and lifted him into the air. He looked toward Heaven and smiled a glorious, joyous smile that lit up his face.

"Mama! Papa!" His arms went out before him, his fingers so eager, reaching skyward, reaching for the love that awaited them. Then he was gone and I knew, I knew with all my heart, with all my soul, that Samuel would never be alone again.

I had to turn away from the grief, from the shattered lives spread before me, a mixture of joy and intense sadness churning my stomach. There would be another star in Heaven that night, a bright and wondrous point of light to guide those souls on earth still in need. It gave me comfort.

The smell was there again, a lingering odour of demon and *him*. I felt my stomach heave with apprehension, my skin crawling with nerves at the thought of his return, so I followed my nose, the smell leading me to a partially obscured trench. The smell was definitely stronger, and a thrill of recognition flushed through my veins, recognition mixed with relief, because I knew then that it had come, that there was no going back. I touched the earth beneath my feet and it filled me, his pain, his agony, his suffering, his abandonment, agonising glimpses of the man Eli had found, and I didn't know whether to weep from joy or sob with sorrow.

My course was set. Heaven would forgive me.

"It is an interesting odour is it not?"

I wheeled around at the sound of that voice. Instinctively, my angel took over, my body lifting into the air in a conflagration of heavenly light. My silver wings blocked out the sun and I was no longer the angel, but a warrior, my silver armour reflecting the sun in sharp unforgiving shards of light, my sword held high in one hand and my shield held before me in the other. I was the wrath of God.

"Oh dear, are we really going to do this?" said the voice dolefully. "Well, if you insist."

White-hot flame hit my shield and I flew backward into a tree, its thick trunk snapping behind my back, sending out a shower of splintered bark. As the pine tree crashed to the ground, it burst into flame, surrounding me in a corona of hell-fire that licked hungrily at my flesh. Out of the flames came the horned beast, its cloven hooves crushing the floor beneath its massive weight as it lowered its immense head and charged.

I threw my shield like a discus straight at the beast, who fell backward, crashing into the burning undergrowth with a terrible roar. My shield flew back into my outstretched hand

and I raised my sword, advancing on the beast before me, my wings beating the flames into a tempestuous fury.

Huge piercing yellow eyes glared at me with such malice and hatred. With a loud trembling *crump,* two pulsing, black fiery wings exploded from its back and in one swift movement the beast was in the air, spinning in a tornado of rage. Its flaming wings collided with my body and I found myself hurtling through the air, shield-less and weapon-less.

With a backward somersault, I landed on my feet just as the beast charged again. I threw myself to the ground, tumbling head over heels, picking up my sword and my shield as the ground spun away in front of my eyes. With a scream of fury, I leaped into the air, arching backward in mid-flight, soaring over the head of the beast, and I swung down with all my strength, the butt of my sword slamming into its back.

With a bellow of anger, the monster fell forward. Its cries tore against the sky, its outrage echoing hollowly through the forest. It ripped a tree out of the ground and turned on me, the tree raised like a club, its terrible features distorted by the fire that consumed the air around it.

"Enough!" I bellowed with my full angelic might, my own anger coursing through the trembling earth beneath our feet. The fire snuffed out instantly with a sad hiss. The beast stopped with a shrug and sent the tree crashing into the forest behind it. Its body began to diminish, folding into itself until there was nothing left but a man.

"Well you started it, dear heart," he muttered wryly as he brushed himself down. "Really, now I'm going to have to get me a new suit. Grass stains are such a bitch to get out, aren't they?"

I calmed myself and put away my angel, regarding the thing before me with disdain.

"Hard to tell on black," I countered sarcastically.

"I like black. Besides, what would you have me wear? Puce? Duck-egg? That would really do my reputation a lot of good now, wouldn't it? You can't beat a beautifully tailored black suit with a crisp white shirt and a black tie. It says professional, it says sharp, it is *so* me!" He bowed with a theatrical flourish, his long, immaculately manicured nails brushing the dirt at his feet.

I was piqued. The sound of his smooth velvety voice was enough to make me vomit. And he was so sickeningly suave with his pearly white teeth, glossy slicked back hair, and his holier than thou smile. I wanted to punch him in the face.

"Are those spats you are wearing?" I laughed incredulously.

He clicked his heels together. "Are they not the *most* adorable things you have ever seen? And so on trend."

"If you say so. What are you doing here, Melek?" My patience was wearing thin, but I knew if I could smell him, he could too. And where there was light, there had to be dark.

"Come now, sweetie. Is that any way to speak to your brother?"

My eyebrows twitched. He had that effect on me. "Brother now is it? It has been a long time since you have inferred such familiarity."

"But I am your brother, am I not? So don't you think you should start using my real name for a change?"

"Please." I laughed. "You have so many names, it's a wonder you can remember any of them."

"Use my name."

"No."

"Oh go on. Please?" He grinned at me with such mischief, his yellow eyes twinkling with amusement.

"I like Melek—it's the less... insidious of your names. And if you don't mind, I really am rather busy."

"Yes, I saw, poor little chap, slim pickings for me though." He sounded disappointed as he swept the area with an elegant arm flourish. Suddenly I felt naked before his gaze. "But that's not what brought us both here is it? You can smell it, too."

"Yes, demon, why are there demons in Paderborn forest, hmm?" Did he know whom Eli had found?

"Oh dear heart, they may belong to my realm, but really, I cannot be expected to keep tabs on all of them now, can I? You know children, they will play."

"And you know as well as I, that they do nothing without your consent, so I repeat, why are there demons here, and what are you up to?"

Melek clasped his hands behind his back and began to pace around me. "Oh you know—I have a few fingers in a few pies, a project here, a game plan there, nothing for you to flutter your wings about. The last time I looked, you had no more say over me and my doings than I over yours."

"Doings?"

"I'm trying to be down with the kids don't you know, do keep up."

"Wouldn't have anything to do with your little war with Father now, would it? Are you still looking for the spear? Tell me, Melek, what would you do with such a thing once you possessed it?"

"Ooo, possess, what a marvellous word."

"Don't push it, Melek."

"Moi? I wouldn't dream of it. And besides, you know what I will do with it."

How I hated his smile—it twisted a thing of beauty into a mask of calculating evil.

"You will have to get Father down here first."

Suddenly he was in my face, wide-eyed and snarling, saliva dripping from his twisted mouth.

"And when he does, I will stick that thing into his fucking heart and watch him bleed out at my feet. His throne belongs to me." He backed away, wiping his mouth with the back of his sleeve. "But how to get him off his ass, how to entice him down here, that is the dilemma, is it not?"

"You know he is not watching. In truth, he has not been the same since you left—you were his favourite, after all, and now he turns his back on us in his despair. We angels weep we are so lonely."

Melek laughed dryly, a cruel sound that brushed against my skin with fingers of ice. "You say *left* as though I had a choice in the matter. Do not forget, Daniyyel, that he made us—he made us all. He is the Father of *all* things, of *all* men. All that has transpired is a direct result of *his* creation, *his* intention. Father needs to man up, face his mistakes, he should forgive them instead of banishing them. He is unfit to rule. It is time for someone with some *real* flair."

"You are sick, Melek, sick in the head. And you wonder why my Father expelled you? You were his greatest disappointment... and his greatest sorrow."

"You know, this is all very interesting, talking about the good old days, but you will not distract me from my question, brother. What are you doing here, Daniyyel, what brings you to Paderborn forest? I know you can smell it, and don't insult me by blaming my demons."

"And your point is?"

"It's him, isn't it?"

It was pointless trying to lie. "Yes."

"Well fuck me sideways!"

"While it is my understanding you like to indulge in such practises from time to time, may I remind you I serve our Father, and as such have taken a vow that prohibits the comfort of others."

"You need a good shag. No wonder you're so uptight. But

then, that's how this balls up started isn't it? Does that mean I can tell Eli? Please, please, please can I tell Eli? Pretty please with a cherry on top?" Melek jumped up and down on the spot, clapping his hands together like a demented child.

"You know better than that, Melek, you cannot intervene, and neither can I, we are bound by the Covenant."

Melek threw up his arms and laughed. "Oh please, rules, do we really care about rules? Come on, brother, surely they both have the right to know. I know *you* think they do."

"But it is not our place, *brother!* You know what happened the last time."

"Oh yes, dear heart, I remember. Father does so have a temper. Poor Noah."

"And the Covenant is there to prevent such a thing from ever happening again." But an idea was forming in my mind, a terrible, dangerous, reckless idea. Heaven needed to heal, and Father needed to forgive so he could start to love again. Neither Heaven nor Hell could break the Covenant and if one party did, Heaven would record the deed in the Book of Transgression, giving the other party licence to commit a single contravention in return, a life for a life. And so the idea formed, coalesced, solidified, an infinite coiling monster of intricate complexity in a never-ending spiral of consequences, with the sole purpose of bringing redemption for all. My mind was set. I had made my choice and I prayed to my Father in Heaven to forgive me.

"Well this is going to be interesting that's for sure. Have you ever thought about what would happen if it went the other way? What would you think of our precious Father then?"

"I don't know." And I didn't. That was the closest I had ever come to fear.

"Oh I do. There would be all out war in Heaven, and

Father would be deposed. So what would *you* do, Daniyyel? What would *you* do if Eli loses? You have been a staunch supporter of him from the beginning, haven't you, but now its decision time — Father will have to make a choice, to stand by his decision or concede, and you have to decide whose side you're on."

"There are no sides in this, Melek, only what's right. He made us, He did, all of us." My rage ripped through my lips, my body trembling with an anger that surprised me.

"Oh dear, touched a nerve have we? You never thought it would come to this, did you, that you might have to make a choice — that you might have to make a stand against him."

"How dare you. I am an angel. I am the word of God. I am the will of God. I will do what is right. And what about you? Did you really think your pathetic attempt would work?"

"Brother, whatever do you mean?"

"You know damn fine what I mean. Gideon."

Melek smirked, like oil splitting over water. "What happens in Judea stays in Judea."

"You should not have encouraged him! It should not have happened!"

"Oh, dear heart, I did not make Eli vampire, you know that, though you might say that it was by Fathers hand, albeit in a roundabout sort of way."

My anger exploded from my mouth and I was in his face, my lips almost touching his as I spat my words into his contemptuous face. "How dare you accuse our Father of such cruelty? Father would never be so vindictive."

"How can you say that, after what he did to me? He lets his beloved humans drown in their own shit and piss and yet you still hold him up as this wonderfully benevolent being? You stupid, pompous cunt."

My wings unfurled and I was above him, my glory

burning down upon his insignificant form.

"Do not forget who I am!" My voice boomed through the forest and the ground trembled. "You who were cast out, Lucifer, the great deceiver, the great disappointment, you who are nothing before God."

He looked up at me then, a supercilious grin splitting his sly face.

"As we are all nothing before our God who no longer cares."

I punched him in the face.

Melek fell backward with a look of utter disbelief. So I turned my back on my brother, on the forest filled with death.

"Rules were made to be broken, Daniyyel."

I didn't look back—I would not give him the satisfaction of seeing the smirk that crept across my lips.

"Yes, Melek, but by better men than we."

Chapter Eight: The Feral

I loved the view, each turret offering a different perspective of the surrounding forest and the sprawling mountain range around me. Cats liked to perch on high. It made them feel superior, it made them feel everything else was beneath them. Up there atop my tower, looking up into that incredible black sky with its untold wonders and innumerable stars, I knew how they felt, superior, unreachable, hidden. But for how long, how long would I remain safe?

There were two humans in my castle. How long before there were more? How long before the pitchforks and the flaming torches? As I stared upon a glowing field of trees dusted with moonlight and stardust, I wondered how much longer I had left to enjoy it, the solitude, the safety, the anonymity, how long before the running started.

When Ethan had cried *monster* I thought it had begun — after all, he saw my monster in the woods, amid the teeth and the blood. But he was screaming at the soldier. It turned out Mal's little plaything was one of the Nazis who attacked the refugee camp, but then Ethan passed out and I had to carry him back to bed and I hoped, beyond reason, my monster remained an enigmatic dream, a fever driven delirium.

And Christ did he feel good in my arms.

"Now there is a look that could curdle milk." Mal rose through the roof at my side and leaned over the parapet. He looked like my shadow.

"What am I doing, Mal?"

"Playing eye-spy?"

"I need you to be serious, Mal, we're in trouble here."

He looked thoughtful for a moment then he hit me with one of his annoying insights. "You are afraid to get involved again are you not, afraid you are being dragged back into the world of humans?"

I bowed my head and sighed heavily. Bilious clouds of cold air should have spewed from between my lips, but there was nothing. I was not human. That really pissed me off.

"I don't want this—I don't want to be pulled back in. I just want to be left alone."

"So why did you bring him back? You could have just left him out there to die in the cold."

"I didn't want him to die."

Mal's eyebrows shot up his forehead and knitted into one killer brow.

"I don't know all right? I couldn't help it, I knew I was going to bring him back as soon as I saw him. It was as if I had no choice. There is something about him, and don't ask me what it is, 'cause I don't know."

"Seriously?" His lips puckered up as though he were sucking a lemon. "Are you telling me you cannot think of one thing to do with him?"

"Not like that." Both eyebrows hit his hairline in unison. How did he do that? "Yes! I mean no! I mean yes, he is good looking but no, that's not why I brought him back, okay? And you can talk, bringing back a bloody German, what the fuck were you thinking?"

"I thought it would be nice for you to have a stocked larder for a change." I shot Mal a look of distaste, but he shrugged it off innocently. "I was just saying, no need to bite my head off."

"Look, Mal, I understand why you did it, appreciate it even, but I don't think you realise what it means, for both of us."

Mal turned away from me so I could not see his face. "I just wanted us to be together." There was pain in those words, a heartfelt depth of emotion that chewed at the lining of my stomach. He turned around, he looked at me, his sweet face full of hope for what might have been, for what he still hoped would be, and I realised then, I would have to hurt him.

"I cannot give you what you want, Malachi."

He moved closer, his fingers brushing the front of my shirt. I could feel them.

"But I am in love with you, Eli. You have to know that. I have always been in love with you. I think you are the most incredible being I have ever met. You are the most beautiful man my eyes have ever beheld. You make me so very happy. Being with you, here in Alte, us, together, I love it, standing by your side — you make me feel so alive."

I made to interrupt him but he silenced me, a single finger placed against my lips. I felt that, too.

"When Daniyyel asked me the question, I knew what my answer would be without hesitation. How could I say yes and lose you? I said no because I want to be with you. I cannot leave you. I would rather dissipate into nothingness than leave you. How can any of that be so bad?"

He was such an eloquent creature, such a wordsmith. I almost applauded. "I'm not saying that it's wrong, Malachi, what I am saying is I do not and cannot love you, not the way you want me to." Pain flashed across his face, but I continued regardless, pushing mercilessly toward my grand finale. "What you have started here may mean that I will have to leave Alte. Mal, I may have to leave my home forever, because of what you have done."

Malachi looked appalled. "I am sorry, Eli. I am so sorry, I did not think, I did not realise..."

"And when Daniyyel asks you the question again, I want you to say yes."

Bingo. That hit home, and the look of optimism slid from his face like shit off a hot tin roof. The light died in his eyes. He could not have looked more hurt than if I had exorcised him myself. I loathed myself for doing it, for hurting him, for causing that look of terrible rejection that washed over his forlorn face, but it had to stop, his crazy, reckless infatuation with me had to stop.

And it was about time Malachi knew the truth about London.

"You want me to leave you?"

I had not expected his words to sting or sound as dreadful as they did, and as he asked that horrible question, I felt my stomach lurch. That was the moment—it had finally arrived, the moment when I would make him want to leave me.

"Do you remember anything about your life, Mal? What is the last thing you remember?"

His face twisted into a grimace of confused bewilderment and I could tell that some distant memory, some half-felt recollection was trying to force its way to the front of his mind. Bafflement gave way to the crushing weight of fear as panic began to tremble through his murky form and I hated my words and I hated myself for torturing my best friend.

"Why would you ask me that, why?" he asked.

"Because you have to remember—I want you to say yes to Daniyyel, and for that to happen you need to remember." I was in at the deep end and I could not swim. My own anxiety began to consume me. I could feel my hands trembling as black spots of apprehension prickled across my vision in a fog of unease.

"No!" he shouted suddenly and I stepped back, surprised

by the anger in his voice. "I don't remember. You cannot make me remember. I don't want to remember."

The sound of glass shattering had us both looking over the edge of the turret, just in time to see a figure slither into the window below. Something moved out of the corner of my eye and I could see another figure, skeletal and repulsive, climbing like an insect up the stone turret toward the broken window. The creature looked up, its smooth head and bat-like ears glistening pale and white in the moonlight, its black eyes shining with malevolent intent. Thin bloodless lips with two overhanging needle-like fangs parted dryly, issuing a sound full of malice and pain and something else, something I knew all too well, hunger.

"Fuck!" I shouted, stunned by the sight of the creature that dared to invade my home. "Find the one that got in, I'll deal with this one." Mal descended through the roof and I leaped over the parapet, clinging to the wall as I scuttled toward the hissing creature below.

The sky lay above my ass and a floor of rough rock lay below my head. If I fell, it would hurt. My fingers dug into stone, my preternatural strength allowing me to defy gravity as my inner vampire awoke and I hissed back at the snarling feral before me. It made a darting move toward the broken window. Half of its grotesquely twisted body disappeared through the hole but I snatched at a gnarled foot and pulled the foul creature out with all my might, glass and wood exploding around me as the feral erupted from the window. Glass tinkled through the air and fell like a lethal shower of snow to the ground below.

The feral spat and hissed as I pulled its long spidery fingers away from the window frame. With a cry of rage, I threw the creature outward and away from Alte, but somehow it managed to twist in mid-air and came to land behind me on the sheer wall. I spun around to face the thing as it landed against the brickwork on its back, its hands and feet twisted impossibly, clinging defiantly to the bricks and mortar. Its head snapped back and glared at me before the entire creature flipped to correct its orientation. It held itself on the tips of its long fingers and toes that flickered and twitched grotesquely beneath it, propelling it backward, hissing and spitting all the time, the gaze of its huge black eyes never leaving me.

We danced around each other, scuttling from side to side like a pair of warring crabs performing some macabre tango. As I advanced, the feral moved back and I knew I had but one chance to dislodge it from my home. I braced myself for the agony about to follow.

I leaped at him.

Strange how moments of such peril seem to pass so slowly. I could see myself launching into the air, a ballet in slow motion, a missile shot toward my unsuspecting target. The feral's withered brain could not comprehend my actions as I plucked him off the wall, like a frogs tongue reaching out lightning fast to catch a fly. In one superbly smooth movement, I held the feral tightly to my chest and wrapped my limbs around its frail body in a protective cocoon as we plummeted inevitably to the ground below.

It did hurt. My back hit the frozen stony floor and my head bounced upon rock with a loud crack. Pain shot through every part of my body as my spine shattered. If I was human, my body and my head would have exploded in a tattered bloody mess, but I was Menarche, an immortal, and at that very moment, I was fucking grateful for it.

The shock rippled through my body in concentric waves of excruciating pain and I lay there unable to move, waiting for the vibrations that shattered my bones to dissipate. The feral lay curled on my chest whimpering. Finally, as the lurching sensations dissipated, I unfurled my broken body to a chorus of brand new pain, allowing the feral to slide away from the crater in which I lay. He never took his gaze off me.

I crawled out of the shallow pit created by my fall, my bones snapping into place as my body healed. My spine rippled and cracked as the vertebrae clicked into position and I closed my eyes to allow the pain to wash away. Slowly, very slowly, I got to my feet, whole again.

I was in fucking awe of myself.

The feral sat cowering on the ground, all thoughts of fighting knocked out of him. He looked pitiful. Filthy rags clung to his skeletal frame and he rocked gently on his heels, his long spindly arms wrapped around his knees.

"Hungry..." he groaned and his voice filled me with sorrow. I could have been born like that mindless creature, skulking in the shadows and the dark recesses of the world only to surface during the night, existing to feed, a savage and uncivilised continuation of skin and bone, the discarded revenants of those vampires who, like me, were born into a higher rank.

All too often I had come across creatures like the feral before me, creatures made in a desperate bid to create companionship, to save loved ones, to continue family, reduced to a loathsome silhouette of those would be creators whose blood was not strong enough, not pure enough, not Menarche enough to bring them over complete. They were our bastard children, the shameful branches of our family tree, and we, the Menarche, we had a responsibility toward them, a responsibility of compassion, of mercy, and no matter how I felt, no matter how much revulsion coursed through my veins at the very sight of them, I would not be cruel.

"Hungry... please..."

"They are not for you," I said kindly. "You must leave

this place, it is not safe for you here, and there is nothing I can give." Veins pulsed beneath his translucent skin and I could only imagine the pain of hunger that coursed through his skeletal frame. I knew how such pain felt, but I could do nothing. I would not let him feed on either of the humans under my roof.

A deceptively frail hand, all fingers and yellowed nails, gripped my hand to brush his dry cheek. Cracked, parched lips kissed the palm of my hand.

"Love... me... feed me?" I felt my chest constrict. The gesture touched me, and I felt more love toward that feral creature than I had felt toward any vampire in a long, long time.

A loud scream from inside Alte brought me to my senses.

"Leave this place," I pleaded but he just looked at me, his black eyes full of sorrow and desperation. The time for kindness was over. "Leave this place! Do not come back." My voice bellowed the command, the command of a Menarche, irresistible to him, and he cowered away from me in a mixture of terror and supplication. "Leave now." With a sorrowful whimper, he fell on all fours and scampered away into the forest, his cries melting into the dark of the night.

Dread invaded my body and made my skin erupt in cold waves of gooseflesh as I ran into Alte, my senses on full alert for the second feral. I could feel his presence—I could hear his pained voice inside my head begging for food, his insatiable hunger driving him toward the humans in my home. He was desperate. He was starving. And he was strong.

Another scream, a sound of pure unrelenting terror ripped through the night and thank God, it came from the basement and not from the upper levels where Ethan slept.

I tore down the stairs toward the desperate sounds and found the feral clinging to the bars of the cell, hands and feet clutching the metal as it tried to force its spindly body through the tight bars. The German stood flat against the wall on the opposite side of the cell screaming hysterically, desperate to keep as much distance between him and the monster snapping at his flesh.

The German's huge fraught eyes saw me and I felt a fleeting moment of sympathy toward him. It didn't last long. "Help me! For the love of God help me!"

Mal was throwing stones at the back of the feral, but to no avail. The feral managed to get an arm and one shoulder through the bars and its impossibly long fingers clawed at the air in front of the screaming German, nails brushing cloth, warm nourishing blood tantalisingly close to its salivating mouth.

I leaped forward and ripped the creature from the bars, flinging the writhing monster violently across the dungeon. Its frail body collided with the stone brickwork and slid to the floor in a heap of dry crackling pain. Black feral eyes bored into me with defiant anger, needle sharp teeth chewing and macerating its lower lip as it growled its displeasure, furious I had denied it food.

I held up my hands toward the creature, pleading for it to see reason. "I do not want to hurt you — please, leave this place, before you force me to do otherwise." I expected the Menarche command in my voice to render it helpless, but to my astonishment it raised itself off the floor, unfolding like an insect, a single accusatory arm pointed toward me.

"You... deny your own kind food." The dry rasping words did not come easily, forcing themselves over vocal cords long dead and barely used. He was defying me, defying a Menarche, and that shook me more than the violence of his incursion.

"I deny you the humans under this roof only — they are under my protection. You must feed elsewhere, away from here and away from me." I spoke the words with as much conviction and with as much authority as I could muster, but I saw his resolve, I saw him trying to stand fast against the compulsion to flee from my voice, and I was gobsmacked.

With an impressive flash of movement, the feral stood before me, his black eyes piercing, his lips almost touching my skin. He was one plucky fucker.

"There is nothing... left. They forced... us... to... leave... they... have forced us out... from the darkness." He pointed toward the German and I understood—I even sympathised. The German war machine marched relentlessly across Europe, destroying so much in its path, forcing the feral from their traditional hiding places. The occasional villager or traveller was no longer part of their staple diet. The feral were predators driven from their natural habitat, forced to hunt in the open in order to survive. They were starving.

"I know you are hungry, but these humans are not for you."

"You would keep... them for... yourself?" His words carried a heavy edge of accusation, but also bitter disappointment.

"I would keep them safe. You cannot have them." I knew I was being harsh and I knew I was condemning him to unending torment but I would not compound an already impossible situation by allowing him to feed.

I was trying to do the right thing.

Suddenly the bastard's hands were around my neck, crushing my windpipe beneath its leather fingers, forcing me to my knees. I was in a state of shock—the fucker took me by surprise.

"You... do not... love us," he spat into my stunned face.

That pissed me off. While I felt sympathy for those pathetic remnants of my species, no feral had ever defied me. I was Menarche, and nobody fucking defied me, least of all in my own bloody house. My vampire erupted across my face in all its snarling ferocity and I ripped his hands away from my neck and raised his frail body, hissing and spitting, above my head. I lost it. Fury and terrible anger burned through my veins and I hurled him with all my might at the stone staircase, where he crashed to the floor with a sickening crunch.

"Leave this place! If I ever see you here again, I will rip off your head and piss in the stump. Leave." The Menarche command spewed from between my lips with full force, a devastatingly irresistible sound that should have sent the creature scurrying for its life. The cheeky fucker just looked at me.

He looked so shocked, so shocked that I would banish him, shocked that I would use such violence against him, he who was one of my own. His eyes flashed with disbelief and something else that shook me to the bone, pure hatred.

But he had left me with no choice. He struggled to his feet, one arm hanging uselessly at his side. Too starved to heal quickly, the feral must have been in agony because of the injury I had inflicted, and the shame of my deed wiped the vampire from my face.

"I'm sorry, I didn't mean to hurt you, but you left me with no choice."

The hatred that bloomed across his twisted features should have burned me to ash.

"And you... have left me with... no choice."

With stunning speed and unhindered by his terrible injury the feral turned around and darted up the stairs. I looked at Mal who shook his head in bewilderment. Then the penny dropped.

"Fuck. Ethan." I shot out of that dungeon as though my ass were on fire. Would he defy me that much? As the stairs flashed past my eyes in a blur, I found myself wondering if I could kill him. Did I have the right to kill him?

Whom was I kidding? If he touched one hair on that hunk of meat's head, I would tear the little shit apart with my teeth until there was nothing left but a pile of wriggling mincemeat.

I reached the bottom of my marble staircase just as the feral reached the top.

"Stop!" I screamed. "Do not make me harm you further."

The feral turned slowly, eyes burning with hunger. The thing leered down at me, its mouth a cruel sneer. Desperation had driven it to the brink of madness, but I didn't care, not while Ethan was at risk.

Suddenly the creature stopped. Its eyes opened wide with shock and its mouth fell open and slack. Blood erupted from its chest in a fountain of black as a wooden spike began to tear its way through the ribs, exploding violently across the marble floor.

A sound issued from between the feral's lips, a mixture of sigh and scream that died in its throat with a gurgling hiss. Its skin began to blacken, spreading outward from the point where the stake protruded, spreading across his dry skin like a creeping black spider web. Black eyes looked at me for help, begging me to stop the entropy that was consuming its body so relentlessly before my eyes.

And then I saw him, the man beneath the vampire, a glimpse of the truth belying the monster. Human eyes smiled with relief and glistened with a thank you unspoken. And then he was gone, disintegrating into a cloud of swirling, glittering dust that danced on the air with a final melancholy twirl.

Ethan stood at the top of the stairs, his left hand bloodied, and the stake fell clattering to the floor from his gory fingers. He looked at me with such anger, but his eyes were hollow and dead.

"One of those bastards killed my mother."

Chapter Nine: The Story of Ethan Part One

As related by Ethan

We Jews never seemed to get a break. Even the press took the piss, depicting us as withering shrivelled monsters that stalked the streets at night, stealing from the pockets of the masses, or stealing the very breath of children as they slept. Stupid, bigoted idiots, as though our lives were not difficult enough. We were just people, ordinary people, wishing to live our ordinary lives.

Except that as a child, I found that my life was far from ordinary.

My parents moved to Berlin looking for a new life, a modern way of life, as did Jews from all across Germany and Eastern Europe. Berlin became the new Promised Land, and we flocked there in our thousands.

Scheunenviertel means the Barn Quarter, and in medieval times, it did indeed house stables. My papa told me that — history was his thing. It was in that old Barn Quarter in the neighbourhood of Mitte where the Jewish people settled and made their home, right at the heart of Berlin, and my parents quickly became an integral part of that community. Papa would declare it was a wonder they had survived for so long without him.

To say he was larger than life would be an understatement — he was a colossus of a man. You would hear him before you saw him, the streets of Mitte would echo with the sound of his raucous laughter. Where there was a crowd there was Papa, surrounded by his adoring flock, always the centre of attention, and he loved it. And they loved him.

Papa was a Rabbi, a man of great importance in any Jewish community. And when he arrived in Berlin, he said it was like some great epiphany, that the good people of Mitte took him into their hearts to be their spiritual and moral leader as soon as they laid eyes on him.

"They recognised my outstanding personality, my son. Always have personality. It will get you far in this life, and who knows, it may even help you in the next."

Papa had an adage for everything. He was famous for them. Things like, *rejoice not at thine enemy's fall, but don't rush to pick him up either.* And his personal favourite, *life should be grabbed by the short and curlies, hair doesn't last forever.* The man should have been a stand-up comedian, but instead he settled for the role of local hero.

That's what my papa was, a hero. It was just that nobody knew it.

Papa existed to serve, and Mitte was a community because of him. He loved his people. Very often, when I was a child, a knock at the door would see him summoned into the night on some urgent errand with Mama by his side. They would leave me in the care of a neighbour, and sometimes they would not return until morning. Sometimes my papa would be gone for days.

But by Christ did he have a temper. It was legendary.

In 1926, Hitler appointed Joseph Goebbels *Gauleiter* of Berlin, the regional leader of the Nazi Party. I was six at the time. Goebbels didn't waste any time and began to spread his message of hate and anti-Semitism amongst the German population using a newly formed offshoot of the Nazi Party called *Der Angriff,* or *The Attack.* I remember a group of Papa's friends coming to the house one evening to show him a booklet handed out by *Der Angriff.* I was in the kitchen with Mama, watching her cook—I loved to watch her cook—when suddenly we heard screams of anger coming from our little parlour and my mama, all rolled up sleeves and floured hands, rushed toward them like the oncoming storm. I clung to her skirts and peeked around her dirty apron, but I was too young to understand what was going on. All I could see was four other men holding down my papa as he thrashed and screamed like a wild man, his face red and puffy, eyes bulging with anger. I thought they were hurting him.

Mama pulled me into her skirts and I sobbed into the fabric as she patted my head, telling me not to worry. But the four men were no match for my papa—he was a big man, and he flung them from his body as if they were rag dolls, sending them crashing all over the room, shattering chairs and breaking ornaments, my mama's prized ornaments.

The sight of her broken treasures tipped Mama over the edge and I felt her freeze, her body rigid and tense with anger. No man was a match for Mama. With a smile that said a thousand reassurances, she gently pushed me back into the hall against the wall. Then she waded into the middle of the brawling men. She just waded straight in there, regardless of the flying fists and tangled limbs. The woman was fearless.

One of the most endearing images I have of my mama is of that moment, when she stood in the middle of a pile of men with her hands on her ample hips surveying their shocked faces. And by Christ did she let rip. That six-year-old child imagined that she must be some kind of angel, because the gas lit chandelier, one of her most prised possessions taking pride of place in our little parlour, cast a bright halo around her head. As she stood amongst the stunned men, my mama glowed. She was, in a word, amazing. They froze in mid-punch and looked up at her with faces that expressed both wonderment and foreboding—they were in deep shit and they knew it. I don't remember what she said because like them, I could not take my eyes off her, the angel with the glowing halo, the angel with her hands on her hips.

What a wonderful, wonderful woman she was.

It was years before I understood what happened that night. The pamphlet called for all those considered to be of *pure* German blood and *pure* German lineage to stand up and rise against the Jew, to shun Jewish businesses, to evict Jewish children from schools and to make life as miserable as possible for the *thriving alien immigrant*. My papa wanted to kill Goebbels that night, and he would have flattened any German that stood in his way. It was all those four men could do to restrain him. They were trying to save him, not hurt him.

The political situation only got worse. Hundreds of Jewish citizens would lose their jobs. Jewish businesses across Berlin were vandalised in a never-ending torrent of violence. Many a night saw a Jewish citizen brutally and indiscriminately attacked in the streets. It was open season on us Jews.

All that was bad enough, but nothing, nothing would be as devastating to me, or to my poor papa, as the loss of Mama.

She was a beautiful woman, inside and out. Plump as only Jewish women could be, she had long bubbly jet-black hair that bounced around her shoulders when she laughed, and she laughed a lot. It was one of her gifts. She had dark brown very wide eyes that always made her look slightly startled, and my papa used to call her *Owl*. Mama loved that. She would chase him through our little house making a hooting noise sending him into fits of tearful laughter and then she would do it even more until he was red in the face, begging for mercy.

For two people who had so much love to give, it always surprised me I was an only child.

Ask anyone in Mitte about my mama and the reply would always be the same, never a kinder person in all of Berlin. Kind of heart and generous of spirit, she worked tirelessly for the community regardless of her own health, regardless of the weather, regardless of her own needs. Soup kitchens, poor-houses, orphanages, youth welfare, my mama had a hand in them all, dividing her time between those who needed it most yet always finding time for me, always finding time to help Papa with his work.

His other work. I do not talk of my papa's duties as Rabbi, or his talks and sermons at Fasanenstrasse Synagogue. Every family has a dark side — mine was no exception.

One of my favourite places was Fasanenstrasse Synagogue, the largest of its kind in Germany. The building itself was an impressive monument crafted by men who loved their work and placed each brick and carved each stone with the care and attention it deserved. It dressed like a Roman but borrowed other structural elements from different cultures to complete its eclectic structure. I loved the three magnificently domed cupolas that crowned the roof, which my papa called Byzantine, but my favourite part, on the outside at least, was the western façade with its three stone portals decorated with columns and statues of lions. I would sit for hours as a child sketching those lions from every angle. I loved them, their artistry, their majesty, they seemed so alive to me.

The inside was no less magnificent. It glowed as the sunlight poured through the many windows and arches reflecting off gold and pale blue motifs that adorned the walls, stretching high into the three domed ceilings of the cupolas. The huge alcove at the end of the long prayer hall radiated a warm orange light, gilded with shiny sheets of the thinnest gold in which was sheltered the Holy Ark, an ornamental closet that held the holy Torah scrolls, the heart of our synagogue.

Fasanenstrasse had another smaller building to the north that served as the everyday prayer house. The basement was huge, used mainly for weddings and other private community ceremonies.

It was also a space used for exorcisms.

One night, an emergency saw my papa called out in a frenzy of hushed voices. I was eleven. I was old enough to look after myself, one would think, but no, my mama was Jewish, so go figure. My parents told me to dress quickly because we had to go to the synagogue.

There was nothing odd about that. Very often, my parents needed to work late into the night, and normally our neighbour, Mrs. Shultz, a lovely woman a little older than my mama, would look after me. She always smelled of cookies and bread. But a few nights earlier, a group of German thugs had beaten Mrs. Shultz, and she was in no fit state to look after me.

They sat me in the main building with my paper and my pencils and told me to draw the Holy Ark. It was to be a gift for Mrs. Shultz on our return, so I had to make it extra special. I loved Mrs. Shultz dearly, so I set about my task with great enthusiasm.

It was funny to sit in that great hall at night and be all alone. The candles glowed like a thousand incandescent suns and cast all sorts of strange and frightening shadows across the walls, figures stretching wildly from every corner, deformed monsters that twisted and flew around the synagogue to torment and haunt me. I was a very nervous eleven-year-old sitting in that cavernous space as the walls moved and danced to the music of the flames.

I felt particularly pleased with my drawing, and it was nearly finished. I liked to use the very tip of a sharp pencil in little scratchy flicks to build up the depth and dimension of my sketches, and I was about to finish a particularly tricky bit when a high-pitched scream made me jump. My pencils spilled all over the floor.

The sound made my skin crawl. The unearthly noise echoed around the hollow interior, and my little heart threatened to burst from between my ribs to join the pencils at my feet. Fear and panic gripped me, and for a moment, I considered running home to Mrs. Shultz where I would bang on the door until she answered. But if I did that, my parents would be worried. Then they would be furious at me for roaming the streets of Mitte alone in the dark, not to mention disturbing a sick Mrs. Shultz. But I could no longer sit in that vast empty space alone. I was too frightened.

I resolved to venture into the ancillary building to find my parents, who would surely understand once they saw the terror written all over my face. So I scooped up my things and ran toward the door hidden discreetly at the back of the hall.

I opened the door slowly, not really knowing what to expect. The synagogue glowed with colour and warmth. Gold, blue, turquoise, green, rich radiant jewel colours that burned with an inner light giving the place a sense of life, but as I opened that cleverly concealed door and squeezed through that opening, it was like stepping into another world. I left the world of colour and stepped into a world of black and white.

Fasanenstrasse Synagogue had been open for only twenty-two years, the main bulk of the money going toward the impressive façade and the main internal decoration. Considering the synagogue relied on community funding, that was no mean feat. But the money had run out, and the ancillary building lay incomplete. The community hall beneath the ancillary building consisted of more modest decoration, but the connecting hall that I found myself in remained naked and bare, breezeblock and concrete, a drab grey corridor unbefitting the splendour of the parent body.

I closed the door behind me and began the long trudge down the concrete umbilical cord. As the door shut, I became aware of a sound, magnified by the unyielding brickwork that surrounded me, a throb that pulsed and undulated. I hurried forward, eager to find the comfort of my parents arms I knew lay just ahead.

And so did that throbbing sound.

It felt like that concrete tunnel went on forever before I reached the heavy double doors at the other end. I pulled on one of the large brass handles, but the door would not budge. I was a weedy little thing, with arms and legs so skinny my mama used to say that one good fart and I would snap. They were very heavy interlocking fire doors, and I pulled on the wrong side. As a result, my sweaty hands slipped from the brass sending me flying backward onto the hard concrete floor.

"Fuck," I shouted and I looked up guilty, half-expecting Papa to be in the doorway with a stern look, angry at my profanity, but thankfully, I was still alone. There was enough trouble coming my way as it was. I didn't need any more.

With a stream of curses—nobody was there to witness my swearing so I felt totally justified—I picked myself up and heaved at the other door. I had to use my entire insignificant body to pull and then push the heavy door open. If I had lost my grip I would have been sandwiched between the two doors like a starfish, but as fanciful as that ludicrous thought might be, I managed to squeeze myself through until I stood puffing and panting on the other side. I jumped out of my skin when the heavy door slammed closed behind me, the spring-loaded mechanism shutting it with a decisive bang.

The throbbing sound intensified. I listened carefully, trying to decipher the alien sound before recognition struck me with a cold chill. It was chanting. The sound unnerved me, the rhythmic rising and falling, the intense passion of voices joined in unison, and it took all my willpower to push myself forward.

Before me lay a curved staircase that led down to the community hall. I hesitated, uncertain, because the voices were coming from below, drifting up the staircase in undulating waves of incredible power, pushing me back. The babble of voices seemed to be reaching a crescendo. Then a single voice, utterly compelling, hollered over the others with a string of commands, demanding that somebody leave. It was the voice of my papa.

I lived a sheltered existence, untouched by the evil of the world around me — my parents saw to that. But my innocence was about to be shattered.

The girl sat in a chair in the middle of the hall. Papa stood directly before her with one hand reaching toward the heavens, the other pressing an ornate book against the girl's head. He was chanting, his voice loud and impassioned, and the girl shuddered violently in the chair, her eyes a terrible glassy white. Surrounding the bizarre scene stood ten figures arranged in a circle around Papa and the girl, each, bar one, clasping an open book from which they chanted versus in perfect unison, their intonation hypnotic in its perfect synchronicity. And one of them was my mama.

As Papa bellowed his commands, the group issued their response. The single figure without a book raised a large highly polished horn to his lips and the note that issued from its curlicue form made me shudder. The sound ripped the breath from my lungs, its long melancholic tone reaching for my soul with cold, indiscriminate fingers. I wanted to run and scream, but the note held me to the spot, and I was hypnotised, cowering behind the banister unable to move.

Suddenly the girl was on her feet, standing high above Papa with her arms outstretched in cruciform. My eyes widened with shock she was so tall, towering above Papa but as my eyes moved down I saw she was floating, her bare feet pointing toward the carpet. My little brain could not comprehend what I was seeing and I kept telling myself it was not real, that it was some dream, a nightmare, but she was there, before my open eyes, floating, and my world imploded around me.

The girl's head snapped up, eyes wide and white, her mouth a salivating morass of black spittle that fell from her swollen lips in thick elastic globules. Long black hair writhed around her head in undulating locks and her throat began to swell, bulging and pulsating until it strained against her white flesh so grotesquely I felt sure it would split. The voice that poured from between her wet slug lips was thick and sibilant, inhuman, the voice of a creature from another world.

"Force me from this whore if you will, this cunt is mine no matter what you do, little man."

Papa began to shout his commands with renewed vigour, the group responding dutifully as the horn sounded, the tone matching the chant of the circle, the note elongated and without pause. The effect on the floating girl was instant and dramatic. She thrashed violently from side to side, spittle flying, her scream a howl of utter defiance. She began to laugh, a deep sickening cackle, black ejaculate splattering across Papa's rapturous face. But he continued to chant Psalm 91 regardless, his voice audible above all else and the horn continued its remorseless cry as the rest of the group took up the verse.

"I will rip this cunt apart with your cock, you flaccid piece of shit! Fuck me! Fuck me!"

Papa slammed the book into her groin and the girl screamed in agony as though the fires of Heaven burned in her womb. He raised his voice, his passion pouring from his lips with every word, the bellowed command a living tangible being as he started to recite the Psalm for the second time.

The girl lifted her clasped hands high above her head. Red trickled down the white flesh, the trickle quickly turning into a steady stream of blood that poured onto the floor beneath her.

"Where do you think you will go when you die little man? Do you think *he* wants you? Do you think there is room in Heaven for your fat carcase? Do you think that *he* loves you, that you are the chosen people? He fucking hates you. All of you."

The steady tone of the horn reached a new, higher pitch, creating a note of incredible purity. Papa slammed the book into the girl, bringing forth a fresh torrent of blood and spittle that rained down upon his open mouth as he began to scream Psalm 91 for the third time, his deep voice booming against the cacophony of vile sounds that erupted from the girl's frothing mouth.

Slowly she sank into the chair and her body sagged, arms falling loosely to her sides, blood soaked and listless. Papa began the closing verse of expulsion, and the accompanying voices started to quieten, their timorous replies barely a whisper. The horn uttered a final soulful cry then fell silent.

Suddenly the girl's head snapped up and she shot out of the chair, gripping my papa by the neck, pushing his considerable bulk backward. As she heaved him violently across the floor, the circle broke, the members shocked and confused by the unexpected show of violence, but all I could see was the face of my mama, her terror, her anger that someone should lay their hands upon her beloved husband.

Blackness filled the girl's eyes, a deep malevolence that consumed her young face in a twisted parody of humanity. Her voice ripped through her throat and tore past her lips filling the space with its fetid reek.

"He is here, the one I have waited for, the Black Messiah and you are all going to die. Even you, Isaiah. Do not think that you are safe, you, or that fat sow of yours. The Black Messiah remembers everything, everyone—he remembers you. The Black Messiah will cleanse the earth of all Father's bastard children. Do not presume to get in his way." The thing threw Papa across the room and he crashed to the floor in a heap. Mama started to move but he screamed for her to stop, to stay away from the creature before them. But Mama, being Mama, ignored his frantic gesturing and ran to his side. She cradled his head in her trembling hands and showered his pleading face with kisses.

A loud crack silenced the room and all eyes fell upon the girl. Her body twisted impossibly, bones cracking and snapping loudly as she swivelled around on her hips in a complete circle. The rawness of it, the brutality inflicted upon her slight frame made me want to be sick, and I tasted bile in the back of my throat.

With a shockingly violent crunch, she snapped, and her hands reached down toward the floor as her upper body fell backward, mangled flesh stretched and cruelly knotted around her torso. The girl was in half but still alive, her black eyes scanning the terrified crowd with sickening satisfaction. The broken form scuttled back and forth on fingers and toes, her head moving from side to side, then suddenly, her head snapped sideways toward me.

The gaze of those horrific black eyes seemed to carry with them a terrible unseen force. My childish body flew against the wall. I could not move, and something akin to recognition flickered across her deadly face and she actually looked pleased to see me. Her lips curled into a cruel sneer and long, blood stained fingers pointed toward me.

"You." The word screamed from its lips with a triumphant howl. The thing turned toward my papa with a contemptuous laugh, but Papa was looking at me, horrified to see me in the room. "That thing is yours?" it demanded.

"Leave him alone, I beg of you, do whatever you will to me but please leave my son alone," implored my papa, tears streaming down his cheeks. Mama covered her face to stifle the scream that burst from between her lips.

"Your son?" hissed the creature. "Ha!" Her black eyes fell upon me and I felt my own warm urine spread shamefully across my trousers. The hissing thing skittered closer. "The Black Messiah will take everything from you that you love, dear heart, and you will be left alone in the dark screaming."

Then the thing began to scream at me.

"Redivivus! Redivivus! Redivivus!" With a tremendous spray of blood and internal organs, her body flew apart, erupting across the room in a shower of red gore. The screaming that filled the community hall was a terrible, painful thing to hear. But it was my scream and I screamed until the blackness consumed me and merciful oblivion stole the world in a thick cloak of suffocating darkness.

Chapter Ten: My Friend Over There Fancies You

Not a shard of light penetrated the fingers clamped so tightly across my face, but not even the darkness could banish the squall that crashed through my mind and blackened my soul. Possessed women tearing themselves apart in a rage of demonic fury, exploding pictures that scorched themselves across my vision in a never-ending mind fuck.

But there was something else. The memory of a horror from a life left behind, a life I had spent sixty years escaping. It gnawed at the corners of my brain with infuriating persistence, a flicker of memory that tugged at my consciousness, an intangible familiarity that screamed at me to open my eyes and see. Every evocative word spoken by Ethan rang in my ears with a disturbing clang of some long forgotten acquaintance. And for the life of me, I could not put the pieces together.

So I buried my head and screamed into my arms, a wretched requiem for the remnants of my isolation. The world was knocking on my door and I would not open it. I did not want it. I did not need it. I certainly did not ask for it. But it was pulling me in with cruel, mocking whispers, taunting me with an inescapable destiny, drawing me back into a world that had already fucked me up the ass.

With every stomach churning thought, the knocking at my door grew louder. If I opened the door, it would be too late, they would see me, they would find me and I would be able to hide no longer.

I needed to hear the rest of his story. Then I would shit my pants.

The Black Messiah—my skin prickled at the name. The words toyed with me, so familiar, yet so lost to the shadows of my mind, lurking at the fringes of my memory. I felt darkness pressing against my back with inevitable certainty, and I was powerless to turn around and face it.

Never was a night so endless.

I felt the edge of my mattress sink. "You know, that trick of yours is starting to wear very thin very quickly."

"Do not mock me, Eli, and besides, I like the feel of the mattress against my bum."

"You like the feel of anything against your bum." Even with my eyes covered, I could feel him sticking his tongue out at me.

"Come on, Mal, spit it out," I demanded, finally uncovering my eyes to look at his translucent face. Butter wouldn't fucking melt.

"So, your new boyfriend is the son of an exorcist. What a marvellous topic of conversation at your next dinner party."

"He is not my new boyfriend." I think thou dost protest too much.

"Oh pull the other one. I have seen the way your eyes linger all over him—your trouser bulges every time you see him. And if I am not mistaken, he can barely tear his fascinating green eyes away from you either."

"You *are* mistaken."

"Really?"

"Really."

Mal harrumphed in an *I don't believe a single word that passes from your lips* kind of way. He presumed too much. It pissed me off.

"So what are you going to do with him?"

"Listen to the rest of his story."

"You know very well what I mean, you stubborn chunk of dead meat, do not be so evasive!"

"I'm not being evasive." My voice was as sharp as the teeth splitting my bottom lip, I was that pissed off. "I'm going to listen to the rest of his story, then we will take it from there. We'll see."

"We will see?"

"Yes goddamn it, we'll see. Christ." I leaped off the bed agitated. "What am I supposed to do? Throw him out into the cold? Let him freeze his bollocks off and take his chances in the wild with a gaping wound in his side? How am I to know what to do? I don't know what to do." Queenie strops were not my thing, but I stormed toward the door, anger exuding from my every orifice.

"I was only asking."

"And I am only saying!"

"Where are you going?"

"Out!"

Okay, so Mal hit a nerve, a very red and pulsating raw nerve. Yes, I fancied him. Yes, he fascinated me. But he also terrified me as well. But nothing was going to happen, nothing.

And I had to admit, the truth of it was inescapable—what man wouldn't look at me? Was I not a stunner? And why couldn't a man love me? What was there not to love? I was funny, I was gorgeous, had a cock that would enter a room before I did and I was intelligent, not to mention my sparkling and witty conversational skills. And why shouldn't I gawp at a piece of eye candy when it was there, so blatantly laid before my deprived eyes? Prick me, do I not bleed? Really. It was the most natural thing in the world.

Natural. And there lay the dilemma. There was nothing natural about me. I was a thing, a supernatural construct masquerading in the shell of a human being with supernatural strength, the ability to fly and an insatiable thirst for blood. I would outlive the planet. Oh, and I could create other monsters too.

Ethan was human. Ethan was a human with all the frailties and limitations that accompanied the species. His bones broke easily, his flesh was like paper and easily penetrated, and if he lived long enough and didn't walk into anything pointy, he would grow old and die. Was that really the lot of a human? To be beautiful, then wither and sag into a limp sack of wrinkled flesh.

I had learned to hide and I had learned to survive, on my own, for a very long time, so why the sudden emotional neediness? I wanted to feel the passion of a lover's lips smashing against my own, to feel the passion of a lover's desires soar through his skin and impart itself within my soul. I wanted someone to love me, and more than that, I found I wanted to love back. The emptiness in my heart was crushing me, making me cold. The lack of existence was crippling me. The pain of loneliness had so settled within my heart, even when I was with *him*, with Gideon, that I knew nothing else. Loneliness felt so natural to me that it had become my normal mode of existence.

Was I ready for that to change? Did I really want that to change? To do so would mean involving myself with another being again, becoming part of the world again, opening my heart again, risk being hurt again.

Fuck that.

So why did I find myself back in that forest amongst the dead? The place drew me back like a magnet, as Ethan seemed to be drawing me to him.

The stack of string-tied diaries lay in the mud next to the trench where I had found Ethan, and I scooped them up. But I was looking for another book, a book that he described in his story, something I remembered seeing lying amongst the discarded dead. I lost sight of it when I ate dinner.

Their bodies still lay where I had left them. The sight of their mangled corpses turned my stomach and I had to look away. Did I really do that?

"Is that shame I see upon your face?"

Daniyyel stood before me in a whisper of disturbed air. He looked magnificent. But I knew the true warrior that lay beneath that face of pure serenity — he wasn't fooling me.

"They gave me no choice." I kept my voice as neutral as possible. It was true they gave me no choice. Ethan or Nazis? I chose Ethan. That sort of behaviour didn't go down too well with those above.

"I know that Eli, I also know what they did here. If you had not dealt with them, then I might have been tempted myself."

My eyebrows shot up. Did I hear right, the angel might actually have taken some action?

"May have been tempted?"

Daniyyel grinned widely and his eyes sparkled wickedly, full of mischief. It was his way of apologising and about as close as that angel ever came to saying *sorry*. I appreciated the gesture.

My eyes scoured the churned up ground. It had to be there somewhere.

"Are you looking for this by any chance?" Daniyyel had the book, of course. He held out the volume toward me, it's heavily embossed binding glinting brightly in the sun. I ran my fingers over the blue gems set into its corners, admiring its beauty.

"Yes, thank you."

"You know what it is of course?"

"It's a Tanakh, a Hebrew Bible. I think it belongs to Ethan's father. I thought..." What did I think? Would Ethan be pleased? Would he be grateful to me for retrieving it?

Why did that matter to me? "I thought Ethan might like it back."

Daniyyel began to pace through the mud, his slender hands clutched behind his back, his eyes fixed on me, burning with a fierce curiosity I did not like.

"What do you intend to do with Ethan?"

And there it was. I knew it was coming. All of a sudden, everybody was interested in me. All of a sudden, everybody wanted a piece of me, wanted answers from me and I was all out of answers.

"You are the second person to ask me that today, although technically, Mal is not a person anymore so does that really count?" The sarcasm dripped from my mouth without thought, but I was beyond caring. His face darkened. That certainly dampened his mood.

"Save your sarcasm for one better served to tolerate such things. What do you intend to do with Ethan? Do not make me ask this simple question again."

The severity of his tone sent a shiver down my spine, but more from sexual attraction than fear of his mood. I should have been afraid, very afraid, but my hormones had a way of counteracting my common sense. Plus I was horny.

"I don't know, all right?" Irritation replaced sarcasm.

"Are you attracted to him?"

The question shocked me so much my jaw hit the floor. "That's a very personal thing to ask, don't you think?" I stammered, hating the sound of my unsteady voice between my lips. "And I fail to see the relevance of that, and to be quite frank I resent the question."

"So you do fancy him." Daniyyel beamed from ear to ear, his smile lighting up the forest around us. He looked fit to burst he was so happy.

So I had a queenie strop, my second one that day. The pile of books I had cradled so carefully in my arms went crashing to the ground and I threw my hands up in exasperation.

"Really? Is everyone interested in my non-existent sex life these days? What does it matter if I fancy him or not? Nothing is going to happen." That only made Daniyyel smile even more. "Ahh!" I screamed at the top of my voice. I curled my fist and punched a tree, sending a chunk of its bark pinging into the undergrowth like a bullet.

Something pounded at the ribs inside my chest, and I gripped my knees as a wave of dizziness hurtled my head into orbit around my asshole. No heart beat within me and yet I felt something churning, pulsing, crushing inside me and I wanted to be sick.

I recognised the symptoms with horror. I was having a panic attack. Me. The notion of wanting somebody again, of feeling so consumed by the thought of them, the look of them, the feel of them, the smell of them... I was fucked.

It was not possible. It was not possible to have such a reaction over someone I had only just met. He was just a man.

Then a thought hit me unexpectedly.

"Do I know him?"

That wiped the smile off his face. Not so fucking smug then, was he.

"What makes you think that?"

That was the trouble. I had absolutely no idea. From the moment Ethan exploded into my life I sensed it, something about him, something so familiar, a nagging sensation in the deepest recesses of my memory. If I closed my eyes, I could almost touch it, but then it would go again, vanishing into the ether of my past.

"Oh I don't bloody know," I slumped onto the ground in a tangle of disenchanted limbs and sulked. "I... I feel something toward him, and that in itself is a load of fucking bollocks because I don't even know who he is. I've only just met him and yet, it feels like I have known him forever. I look into his face and it fits. He just... fits."

Daniyyel knelt down beside me and placed a comforting hand on my shoulder. A tingle of energy flickered through my upper body at his angelic touch and I shuddered. I was doing a lot of that lately.

"You, of all people, should know by now you do not have to justify your feelings toward another, regardless of whom or what they are." I looked into his deep fathomless eyes, and the compassion that radiated from those clear bottomless pools touched me.

"It's not that, Dan, it's just that... it's just that after Gideon, I swore I would never put myself in that position again. Then ding-dong along comes Ethan."

"Those who hurt the most also love the most — you cannot have one without the other."

"He just *feels* so familiar to me... I can't shake it. The moment I saw him over there, dying in the mud, it hit me. And just for a second, the tiniest second, I felt happy... like when you meet someone you haven't seen in a very long time... it overwhelmed me, *he* totally overwhelmed me. I can't explain it. No one has ever done that to me, not even Gideon. So tell me, Daniyyel, my friend from Heaven, do I know him?"

Daniyyel got to his feet and for a moment, one foolish moment, I thought he was going to say something momentous, something profound, but then I saw the reluctance cloud his eyes and the moment was lost.

"You want to help him." It was a statement, not a question. But the key word, the word that always meant a great big pile of steaming shit was in there, the word I had been dreading.

The last time I *helped* someone, it opened all sorts of doors that led to all sorts of Hell. I lost everything because I helped. I lived in self-imposed exile because I helped.

"You know who these people are?" Daniyyel said, his arm sweeping across the bloodbath that surrounded us.

"Surely who they are is irrelevant. They were people, people who did not deserve such brutality. Look at them, a waste of precious life."

"You misunderstand me, but it is good to hear such compassion in your voice."

"Then just for one minute, can we please pretend that I am not a vampire and you are not an angel and that we are just two people speaking plainly?"

"Then plainly I will speak. All humankind is beloved to my Father, but the Jews hold a special affection in his heart. The atrocity that has occurred here is but a tiny fraction of the slaughter being committed across the world in a war that is on the verge of splitting this planet in half. We sit and we watch, unable to intervene as they die in their millions, and all at the whim of a single lunatic, a true monster."

"Then *do* something about it!"

"We can't!" The anger and frustration in his voice surprised me. "Father forbids it. The consequences of such actions would be catastrophic. Consequences, Eli, always consequences. So we sit and we watch. Heaven weeps and the rivers of our tears threaten to drown us in our apathy. Father insists that the human race sort out its own problems, for better or for worse, and while there are many of us who disagree, none will stand against him. Remember what I said about rules?"

Fuck me, I was stunned. In all the years I had known Daniyyel, he had never opened up to me in such a way. But the thought that Heaven could stand by so callously and watch the human race tear itself apart shocked me even more. That God would allow such a thing filled me with a profound sadness, because if he didn't care, why the fuck should the rest of us?

"And yet you are here, telling me this, is that not breaking the Covenant?"

"A nudge, a little encouragement is not the same as outright disobedience. Man started this war and man must finish it. We cannot get involved. But you have shown an interest in Ethan and his plight, indeed you saved him from the Nazis, so does that mean you want to get involved in this? Are you coming out of hiding?"

"I'm not hiding." How dare he?

"You have been hiding for sixty years. You may be able to convince yourself otherwise, my friend, but I know you better than that. The world is at war. Are you prepared to get involved in that?"

"The world has already taken everything I have. It is a better place without me in it. Okay, so I have been hiding for sixty years, but I have been running on empty for far longer than that. I just want to be left alone."

"And yet you brought Ethan back to your home. Is that not getting involved? Does that not illustrate a desire to re-emerge into the world of the living?"

"Oh fuck off, you bloody hypocrite. Go and drown yourself in that fucking river of apathy, why don't you. How can you stand there and goad me for not getting involved when you lot won't lift a fucking finger to help anyone?"

Blinding white light burned across my vision and I cried out in pain. My head filled with the sound of clashing steel and all I could see was blood. Agony crippled my limbs and blinded my senses. All was lost in despair and hatred.

Suddenly Daniyyel was holding me tightly to his slender chest.

"I'm sorry, I am so sorry," he whispered, "I lost control, forgive me, my friend, forgive me."

"It's okay, honestly, don't worry about it, I deserved it." I knew how to push his buttons, so I had it coming.

"No, no you didn't. It's true what you said—we are hypocrites. I am a hypocrite."

"No, Dan, no, you are just like me, that's all, afraid, we are just afraid."

"I hate this, Eli, I can't stand it. Heaven is supposed to be more than it is, we are supposed to be more than we are. I don't know where it went wrong, or what to do. I don't know what to do."

"Welcome to my world."

Daniyyel laughed suddenly and I felt the mood lighten between us.

"For once, my friend I agree!"

"I have seen war before, but this one… I don't know what to think of it to be honest. I need to hear the rest of Ethan's story—maybe there will be answers there, perhaps for both of us?"

"If mankind survives this, there will be more wars in the future. While men have ideas, there will always be conflict and bloodshed will always be inevitable. But it is the ideas behind this war that make it so different. One man's desire to stamp out all that is different from him and his personal ideology may well result in the extermination of all that is beautiful and individual in the human race. Something I would have thought you would well appreciate?"

"Meaning?"

"That it is not only the Jews who are being systematically slaughtered."

I understood his meaning—his subtleties were not lost on me. What was more pertinent though was the meaning behind his words.

"So what you are saying is that you *want* me to get involved. You think I *should* get involved."

Daniyyel smirked. The audacity of that angel.

"You might well think that, but I couldn't possibly comment."

It was my turn to laugh. I had always thought myself above such manipulation, but against the angels machinations, I had no defence. In one swift and insidiously clever move, he had me fighting the Nazi war machine. I went back to that forest to find some books, but he would have me leave a freedom fighter.

"But mark my words, Eli." His sudden solemn tone chilled me. "This will be a game changer. Once you start down this path, there will be no ruby slippers to take you back to Kansas."

I let his words sink in, smirking slightly at his Judy moment. Then I looked into his beatific face and beamed at him. "And maybe you will ask me the question if I get through this? Assuming I still want to go."

"Cheeky."

"Of course."

"Who knows, my friend, if you get through this, then God himself may ask you. Tell me, that book, have you ever read it?"

"Hell, no."

"There are many angels and demons in that book, many stories. You may wish to read it sometime. It may be of interest to you. May I accompany you back to Alte? I would also like to hear Ethan's story, plus it would give me an excuse to fly with you once more. It's been a long time."

"It would be my honour."

I felt somehow that something had changed between us — I just wasn't sure what it was. But something had shifted. Perhaps we found a deeper understanding of each other, a more thoughtful appreciation of each other. As we rose into the air, we clasped hands, the vampire and the angel, flying through the air like old friends, hand-in-hand as though it were the most natural thing in the world.

Chapter Eleven: The Story of Ethan Part Two

As related by Ethan

The more I worked my body, the more I liked it. Paint cans, bricks, anything to push my muscles to their limits, but as I pushed my body, I also pushed my mind, absorbing all the information my parents could give me like a sponge, reading every book in my father's extensive library. I would never be weak again, physically or spiritually.

Within the year, that child who saw the devil became a man, but the man became something else altogether.

Papa was a Rabbi, but he was more than that, he was Baal Shem, the master of the name. The Baal Shem is a master of the Kabbalah and seeks to bring harmony and understanding to the universe through his teachings and, as the stories go, has a direct line to God. As such, the Baal Shem is the head of the ritual Quorum, a group of ten individuals known as Minyan who surround the Baal Shem during exorcism to give spiritual strength. My mama was the only female I had ever heard of to hold such a position.

I was so proud of my parents and so very grateful. That first night when I lay screaming on that carpet, instead of hiding me away, shielding me behind a wall of cotton wool, they took me into their confidence. They told me everything. They taught me about a world of demons, monsters, possession, ritual exorcism. A world constantly at war with the devil, and it frightened me at first, but I listened and I learned. I felt closer to them after that night than I ever thought possible, the bond that had cemented itself between us three a tangible thing, unbreakable. We completed each other. Those few fragile and precious years together defined my very existence, defined the shape of my body and the shape of my mind, and I saw my future laid out before me with clear purpose. My parents trained me so that one day I could take over as head of the Quorum and I could think of nothing more fulfilling.

Of all the exorcisms I attended, none ever reached the intensity of that first one. We never forgot it, particularly Papa. I could see the torment hiding behind his eyes, that maybe he could have done more, the teasing agony that maybe he could have expelled that vile force earlier. Mama tried to comfort him, sometimes with a word, sometimes with a gentle touch. I could see the relief, all be it brief, flicker across his troubled brow and the guilt would lessen, only to return with renewed intensity. I knew deep down he blamed himself, every minute of every day.

Redivivus, that was what it screamed at me, an ancient Latin term meaning, *to be reborn.* It also mocked me for being my papa's son. All part of the demon's twisted mind games, my parents said, but it always bothered me because that thing spoke to me as though it knew me. It bothered them too, though they tried not to show it, eating away at them silently every time they looked at me. I always figured one day they would explain, when they were ready, but time is a funny thing—we never seem to have as much of it as we think.

Many a night I lay awake, the demons words tormenting me, how I would lose everything, how the Black Messiah was coming to take everything away from me. That I would be alone in the dark screaming. My parents were my world and everything that was dear to me, and that monster threatened to rip them away. I lived in stark fear of that threat for most of my early life.

In February 1933, my nightmares came true.

On the 30th January 1933, Adolf Hitler became Reich Chancellor, effectively sealing the future of the Nazi movement and assuring his rise to the ultimate power in Germany. The SS took to the streets with torches, marching triumphantly through Berlin. We fled to our homes, terrified for our lives, and I think we knew then our time in Berlin would soon be at an end. January 30th 1933 was the turning point for everything.

The next day, the strangest sight greeted our eyes. Not one prone to dramatics, I considered myself to have a reasonably level head, but when we dared to venture out into the day it was as if some terrible foreboding hand reached across the city to wrap its fingers around our unsuspecting throats. The atmosphere was tangible. Something had descended onto the streets of Berlin, something dark and sinister, and it brought with it a deathly, silent pallor that clung to brick and flesh alike. We all felt it.

I found myself transported back to that night as a child when I opened a door from colour into a world of black and white, for that was how it felt walking onto those desolate streets that morning. A world filled with a painful silence and a profound, deadly stillness, no traffic, no birds, not even a breath of wind to ruffle our hair. We all looked at each other puzzled, each of us feeling that same stomach turning dread.

Then we heard it, the sound of horse hooves, heavy and laboured, dragging against the concrete surface of the road. The sound of pain personified.

We huddled together into little sporadic groups and stared transfixed as the first animal rounded the corner.

Two enormous black horses each pulled a black cart.

Huge, shabby, unkempt creatures, they seemed to heave their bulks down the street rather than walk. Steam and mucus leaked from their ears, their eyes bulging black from their angular heads under the strain of pulling their unearthly loads. The horses didn't make a sound, not a snuffle, or a toss of the head — they remained steadfast and silent, with just the grind of their hooves sliding against the road surface to disturb the hush. A Nazi flag wrapped the sweaty carcase of each beast. The swastika stood out like a beacon of hate against their jet-black bodies. The sight of it repulsed me.

Each cart carried a cluster of tall boxes, at least eight to a cart. Each box stood roughly the size of a man, bizarre coffins constructed of wood, pine monoliths each emblazoned with a swastika. The sight of those boxes sent an irrational chill of fear through my body. I could feel the malevolence oozing from them, leeching through the timber toward us and I knew they concealed something terrible.

As the first cart drew level, the Nazi clutching the reigns in his black leather clad hand sneered down at me. Never had I seen such a look of contempt written across a human face. Dressed from head to toe in black, he cut a formidable figure. Not all Germans were Nazis and not all Nazis were monsters, but those black pariahs were SS, an evil rooted deep at the heart of the Nazi Empire, and one whose reputation we rightfully feared. With growing unease, we stepped away from the carts for fear the whip clutched in the bastard's hand might find a place against our faces. He knew what we were thinking, and he smirked. I wanted to punch that triumphant look of superiority from his lips, but not even I was that stupid.

The procession moved painfully slowly, but as the last two carts came into view, another sound began to overpower the dragging staccato of hooves. Bilious clouds of steam hissed into the sky accompanied by a whirring, clicking mechanical noise that screeched above all else.

The engine that appeared resembled something from an H.G.Wells nightmare. The thing crawled through the streets like a tank, for it moved on casters and tracks like a regular vehicle, but that was where the similarity ended. Atop the tracks spewed a seemingly chaotic array of tubes, pipes and pistons that moved and hissed, spitting copious amounts of steam amid a complex collection of clockwork mechanisms that defied understanding. Cradled in the middle of that cacophonous pile of technology sat an enormous block of ice, draped in a thin veil of mist that swirled and coiled around the many tubes and wires that pierced its cold surface. I had never seen anything like it.

Something sat within the ice, something large and dark at its heart though the ice and mist heavily distorted the image and I could not be sure. I could see however, that the tubes and wires seemed to converge on or into its form. Curious still, I saw a large brass tube protruding from the ice, ending in a tap.

As the thing moved past, my flesh crawled, and it wasn't just because of the cold. Some of the women around me looked faint and the men hurried them back into the safety of their homes, but I stayed until the thing was out of sight, unable to tear my eyes away from that block of ice and its mysterious contents. Eventually it disappeared, the sounds of its mechanics fading.

"Papa, have you ever seen anything like it?" Papa looked dreadful, white and trembling where he stood. The look of despair and terror upon his face frightened me more than anything I had just seen. "Papa?" Without a word, he turned his back on me and walked into the house. I stood there for a moment shocked, unsure what to do. I jumped as a hand rested on my shoulder.

"Mama. What's wrong with Papa? Did you see him?"

"Leave him, Ethan, just leave him be." Her eyes, red and puffy, betrayed her concern.

"But Mama..."

"Leave him be, Ethan," she demanded, her words hard as steel. I reeled back, stunned by her tone, shocked she would raise her voice to me. She must have seen the hurt flicker across my face because she swept forward, scooping me into her ample chest until all I could smell was freshly baked bread.

"Promise me, Ethan, please, do not question him, please, please just let him be. Papa will be fine, just fine."

"Yes, Mama." Nothing more was said.

The deaths started that night. The first one hit very close to home and by rights, we should have left Berlin there and then, but Papa would not abandon his people, even though God abandoned us that night.

We awoke to the sounds of shouting in our street and we rushed outside to find Mr. Shultz, our neighbour, screaming as half a dozen SS troops loaded what looked like a body bag into a large black van. His sons held him back but the poor man was inconsolable. Two of the men in black had rifles pointed at Mr. Shultz and his sons, keeping them away from the van, and Mr. Shultz was literally out of his mind pleading for them to return the body of his wife, begging them to understand she did not commit suicide.

I stood rooted to the spot, my mind a frenzy of shock and confusion. Mrs. Shultz was dead. Suicide? Why were they taking her body? Did they not understand our ways? Where were they taking her?

Mr. Shultz broke away from his sons and flung himself at their mercy, kneeling on the wet ground before them, begging them to listen, his pleas pitiful to hear. The soldier laughed, lifted his rifle and hit him across the head with the butt of the weapon. He crumpled to the ground. We rushed forward, but the guns lifted toward us instantly and we had no choice but to obey. The SS troops backed away into their van, still aiming their guns at us as they drove away.

Aided by his two sons, we picked up Mr. Shultz's body and Papa ushered us all into our house, where we laid the barely breathing man on our threadbare sofa. He was bleeding heavily from a deep gash on the crown of his head, but Mama was expert in such things and immediately began to tend to his wound while his sons explained what had happened.

The boys, grief stricken and terrified, told us of the events that transpired. Mr. Shultz woke to an empty bed and heard a strange moaning sound downstairs. He ventured down, worried his wife might have fallen and hurt herself. As he reached the bottom of the stairs, he saw his wife lying in the arms of a sinewy black shadow, but it was dark and he could not see clearly. The shadow unfurled from the body of his wife, then dropped her before leaping out of an open window. Mr. Shultz, shouting for his sons help, ran toward his wife, but he could see that she was already dead. Her eyes were wide with terror. Before he could pick up her broken body, the SS burst through the door, bagging the corpse while fending off the family at gunpoint. One of the troops claimed suicide was against the law and declared the confiscated body belonged to the German Empire.

Two other members of the Jewish community died that night in similar circumstances. The Germans reported both deaths as suicide. The SS took away both bodies.

Mr. Shultz recovered enough to go home. The next night we heard him screaming through the walls, a terrible agonising sound that would forever haunt my nightmares. Thinking we could help, we rushed next door, where his sons told us Mr. Shultz had dreamt his dead wife had visited him. We did not see Mr. Shultz, but we could hear him crying as his eldest son tried to calm the frail man, but his agonised pleas echoed through our thin house as though the walls did not exist. He kept calling out his dead wife's name, begging her to come back to his bed.

Mr. Shultz died the next night, his body also impounded by the SS. The official explanation cited overwhelming grief leading to suicide. One week later, both sons were also dead. In a space of two weeks, some twenty Jewish souls, twenty friends, twenty God-fearing beautiful souls were dead, all by apparent suicide, all linked by close relatives, entire families gone. Names that should have perpetuated through time vanished, names that no human lips would ever speak again, lost to us by some unspeakable, unholy massacre. The world became a sadder, darker place for the loss of those names.

Our community fell apart. Superstitious rumour spread like a cancer, eating away at our hearts and our souls. We heard talk of monsters, demons that sucked our lifeblood, but no one survived to give a full and proper account, and with every night came the report of more deaths, of more bodies stolen by the SS.

We feared the night. Sometimes we would hear screaming in the darkness, and we three would sit at our kitchen table, terrified and powerless. Something was hunting us in the darkness and one by one, our people disappeared. Death lurked in every shadow. We felt as though we had been marked, singled out for punishment, abandoned by God. We felt unclean. Our normal everyday lives no longer existed, and though we remained safe by day, once the sun set, we would huddle together in groups, fearful of sleep, fearful of every sound, fearful of what may visit during the night.

It had a profound effect on Papa. The cheerful, joyful soul that filled the community with so much happiness withered before my eyes. For every death a little more of him died. Never had I seen him look so powerless. He would not speak to me. He found it difficult even to look at me. Mama, poor Mama, all she could do was sit at his side cradling his hands in hers, hands that trembled constantly. She tried to reassure me with her smile, but I felt the desperation that poleaxed them both.

Where had his fight gone? I could not understand it. That was not my papa. The grey frightened man sitting with his head hung in defeat at our dining table was not my papa.

People left. I could not blame them. Families evacuated with as much as they could carry on their shoulders and within a few short weeks, the Jewish community in Berlin had dwindled to barely half. I could not begin to number those that left and those that disappeared. It all happened so quickly, friends I had grown up with, people I had known my whole life gone, the bags upon their backs a pitiful reminder of that which they left behind, and sadder still was the knowledge we would never see any of them again. We were a decimated people.

Then the first non-Jewish suicides began. I suppose with so little kosher meat available it was only a matter of time before the plague extended to those other members of the community considered undesirable. Anything non-Arian seemed to be fair game. Even those Germans considered ... different... began to disappear.

I had a friend, Karl. His parents owned the lumber mill where I had worked many a happy childhood hour. One day when I was brushing up the sawdust, I found him hiding behind a pile of wood I was busy sweeping around and he was crying. Karl's father was a monster, a first-degree bully who thought nothing of beating the German way and German discipline into his child. I noticed the red welts across Karl's knees, freshly inflicted. I sat with him for a little while until he calmed, and we became friends from that day forward. Over the years, our friendship grew stronger, even though we both knew it was a friendship condemned. We dared not speak to each other in public never mind hang out together in public, the Jew and the German, a friendship forbidden, on so many levels.

Karl was dead. I saw them take his body. Moreover, his father seemed to be pleased about it. I cried over his loss, I think it broke my heart a little. But he was the first non-Jew taken by the SS, and the rumours of his suicide quickly spread through the community. I heard voices claim that Karl deserved it and it served him right, and they were not just German voices either. I wanted to ask them where their humanity was, where was their compassion, but I kept quiet, ashamed, frightened. Karl was the first, but he was by no means the last.

I could not help but wonder when my turn would come.

By mid-February, the Jewish community had dwindled so much that those who remained, had taken to congregating at night in the synagogue. Our place of worship had now become a place of shelter, but the blight that was stealing our families and friends showed no sign of abating.

So many elderly packed into that synagogue. Grandparents, great grandparents, the wisest of our generation, all crammed into the one space, each with their own opinion and theories regarding our plight. Sheesh were they vocal about it. Many a heated debate broke out in a space already charged by fragile emotion, a tinderbox on the verge of exploding.

It was during one such spirited conversation that poor Mr. Weitzman died. Bless him—at the age of eighty-six he saw his family destroyed, one by one, hauled off in body bags by the SS. I think they also took his will to live. As he struggled to his feet, his voice impassioned, he suddenly

Dead Camp One

clutched his chest, and the realisation of his looming death bloomed across his ancient face. There was not the grimace of pain or even the look of fear, just relief, relief he was about to leave a world that had betrayed him so very badly.

We carried him into the annex, where we placed his body on a table and covered him with a white sheet. Our tradition meant that a member of the family stay with the deceased until burial could take place, but in that instance, no family remained, so my beloved mama opted to stay with Mr. Weitzman. I was to organise the preparation of the body, the Taharah, in accordance with our customs, of which there are very many different processes, from cleaning the body to purifying the flesh with water. Mr. Weitzman was devout in his beliefs, and he deserved to have those beliefs upheld, no matter how dire our circumstances.

The last time I saw my lovely mama alive was at that moment, in that hall sitting next to the shrouded body of our friend. Her long hair, still vibrant and glossy for a woman her age, sat atop her proud head in a curled bun, held in place by a knitting needle, of all things. Her cheeks glowed red and her eyes glistened with steely purpose. She wore her favourite black housedress, knee length, trimmed around the hems and cuffs with ivory lace, pinched in at her ample waist by a thick leather belt. She had owned that old belt forever. The last image ingrained into my heart is of that final smile and the flick of her hand as she sent me to find Papa, who would have Mr. Weitzman's Tallit.

If you knew that one moment, that precious unique instant of time was the last time you would ever see your mama alive, what would you do? Would you rush up to her and hold her tight? Would you tell her how much you loved her? Would you thank her for your life, for her love, for the joy she instilled into your very being, would you thank her for making you the person you are? Would you try to stop her dying somehow? Would you die for her? If you knew that you would never see her alive again what would you do? All I knew was that I winked at her. My mama was about to die and I winked at her.

Papa and the others crowded around the doors to the synagogue, craning their necks into the outside world. The streets were crawling with SS troops and fire engines.

"The Reichstag building is on fire." He didn't need to say anything else. The Nazis would see the destruction of such an important German building as an act of terrorism and the whole of Berlin would suffer the consequences. Jews would suffer the consequences.

Transfixed by the chaotic scene unfolding before him, he thrust something into my hand and I realised it was Mr. Weitzman's prayer shawl.

"Your mama will want this." Trust him to know what Mama needed.

I hurried back down to the hall, eager to tell her of the events unfolding outside. I rushed through the door breathless, words spilling from my lips before my eyes had the chance to see the horror before me.

It looked to me in those first few seconds that the two figures before me blurred together as one, the monster and my mama. The creature wrapped itself around her body in a tangle of gangly limbs, and a dark lump lay snuggled into her throat. At the sound of my arrival the creature looked up, unfurling its vile head from the neck of my mama with deadly poise. Its eyes blazed red from a long white face and I glimpsed something on its back, clinging to its shoulder, squirming darkly, but I could not be sure. The vampire opened its cavernous mouth that dripped with the blood of my mama, its two long white teeth flashing in the dim light as it hissed at me.

My tiny human brain could barely understand what I was

seeing. My head screamed in agony at the sight of her limp body clutched in its hands, but my voice caught in my throat, a strangled groan that died along with my heart. Fear froze my crumbling legs to the floor, a cruel relentless fear that tore my body apart, fear she was dead.

The creature dropped her limp form to the floor and I gasped with horror, that single careless act repulsive to me. I screamed something—I don't know what—and the thing actually smiled. It stepped over her body, moving stiffly, its limbs elongated and bony, and the whole creature moved in a haunch, hands curled up under its chest, fingers dangling loose beneath it. Then I saw it, flashing across its grotesque face and I felt it too, a dawning recognition. The monster knew me, and I knew it.

It was Mr. Shultz. Terrible blood slathered lips parted and a voice, so dry and dead, hissed through the cracked gore-smeared slit.

"She is ours now, she will receive the child of our mother, and she will do her bidding. Can you hear his voice, human? He speaks to us in our heads, our Black Messiah commands us and we go where he bids, gathering his chosen into our collective. She is ours."

The rage hit me with tremendous force and something inside me snapped. Without a thought or care for my own life, I launched myself at the monster, my hands outstretched for its wretched throat, but before my fingers could wrap themselves around his neck, the creature roared, a dreadful bone-shattering sound that drowned out my own screams as it swatted me aside like a fly. I hit the far wall hard and slumped to the floor, my breath knocked from my lungs. I looked up quickly to see the Shultz thing scuttling toward me, its arms flailing from side to side as it swept through a group of chairs that shattered at its touch. I half ran, half-slid along the wall and grabbed a chair, hurling it uselessly at the thing behind me. All I could think of was the body lying on the floor, my mama, my dear precious mama, my beloved dead mama.

I changed direction suddenly and dived at the creature, sending us both tumbling to the floor. As we rolled through the wooden debris, I grabbed a broken chair leg and plunged it down with all my might into the chest of the writing creature beneath. It cracked through the rib cage with a sickening crunch and blood pumped thick and black into my face. It was cold, so cold. But I was beyond caring. I pushed and I pushed, screaming through clenched teeth as the wood penetrated deeper. I placed my whole weight above the stake, and with a sudden explosion of blood and bone, the wood hit the floor beneath the monster. It hissed and screamed, thrashing from side to side then it stopped, its grotesque jaw slack, its cruel fingernails buried deep into the floor at which it clawed.

Still screaming I stepped back slowly, hardly able to believe what I had done. I held my hands before my eyes, my fingers dripping with its blood, blood that mingled with that of my mama, and I screamed my horror through my fingers until my voice ran out of breath.

It was dead.

I had killed it.

And I died along with the bastard thing.

My eyes could barely accept the motionless mound lying where she had fallen. I wanted her to move, some flicker of hope to tell me she was still alive, just a little sign to tell me I had not lost her. I was desperate, hysterical because she was not moving.

Please, Mama, move, just move, move. The words screamed and screamed in my head and reason abandoned me.

And there was movement, but not from her.

Mr. Shultz sat up sharply like a puppet pulled by

invisible strings. Blood-encrusted hands moved involuntarily, grasping at the wood embedded in its chest and again I glimpsed that strange humped shape on its back, just a suggestion of movement over its shoulder, something alive there but always just outside of my perception. Withered hands pulled the wood from its chest in an explosion of gore and a sigh hissed between its ragged lips as it fixed its deadly gaze upon me, red eyes burning into my soul. The monster snapped to its feet with terrifying speed and a clawed hand flashed out suddenly, hitting me in the chest to send me crashing against the opposite wall.

The rest happened in slow motion, at least that's how it felt, the slow inevitability of impending death.

I saw the monster rise into the air, legs curled beneath it, arms spread wide to embrace me, and in one fluid movement, it was sitting on my chest, my hands pinned beneath its knees. A thick, sickening gurgle erupted from its maw as it lowered its head toward my neck, saliva and cold blood bubbling around its trembling lips. I felt the twin points of its teeth brush against my flesh. I felt anticipation tremble through its body and slowly, oh so fucking slowly, the teeth pressed down.

At that moment, I knew I was going to die. All I saw was blazing red eyes and blood-encrusted lips.

As death bore down I saw her, my mama, floating over me, and I could see straight through her. The thing at my neck knew she was there because it reared backward in an impossible display of contortion that sent its bones cracking, its head nearly touching its spine, hissing and spitting at the apparition that shimmered behind it.

I struggled out from underneath the vampire and scuttled backward. I couldn't take my eyes off the spirit floating before me. She was so radiant, so beautiful. Her eyes said everything to me, so much love and so much sadness,

sadness to be lost to me, sadness she was lost to her husband. The depth of feeling in that one glance filled me with overwhelming grief—it was all I could do to stifle the sob that erupted from my throat and I had to clamp my hands over my mouth to quell the terrible sound trying to break free. Tears streamed down my face as my body shook with uncontrollable emotion, my heart and my soul laid bare in all its shattered pieces.

With a sound I felt more than heard, the spirit entered the furious creature before me. My ears exploded with a violent pop as the air pressure plummeted. The vampire screamed in agony, writhing on the floor, its painfully long limbs slapping the ground so violently I thought they would snap. Steam began to issue from its mouth, from its ears and eyes and blood began to leach from its flaccid grey skin. A wave of heat slammed me against the wall as the vampire began to disintegrate, huge chunks of flesh falling from its bones and turning to ash as it hit the floor. A loud whistling noise filled the air, its pitch rising higher and higher until it became intolerable. And then it was gone.

She knelt before me, a shimmering vision I could not touch or embrace. Our fingers reached out toward each other but I could feel nothing. But I felt her inside. I felt it ripping at my heart, I felt it tearing the joy from my soul, and the feeling of loss and overwhelming pain was more than I could bear and I wept, tears falling freely, great gulp-inducing sobs heaving at my shoulders. Even in death, Mama had saved me, as she had always saved me in life. Her smile hurt me even more because I knew it was a thing I would only see in my nightmares from that moment on, that she would never be able to give it to me again. I did not want that smile to fade, I wanted to commit that smile to everlasting memory, to remember every single crinkle and crease that formed around it. But all too quickly, her image began to fade.

"Mama! Don't go. Please don't go. Please don't leave us." My sobs were pitiful and useless. Her lips moved, but the words had no sound—but the shapes of those words were unmistakable to me, because I had heard her say them to me so very many times.

"I love you."

With a final heart-wrenching smile she faded away, back into her lifeless corpse, and I stared at the empty space before me in utter horror and despair. Mama was gone.

Then I lost it. I crawled over to her body and clutched her to my chest as my grief filled the great hall. Blackness seeped around the corners of my eyes, but I didn't care if my misery stole my sight or if my heart stopped beating within my chest, because my heart already felt dead.

A wretched cry echoed through the hall, but not from me. A hand gripped my shoulder and Papa knelt before me, staring at me in wide-eyed horror and disbelief, his mouth open in shock. I screamed at him, holding my dear dead Mama out to his trembling hands and he gripped my shoulders, his fingers digging into my skin, but I did not feel the pain. He began to moan, looking at the body I clutched so desperately, his mind unable to accept what he was seeing, and Papa fell apart before my eyes.

As the streets of Berlin erupted in violence and the Reichstag building burned, we carried her body back to our house. In the confusion and the violence no one tried to claim her body, and I think Papa would have ripped them apart with his bare hands if they had tried, such was the ferociousness that burned in his eyes. It frightened me.

I carried his dead wife across my shoulder, wrapped in a blanket, but he did not say a word to me.

When we reached our home, a moan escaped his lips as he opened the door, a sound that caused the tears to roll from my eyes. He turned to me as I walked into the hall, his entire body shaking, his face wet with spilled tears. He took his dead wife from me. He carried her into the parlour and laid her on the table, so gently, and his hands hovered briefly above the cloth as though they could not bear to touch her.

"Papa?" I whispered, desperate for him to speak to me. "Papa? Why will you not speak to me, Papa? Papa, can you hear me?"

He turned, and the look on his face made me step back in fear. With long purposeful strides he crossed the short distance between us, his hand outstretched flat against my chest and pushed me out of the small room, closing the door in my face without a single word.

I sat at the kitchen table for the rest of the night. I could not bring myself to close my eyes, because every time I did, I saw that thing at Mama's throat and I heard its monstrous voice taunting me. The vampire spoke as though it had purpose, as though directed by a higher power, as though it expected Mama to rise from the grave and join it, to join his collective.

It expected Mama to rise.

The words echoed around my skull, paralysing me with horror. I looked toward the parlour door as if expecting her to shamble through it, the blood of my papa dripping from her dead lips. I screamed, the word escaping from my lips before I had time to temper the terror that fuelled it.

"Papa!"

I shot up from the table, the chair overturning as I darted toward the door. I pressed my ear against the wood and listened for any hint of movement within, but only the sound of my own pounding heart echoed back at me.

My unsteady hand reached out and turned the knob, my fingers tentative as my whole body thrummed with the apprehension of what lay behind that thin wooden barricade. Slowly it opened. I held my breath, willing my limbs to push me forward. I walked into darkness.

It took several seconds for my eyes to become accustomed to the gloom, several heart-stopping seconds immersed in inky blackness, unable to perceive the wretched hands I felt sure were reaching for my throat. But nothing stirred. Shapes began to materialise as my eyes adjusted to the darkness and I could make out my poor exhausted papa slumped at the table with his head in his arms, shoulders twitching with troubled sleep. Mama's body lay next to him under a white tablecloth, her livid white feet sticking out from the bottom.

Morning began to struggle through the thin curtains, lifting the death shroud that hung heavy upon the scene. One of her arms, limp and flaccid, lay dangling toward the floor.

There was something wrong with that hand. Mama had workers hands, rough skin, stubby fingers and very short clipped fingernails. She hated the thought of bread dough lurking beneath her nails so she always kept them brutally short. All the easier to clean, she would say. But those fingers dangling beneath the table were long and skinny, like articulated twigs that ended in equally long, viciously sharp nails and I rubbed my eyes, uncertain of what I was seeing because those fingers and nails seemed to grow as I watched.

My stomach lurched and squeezed as bile gushed up my throat and filled my mouth. I felt faint. I fell to my knees gasping for air, slamming my hands against the floor, my throat tightening, suffocating me with fear.

The sound of rustling fabric above my head and the groan of wood complaining beneath a shifted weight turned my pounding blood to ice, freezing me to the spot. Blackness seeped around the corners of my eyes and the world swam before me in a perfect storm of madness. I forced my head up, just enough to see the legs of the table. I didn't want to see, my god I didn't want to see and I didn't want to hear, I didn't want to raise my head and I didn't want to witness Mama's bare legs reaching slowly toward the floor, long ugly toes digging into the thread bare rug. My eyes refused to see the trembling white flesh, the blotchy patches of purple blood, or the black insidious veins that pulsed with undead life.

But I did see them.

I looked up, may God forgive me and rip my eyes from my skull, I looked up. My mouth fell open and I heaved. Warm urine trickled down my leg. I wanted to scream, but my voice died in my throat as my mind withered at the sight that assaulted my eyes, and something inside me snapped — something inside me broke.

Mama looked down on me with black eyes, her face a mere parody of the one I loved. White, blue veined, translucent skin stretched over high gaunt cheekbones and pointy ears gave her a vaguely animalistic appearance. But the mouth was worse. Thin languid flaps replaced her once plump ruby lips, and sticking out between those lips, almost piercing her chin were two long teeth, very close together and very sharp. Saliva dribbled from the corner of her mouth.

She held her long hands up toward her saggy chest, left hand wrapped over the right wrist, those terrible fingers dripping down, twitching slightly. Her dress, her wonderfully familiar black dress, hung like a rag on her emaciated body, the fabric stained and wet with body fluids. She stood with a slight stoop, as though her hands, which she held so close, were too heavy for her to hold.

Mama had been dead for only a few hours, but the

shivering, putrescent corpse standing before me had the stench of week-old death.

No one should ever have to witness such a thing.

I thought it couldn't get any worse. I thought that monstrous apparition was the absolute apex of terror that I could possibly endure. I thought God would not be so pitiless as to inflict yet more cruelty upon me. My eyes had been defiled, but then began the corruption of my ears.

Her lips quivered and parted with a dry crack and a desiccated voice squeezed from between them. The sound was painful and disjointed, as though the words themselves were difficult to string together, but it carried with it a tone of desperation and pity that made the tears tumble from my eyes.

"Hungry... I am... so... hungry."

A tremulous hand reached out toward me, her entire body beseeching me, her face imploring me. It was a look of such total pain and such desperate sorrow, despair given form. She snatched her hand back sharply and staggered back into the table. She was trying to resist me.

"It... hurts. I feel... pain... Feed... Me... Feed... Me?"

I had to help her. I had to help my mama. I held out my wrist, hesitant, desperate. But that was my mama and she was asking me for help, so I thrust my bared flesh toward her quivering lips.

She looked at my wrist, her black tongue flicking against the points of her monstrous teeth. Her mouth opened and closed, but then she looked at me, and it was a look of utter pain and confusion. I could see the conflict raging across her dead face. I shook my wrist at her gently, trying to tell her it was okay, that I would do it for her, only for her, always for her.

Something akin to lust overrode her caution and slowly she slithered toward me, her hands held up at the level of her eyes, fingers twitching excitedly. Her movements looked jerky, stilted, and it repulsed me. But I could not resist my mama.

My voice exploded inside my head.

She is my mama and I love her.

She is my mama and she needs my help.

I am my mama's son and I will die for her.

"Feed... Me..."

Bones snapped and cracked as she bent down toward my wrist, her back bending in unnatural places, but I clung to the living memory of my mama and to her love that still filled my heart.

Fingers brushed my skin. My flesh erupted with goose pimples. For the second time that night, I felt the teeth of a vampire caress my flesh.

I saw him then, over her shoulder, Papa staring wide-eyed at the scene before him. I saw the terror and the disgust written on his tear-stained face. I shook my head at him sadly, hoping he would understand, hoping he would not hate me for what I had to do.

He moved with a speed that belied his age. With a roar of fury, he gripped his dead wife around the waist and flung her to the far side of the room. Without so much as a missed heartbeat he turned and the palm of his hand lashed out across my face with a force that found me sprawled across the floor.

The situation hit me with instant clarity. My head cleared, and in those precious few seconds I realised the creature had ensnared me in its thrall. And it was a creature, a vampire — it was not my mama.

"Take me, my beloved, not our son, he is so young and I am so old, and I cannot exist without you by my side, the pain of living without you is too much for me to endure. Take me with you. Let me die at your side."

To my utter dismay, Papa moved to her crumpled body, his intention horrifyingly clear. He wanted to be with her, he wanted to go with her into eternity, an eternity of death. And I knew he was not under her spell — she had not spoken to him or looked into his face as I had. His decision to die by her hand was his own. Nothing could have frightened me more.

There was no time to think. I threw myself at the curtains, grabbed the thin cloth with both hands, pulling them away from the window. Sunlight flooded the room.

Bright white light, the very fingers of God himself hit the corpse that had once been my mama. She did not cry, not a single sound escaped from her dead lips. I stared at her, unable to tear my eyes away from her morphing features as the vampire that ravaged her dead corpse evaporated in the sunlight, leaving behind the wonderful, kind face of my beloved mama. Her beautiful eyes, her glossy hair, her ruddy complexion, the smile that made the skin around her eyes crinkle the way I loved. And it was a face filled with such relief, such peace. Tears streamed down her cheeks, cheeks that were beginning to crumble, sending out plumes of twinkling dust that danced in the sunlight.

The look in her eyes said so much, but most of all, they said *thank you*. I watched my mama die for the second time as her body crumbled gently into ash and the ash itself became fine dust that turned and spiralled with a life of its own. I thought I saw a hand holding hers, I thought I saw someone guiding her away into the afterlife, but all was lost in dust.

She was gone, everything that she was, all that she had been, all the love and all the kindness in the world, gone.

Papa began to scream. And he did not stop screaming for hours.

He locked himself away in his bedroom. I slumped onto

the floor and listened at his door for hours, listening to the agonising sounds of a man grieving, my own silent tears soaking the wood as I pressed my face against the door, willing myself to be close to him but feeling so very far away.

I couldn't cope, seeing her die twice, once by my own hand. Witnessing my papa fall apart, feeling that he had abandoned me and with nowhere to turn, it was more than I could bear. I had always believed that grief brought loved ones closer together, but it can also push you apart. I sat on my bed with my knees tucked under my chin and let my despondency consume me in an overwhelming crescendo of grief, pounding my broken heart with wave after merciless wave of despair and pain. Never had my soul felt so black. Never had I been so alone. My tiny bedroom became my prison and my head became my cell. I closed my eyes and wept.

The next few days were like that. I ate in my room, what little my stomach could tolerate. I left food outside of Papa's door, but it always remained untouched, and I feared for his health and his sanity. I barely held onto my own.

I lasted three days in that state, but then I could not endure my own stench any longer. The top of my shirt and my sleeves felt crisp with dried tears and snot and my skin crawled. I stank. Mama would be so ashamed. That, more than anything, roused me from my stupor. So I bathed, the water icy against my flesh, but I lathered the soap onto my body and I scrubbed away my pain, vigorously. I scrubbed with anger and with bitterness until my flesh lay red across my body, until I had exorcised every particle of dirt and every follicle of stubble from my very being.

When I stepped outside the house, the bitter cold felt invigorating against my skin, and I inhaled lungs full of super chilled air that stung my throat and burned my chest.

It made me feel alive.

That once vibrant, bustling suburb of Berlin lay open and wounded like a war zone, grey and stark against the blueness of the sky. We were a people cursed, in hiding from a world that rained death upon us from wooden boxes, hiding from the Nazis that now patrolled the streets in force after the chaos of the fire, for our own protection, of course.

The boxes stored in the Reichstag building left the day after the fire. I heard endless stories of soldiers dragging them from the blazing ruins, of screams filling the night sky as those same soldiers fell victim to the monsters they were trying to save.

Stranger still were the stories regarding the block of ice. At least two reliable witnesses said that fire had started to melt the ice and that the thing inside could be seen more clearly, a humanoid figure with numerous tubes exiting its body, converging on a tap.

Far more boxes left Berlin than arrived. The block of ice remained covered when it left. Hundreds of soldiers, an entire battalion of SS, escorted the procession.

When I got home, I was surprised to see Papa out of his room. He was like a man possessed, pouring though reams of papers strewn across the kitchen table.

"Papa? What are you doing, Papa? Can I help you?" He ignored me, running his stubby fingers through his wild hair, almost tearing the delicate strands out by the roots. "Papa?"

The man before me was not my papa. My papa was a kind, thoughtful, considerate man. The man before me was a spectre, a pale white shadow of the man I loved and respected, a man filled with hopelessness and desperation.

"Papa!" My father looked at me with surprise. I shocked myself. "Papa, you are scaring me, please, talk to me."

"I have to leave for a little while, Ethan," he mumbled as

he began to ram sheets of paper into his brown leather satchel. "You will stay here and wait for Mama to come home."

My skin turned cold and my stomach churned. Papa was broken, and Mama was not there to fix him.

"Mama is dead—she's gone, Papa." My words caught in my throat. He looked at me with eyes of barely contained anger but he had to accept the truth, no matter how difficult.

"She is gone, Papa, Mama's gone."

He slammed his fists down violently on the table and his voice hit me like thunder, spittle flecking against my reddening cheeks.

"Don't argue with me, Ethan! I know exactly where my wife is. And you will obey me in this."

Obey? That was a word I had never heard him use before. I backed away, nervous of the man that stood before me.

"I am going away and you *will* stay here and look after our house, do you understand me? I have to find it—it's the only thing that can save us..."

His shoulders slumped and suddenly he was a tired, grief stricken old man again. Trembling fingers fumbled with his satchel and he turned away from me, his gait sad and weary as he walked to the front door. I ran after him, I didn't want him to go, I couldn't stand to lose another parent.

"Papa, please."

He opened the front door, but then he paused.

"It's coming, my son... the end of days is coming." He turned to look at me and his face, the fear in his eyes, the tears streaming down his cheeks, chilled me to my soul. "The Black Messiah will kill us all. He will scorch the earth with his evil, and I have to stop him. I need to find the spear—it's our only hope."

Papa walked out into the winter sunshine and the door closed behind him. That was the last time I saw him for over a year.

Chapter Twelve: To Read or not to Read

"Good grief, I need to sit down. That poor dear boy." Mal fluttered over to a dining chair all a-quiver.

Drama queen.

The diaries sat on the table, taunting me. "I have to read them." My fingers brushed their aged surface, and it was all I could do not to tear them open.

Almost sixty years had passed since I had to deal with that demon shit, and there it was again, sitting in my face like a great big wet asshole waiting for me to lick it.

"They are not your diaries to read," said Daniyyel in a voice so calm and reasonable that I wanted to smack him in the face. Or kiss his lips, I never could tell which.

"Oh, but they are just sitting there on the table," declared Malachi innocently. "It would be rude not to."

"It should be Ethan's decision who reads them. They are his to do with as *he* pleases."

"Oh fuck off, Dan, you patronising bastard. You knew about all this, didn't you, you knew this was coming, that's why you're here."

"Please, let us not start that argument again."

"Start? We have barely fucking begun! How convenient that you turn up and then all this shit hits the fan again. The Black Messiah? The fucking spear? You going to tell me that's coincidence?"

"As you said, *vampire*, this is your shit. Perhaps if you had dealt with it differently in London, none of this would be happening now. It's about time you stopped blaming others for your mistakes."

My anger exploded from me like an unexpected fart and before I knew it, I was in the angel's face, my eyes black and my teeth extended.

"Are you saying this is my fault? You, who dare not lift a finger for fear that your Father may find out? Hypocrite." He simply looked at me with his impenetrable blue eyes and I wanted to piss on him, he pissed me off so much. I opened my mouth in preparation for my next tirade when suddenly a massive whoosh of energy pushed me away from the stoic angel as Mal — bless him — darted between.

"Boys, please! Put the testosterone away and be reasonable. Really. I do not know what is going on between you both, but this incessant bickering must stop before one of you regrets it."

"Reasonable? There are demons knocking on my door and this heavenly piece of shit knows it and you expect me to be reasonable? So come on Dan, what's it to be? Am I to get involved or not? Do I do all this again? And why the fuck should I? What do I have to show for my efforts? Fuck all, that's what."

Blinding white light blasted my body as his wings distended, sending me flying across the floor. The pain sliced through my body and my flesh burned as I covered my eyes to avoid the searing light.

"That was no mistake this time. Sit on your fucking ass while Hitler murders the world around you. *Then* wonder why I do not ask you the question." I felt the light blink out from behind my clamped fingers, taking my anger with it, leaving just a hollow space in my heart that filled my existence with utter emptiness.

"It's happening again isn't it? London. I don't know if I can... if I have anything left..." Frustration rippled through me as I felt the bitter sting of tears stabbing at my eyes, my own inadequacies pouring down my cheeks in rivers of unyielding shame. I bowed my head. I did not want him to see my tears. Gentle fingers stroked my hair, but I could not look at him, I could not bear to see the sympathy nestled within his fascinating eyes. I had no need for sympathy, only a way out.

"We will always be faced with difficult choices, Eli, be they for the good or the bad, but it is the choices we make that define the beings we become and ultimately, only we can choose our paths. It seems that Ethan's path and yours are linked, and that maybe, for the first time in your existence, you may get nearer to the truth of things."

"I don't know what that means." He was trying to tell me something, I knew he was, but his words were so jumbled in angel speak they defied me.

"No, my friend, I know you don't, and that is why you have never been asked the question."

"Phew, I am so glad that is over, now, what about the diaries?" Trust Mal to bring me back to reality with a bump. With a heavy heart, I picked myself up off the floor and placed a hand atop the volumes, feeling the answers rippling through the palm of my hand.

"Read them."

The voice from above startled us and we all looked up to see Ethan descending the stairs, a vision in white linen. My, he was quite a sight. Muscle rippled through tight cloth. Tight cotton trousers outlined a magnificent... I pulled myself together, too many tight things.

"I want you to read them."

"You should not be out of bed. Your wounds have not fully healed." Even my voice was drooling.

"I have slept long enough. I need to find Papa, and those books may give me a clue as to why he was taken."

"Taken?"

"My father was taken from me in 1938. I have been searching for him ever since. Those diaries are all I have left. I know what you are. I know what all of you are." He was so direct, so fucking sexy.

Mal floated forward, his face agape with incredulity while Daniyyel remained as impassive as ever.

"You can see me?" squealed Mal excitedly.

"My papa taught me that once you have been touched by darkness ,your eyes are opened to the truth. So yes, I can see you — you are a spirit, and you are bound to Eli." He looked toward Daniyyel, an unspoken reverence burning in his green eyes. "And you are an angel — it was you who took my mama to Heaven, was it not?"

I shot an accusing glance at Daniyyel and he looked away, suddenly very sheepish. Fucking liar.

"And you are something new to me," Ethan continued, his gorgeous eyes boring into my soul. "You are a vampire, though I have never seen one like you before."

"You know all this, and yet you are unafraid?" I tried not to sound horny.

"You saved my life. You have nursed my wounds and you have given me a place to rest. That does not seem to me to be the actions of a monster. I stink. Is there somewhere around here where I can bathe?"

We were all too stunned to speak. He looked into each of our astonished faces, and as his gaze moved over me, I felt my flesh burn. I felt those eyes appraise me, I felt their focus move down my body, hesitate, then move quickly back to my face. I think my jaw fell open.

"Bath? Water? Soap?" He laughed. Still unable to make my vocal cords, work I pointed to one of the concealed doors behind the staircase and led him toward my homemade shower.

His big green eyes considered the ramshackle set-up

approvingly, then suddenly and without any preamble, he began to strip down in front of me. I turned quickly intending to walk out but he stopped me mid-stride.

"Please don't leave—stand and talk with me?"

Okay. He was about to get naked and I was acting all embarrassed. What was that all about? I had already seen most of his body anyway, even if he was half-dead at the time. And boy did I really want to get another eyeful. So why was I behaving so strangely? Bashful I was not.

"Sure, why not," I mumbled awkwardly as I pulled up a chair. I turned the chair around so I would face away from him.

"I would rather talk to your face than the back of your head."

Shit. After turning, I had to cross my legs and fold my arms on my lap. I didn't want him to notice the growing bulge developing in my pants.

"So what would you like to talk about?" His naked body glistened with perspiration, every part of him defined and hard. My eyes could barely believe the astounding beauty of him. I forced my eyes to look away as he stepped into the copper bath, then I glimpsed his manhood falling between his thick muscular legs. Bloody hell. More than a mouthful was a waste. I had a big mouth.

"I'd like to know a little about the man who took me home. You know more about me than most, and I know nothing of you, other than the fact that you saved my life and I thank you for that. What you did out there was quite... something."

The sound of gushing water made me glance in his direction. Mercifully, he was in mid-turn, but the sight of the water pouring over his hard, perfect torso just made me squirm even more. And his bum, surely, bum cheeks should not be that high, or that hard. Or that smooth? Even the water could not cling to them.

"Not much to tell." Ouch. That was pathetic and uncharacteristically coy of me.

"I find that hard to believe."

Hard, oh yes, definitely hard.

"How old are you?" he asked.

"Age is such a bore don't you think?" That was truly feeble of me. "Let's just say I was there when Shakespeare had the idea for Macbeth, I told him a few stories that may have contributed to the final act."

"You're looking good for your age! You must tell me your secret sometime."

"Doesn't look like you need any help on that score."

"Thank you."

Were we flirting? Why were words of such insuperable dribble issuing from between my sorry lips? My gaze wandered over his lathered magnificence and it took all my willpower to stop myself from leaping out of my chair to grab his loofah.

"Okay, so we've done the age thing. And I know you are a vampire. So who are you? Who were you, before you became... special."

He called me special. That thrilled me more than it should.

"I don't know who I was before this—I have no recollection of having been human."

"Nothing at all?" He sounded genuinely surprised, shocked even.

"Nada, diddly squat. I have searched the world for memories, for anything that could connect me to a human life, but I have never found anything, no answers, no relatives and no record of birth or mention of my name. I remember eyes, I remember something forced into my mouth and a whole world of pain, and that is it. As far as I am aware, I was born vampire, it is all I know."

"Is that why you are different?"

"What do you mean?"

"I have never seen a vampire that can walk in the sunlight before, so clearly that makes you different, but the thing I don't understand is you yourself. The vampires I have killed were monsters, they looked like monsters, and they acted like monsters. But you, on the other hand—you look human, you sound human, you are civilised, and since you saved my life you are obviously compassionate, and yet within you the vampire dwells with you at all times. I have seen it."

He had intelligence as well as good looks. One stroke, just one stroke, and I would be there.

"The reason you have never seen anything like me is that we are very rare..."

"I should say so."

"... I have only ever met a couple like me in the entire world." It was hard to talk between smirking lips. "I am an original being, Menarche, and don't ask me what that means because I don't really know myself. I am Menarche, and my blood is stronger than that of the feral you have encountered. The one that you killed on the stairs was a feral, like the ones in your story. If I were to turn you, essentially you would retain much of your humanity."

"Turn me? Hmm." He smirked and I felt my cheeks flush. He must have seen it because his smile widened and his eyes glittered mischievously.

"The Menarche blood in my veins would prevent you from devolving into the creatures you have seen," I continued, trying hard to keep a straight face. He really was rather cheeky. "Regular ingestion of my blood would even allow you to walk in the sunlight, for short periods at least. But if you were then to turn another, without my blood, without the bite of a Menarche, they would become an animal, a feral, a creature formed of instinct and the desire for survival, the desire for blood."

"Desire? It's getting better by the minute."

"Don't be cheeky."

"Spoilsport. Sorry, carry on."

Wow. I felt dizzy, intoxicated.

"All remnants of humanity would be corrupted by the need to feed—they become scavengers, so impure is their blood as to be burned by the sun. They are to be pitied rather than feared, vermin that are shunned from the light through no fault of their own."

Silence. No running water. No cheeky comebacks. I realised I had been staring at the floor between my feet the entire time and I looked up then to see why he was so quiet. He sat on the edge of the bathtub, a towel draped across his lap, and he, too, was looking down at the floor. I knew what he was thinking. He saw his mother killed by a feral, he saw his mother turn into a feral, a starving desperate monster, a pitiful heap of reanimated skin and bone. The pain of it tainted his green eyes. So the question that formed on his lips was only natural, he could just not bring himself to ask it.

The thing on its back, the feral's disquieting intelligence, its ability to converse cohesively, none of it was right.

"Yes, I have turned someone," I answered his silent question, I thought I could save him that much at least.

He looked up at me then, eyes sparkling with such sadness I wanted to reach out and wipe it away.

"I suppose it would be too much for me to hope otherwise." Poor boy, he was in a great deal of pain. All of his beliefs, all that he understood of this world and the next called into question, and he was looking to me for understanding, when I did not understand it myself.

"Let me speak plainly to you, Ethan, it is important for

you to understand." Why was it important for him to understand? Why did I feel the *need* for him to understand? Did it really mean that much to me? Was *he* beginning to matter that much to me?

Slippery slope, Eli, slippery slope, I told myself.

"I need to drink blood in order to remain... myself. I can go for long periods without doing so, but never the less I do have to feed. But I do not kill my victims. I consider my Menarche condition to be a curse, and I do not wish to inflict this state on anyone else. Yes, I have turned a few, but not by my own choice, and I hope you believe me when I say that. None of this is by choice, not my choice, and if I could wake up one morning, wake up human, then no one would be happier than I would. But I am not human—I never will be human, no matter how much I may want it. I am vampire, but I am not a monster. I fight monsters—I do not create them."

He looked at me, his penetrating gaze unwavering, searching my soul for the truth, and I laid it bare for him to see. A single tear spilled down his beautiful cheek, and from that moment on, I loved him. My heart was his to do with as he pleased.

"I believe you."

Relief surged through me like an electric current. It was an unusual experience for me.

"Thank you."

"And I trust you, which is why I would like you to read the diaries with me. I don't have a clue what lies in those pages—they have only just come into my possession. But I heard some of your conversation downstairs and, I have the feeling their contents will be just as important to you as they are to me. I think it's about time I knew all about my papa."

"Time?"

He stood up, the towel falling into his hand and he began

to scrub his hard flesh with the soft absorbent cloth. His arms bulged, muscle flexing beneath taught skin. His hands worked the towel lower, between his legs. I looked away.

"Papa used to leave us for weeks, travelling the world on the behalf of a group of scholars I never met and never saw. Mama always looked so sad when he left on those mysterious trips, but she would smile and say he would be back soon. To this day, I still don't know what he did for them, or who they were. I have gone beyond waiting for him to explain that to me."

"You sound as though you have lost your faith in him."

"No, no, never that. Papa is a broken man—he has had everything he loves taken from him. I need to find him so I can mend him, mend us both."

"I know that feeling well."

"Then read the diaries with me."

"I don't know if I can. I've been alone for so long..."

"So have I."

"Then why do you want me to read them with you?" I wanted to read them—I needed to read them, but to involve Ethan, to be involved with Ethan, that was another matter.

Those green eyes bore into me, penetrating me, fucking me hard and deep.

"Because I no longer feel alone."

A sudden knock at the door disturbed our eye fuck, and Mal's high-pitched voice floated through the wood. Usually he would just barge in, or float in, so his discretion came as a refreshing change.

"Are you going to be much longer in there? What are you doing?"

"Talking," we both shouted at the same time. We looked at each other and laughed, the sound filling the small space. Suddenly I felt very close to Ethan. We understood each other, respected each other even, and I saw within him the germination of a friendship, of something shared. It was the most encouraging interaction I had had with another being in a very long time, and I liked it.

Mal's disembodied face materialised through the door. "What are you laughing at? No please, tell me what you are laughing at?"

"Mal," I said, unable to resist the temptation to tease. "Did you know that when you sleep, spiders rub their willies on your face?"

"What?" he hollered hysterically. "Why would you say that? Really. Is there any need?" His piqued face squealing through the wood made us laugh even more and I felt... something. Something was stirring inside me, something I had not allowed myself to feel for a very long time. And there was absolutely fuck all I could do about it.

Chapter Thirteen: The Diaries of Isaiah Nathan Silberman

March 3rd 1909 Vienna

What a wonderful city this is, so alive, so vibrant. Today I indulged myself and I sat in the glorious winter sun and sketched a most magnificent woman. I think the kind thing to say is that she was large and I am beginning to think it's a prerequisite for the trade of a Street Fruit Seller. And a finer specimen I have rarely seen! She carries a huge basket strapped around her ample waist, and sitting on this basket is a long bowed piece of wood like a giant ladle which itself is laden with fruit and vegetables. And mind you, the weight of this arrangement must be immense, because she regularly refreshes her wares from the basket below the huge ladle. She made a fascinating study in charcoal, and I was able to capture the folds of her scarf quite beautifully, though what my tutor will think of this at the university I cannot guess. Our study should be architecture. I will have to persuade him that the cantilever of her breasts fulfilled the brief. Surely, this beast of the streets is architecture enough.

I saw him again today. That's three days in a row now, and every day last week. The Hofmuseum is rapidly becoming one of my favourite places to visit, and I find myself wandering its massive halls almost on a daily basis. There is an area open only to scholars and lucky students like myself from the Vienna Academy of Fine Art, the Hapsburg's treasury displaying many of the most valuable treasures. He is always in the same place, sitting on an old wooden chair in front of one particular display case. He has a sketchbook on his lap, but in all my observations, I have never seen him put pencil to paper. The young man just sits there staring into it, as though waiting for some earth shattering epiphany. I don't know what is in the glass case, as I have never approached it or its observer. Somehow, it would feel rude to do so.

Something about that lonely figure saddens me – he is so unkempt and so very... scruffy, like a vagabond off the streets. He is unshaven and his hair is a tight mass of grime that no comb has visited in an age. And he is most certainly malnourished, for his cheekbones protrude through his gaunt flesh in an alarming manner. He has the visage of a street beggar, a vagabond and yet the authorities allow him into the inner sanctum of the museum, so he has to be a student, though I have never noticed him at the university. But it is too glorious a day for me to dwell on such things, and my sketchbook is full! Time to face my tutors I think.

3.30 AM

I cannot sleep. Two things have kept me awake, gnawing incessantly at my mind. The first is that my tutors were not amused. I explained my reasons for sketching the large woman, I even gave them the cantilever line, but sheesh were they unhappy and scolded me in front of the entire class for wasting my time and the time of the university. I declared that even the grand masters themselves could not resist rendering the fine figure of such a woman, to which I was reliably informed that the figure I had committed to paper was neither fine or womanly by any meaning of the word. Now I will have to work doubly hard to make up for this lost time.

The second thing, and if I am going to be honest, as one should in the pages of one's own diary, the thing that bothers me the most, is the enigmatic stranger I have seen almost every day at the museum. There is something about him, something... magnetic. It's not pity I feel, at least I don't think so, but I really need to know who he is, why he just sits there, what is it in that case that so fascinates him? Questions, questions, questions. I will find out, tomorrow I will make it my one mission to find out. Then I will sketch every damn arch and colonnade the city has to offer.

March 4th 1909 Vienna

I did it. I met him. Never let anyone say Isaiah Nathan Silberman is not a man of his word. If I thought him enigmatic before, I don't know what to think now. What a strange little man, what a puzzle he is. So full of passion, so very intense, and yet he seems filled with doubt. I shall make him my friend.

My intention was to waltz into the Hapsburg's treasury, straight up to the sallow chap, and introduce myself with an outstretched hand, thus forcing my beguiling charms upon him. But when I entered the area, something stopped me, a feeling, an omen, telling me to take my time, telling me to look before I leap.

So I looked.

He was sitting in his usual place, sketchbook unused on his lap, staring at the cabinet in front of him as though in a trance, nothing unusual there. But then I happened to look beyond him to the furthest corner of the room, and the shock of what I saw, or what I think I saw, nearly made me stumble backward. Another figure was watching the stranger on the chair, but the shadow that fell upon the wall behind him looked nothing like the man casting it. In all outward appearances, he was a normal looking man wearing a black morning coat and grey stripped trousers with a high-collared white shirt and sky blue tie, nothing untoward, albeit a tad smart for so early in the morning. But his shadow, it crept across the wall behind him, huge and elongated with impossibly long arms and fingers that crawled across the ceiling. I saw it only briefly, and I blinked, thinking it some horrendous trick of the light, but when I opened my eyes, the man with his impossible shadow was gone. Surely I had witnessed some unusual trick of the light, some bizarre ocular illusion. What else could it have been?

I rushed over to the man in the chair.

"Did you see that? There was a man standing over there, and I *think he was watching you, but his shadow... it looked like it was crawling all over the wall and the ceiling behind him — I've never seen anything like it. The incandescent light bulb is truly a modern marvel! Hi, my name is Isaiah. What, may I ask, is yours?"*

He shot out of the chair clasping his sketchbook and ran. I was so taken aback that it took me a couple of seconds to realise what was happening. And then I did the only thing I could think of, I gave chase.

For somebody so impoverished, he certainly moved fast. I swear he had the wings of Icarus himself sewn to his feet. I barely glimpsed him darting into the freedom of the outside world, and I literally had to plough through the indignant figures around me to keep up. The bright sunlight that assaulted my eyes after the varied interior lighting caused me to blink furiously as my eyes filled with water. I nearly lost him, and I ran headlong into the bustling streets without a clue of direction. Then I glimpsed him looking at me through a group of market sellers, and he shot off again. Encouraged by this glimpse of my prey, I followed, running faster than I have ever done before. I have never considered myself an overweight man, and I am of average build, but this chase, this relentless running. I could hardly catch my breath, and I realise now just how unfit I am.

The imposing arches and colonnades of the Horse Sales Arena reared up before me. Then I saw him, standing at the edge of the green lawns before the Arena watching a group of children playing Diabolos. Children tossed wooden spools into the air so that another child, holding identical pairs of sticks with string tied between them, might catch them. The scene was almost hypnotic, and the skill of the children making the spindles spin on the string was quite beautiful to watch. But even more bewitching was the look on the stranger's face as he watched those lovely urchins play. I edged toward him carefully, not wishing to frighten him or disturb his reverie. I stood beside him, finally getting a good look at his slight frame. I was sure he was no older than I was, but his circumstances were obviously in complete opposition to my own.

Suddenly he spoke, and the sound came as such a surprise that I nearly jumped out of my skin. His voice was rich and deep, commanding, even, and I found myself clinging to his every word.

"The word Diabolos is derived from the original Greek meaning the liar, and later became to be used by the Christian faith to mean the liar that speaks against God. Many of today's civilisations credit this for the origin of the word devil. These children are playing with the devil."

There was not a lot I could say to that, but there was one thing it taught me about him immediately. He was obviously a learned man of some intelligence, and I warmed to him immediately.

"May I buy you a cup of tea?" Now I am not in the habit of inviting strange men for tea, but I had the feeling this man, this hypnotic stranger, had a story to tell, and I wanted to hear it.

"Why?" He said this without as much as a glance in my direction. I thought him to be watching the children still, but then I saw, lurking in the shadows of a stone niche set into the Arena, the same well-dressed figure from the museum. I am not a superstitious man, but the hairs on the back of my neck bristled with a sudden cold chill.

"Do you know him?"

"No, but I will do. Adi."

"I'm sorry?"

"My friends call me Adi, and if you are taking me for tea, then I assume that for some reason you wish to be my friend. You have been observing me for the last two weeks, have you not?"

He looked at me then and I could see the beginnings of a sly grin at the corners of his unshaven face. This strange, quirky, intense young man had a sense of humour, and I clasped his outstretched hand enthusiastically, laughing as I did so.

"And I am Isaiah, Isaiah Nathan Silberman, and I am delighted to meet you."

I led him to a nearby café where we sat outside in the gloriously cold sunshine and I ordered us both a pot of tea and chocolate cake. There is always room for chocolate cake. We sat in silence to begin with as we waited for the treats to be brought to us. My newfound friend, Adi, watched wide-eyed as the world went on with its daily routine about him. He seemed fascinated by everything, constantly swivelling around in his chair to afford himself a better view.

Finally, our order arrived, and Adi looked at the chocolate cake before him as though presented with a golden ingot. He looked at me, and I'm ashamed to say I felt overwhelmed by pity. He looked so very happy, as though I had given him the most tremendous gift, and his fierce blue eyes bore into me with such hypnotic intensity as to bare my very soul. Then he attacked the chocolate cake, positively ripping it apart with his grubby fingers, shovelling it into his mouth, words pouring out of him at such a fast pace I could barely keep up.

"I thought you were a debt collector, which is why I ran from you. You have been watching me for some considerable time, and I thought you were waiting for an opportune moment in which to arrest me." He barely paused for breath as he shovelled in more cake. "You see, my mother died not long ago and everything was lost, not even enough money to pay for her funeral, so I had to escape into the streets, as her house was re-possessed, together with all of her belongings. I took nothing. I wanted nothing, and now I live for myself and answer to nobody."

I was horrified. Both of my beloved parents still walk this earth, and I have never known poverty or been deprived of comfortable accommodation. To be lost in these streets, in this cold, with nothing but the clothes on one's back was anathema to me. I felt my compassion moisten my eyes, but I tried very hard not to show it.

"Then where do you sleep? Eat?"

Adi shrugged, as though this were of no great concern.

"I sleep most nights on the floor of the Hostel in Brigittenau or sometimes the public rooms at Warmestuben, where I may find protection from the cold huddled amid the numerous displaced families and human detritus. It is like a giant coffin filled with the living. It is amazing what comfort and warmth may be gleaned from the bringing together of so many bodies huddled together in such a small space. I garner what sustenance I may from the bread and soup they so kindly provide once a day, or I visit the soup kitchen at Meidling, where the Nuns and volunteers are most kind. I have much to be grateful for to your kind sir."

"My kind?"

"You are Jewish, are you not? My mother's doctor was a Jew, and never a finer man have I met. When the cancer began to consume her body, he worked tirelessly to ease her pain and give her what quality of life he could. And the hostels and soup kitchens are operated on the whole by the Jewish community, and they also provide the funds to keep such things functional."

"I had no idea." And I didn't. I lived in my own Isaiah bubble. "I think it time that I had better acquaint myself with the world."

"Then you should!" His eyes burned with passion, and it startled me somewhat as his voice rose to almost embarrassing levels. "Always be aware, my friend, of that which goes on around you, of your position in society, of your contribution to the German way of life! It is your duty as a Jew and as a German!"

He calmed down and licked the chocolate off his fingers, downing the last of his tea noisily.

"History will be written by the likes of you and me, Isaiah — never forget that."

"I assumed because you were in the Hapsburg treasury you were a student. I saw your sketch book..."

He slammed his fist down on the table so loudly and so violently I nearly fell backward off my chair. Passers-by stopped and looked, while fellow customers paused with their cups in mid-air. I smiled at them with barely concealed embarrassment.

"They do not see talent when it is presented to them! Twice I applied. Twice they rejected me. They are nothing more than a narrow minded group of snobbish miscreants."

"I'm sorry, I just assumed..."

"Assume nothing! From one cup of tea and slice of cake, you presume to know everything about me. You know nothing of me!"

I will admit that his violent outburst startled me, but I was too intrigued, my emotions too committed, to back down. We sat in silence for a few minutes as the scene around us returned to its normal humdrum. Adi eventually calmed and slumped back heavily into his chair.

"I am sorry, you did not deserve that, you have shown me nothing but kindness, and I have acted like a petulant child."

"May I see them?" I indicated his sketchbook and for a moment, I thought he was going to shy away. Then, albeit reluctantly, he handed me the string bound folder of papers. I flicked through slowly while he sat nervously watching my every move, my every expression. Each page had a small postcard stapled to the corner with a skilfully rendered enlargement filling most of the paper, some in watercolour, some pencil, or charcoal. I stopped at a beautiful copy of a postcard exhibiting the Maximillion Platz Church with its imposing granite spires reaching into a cloud-laden sky. Sunlight streamed through gaps in the clouds to caress the spires like the fingers of God. So maybe they were not the most original or the greatest works of art I had ever seen, but there was definitely some talent there with distinct commercial possibilities.

"Have you ever thought of selling these?"

"Who would want them? They are just copies, replicas of photographs taken by those more skilled than I. Always I find one's subject for painting the most difficult to attain, so I resort to copying the work of others."

"Do not put yourself down, Adi my boy. Okay, so you have been turned down by the Academy..."

"Twice!"

"Yes, well let's not dwell on that shall we? That place wouldn't see talent if it hit them square on the jaw. You should try selling these. Honestly, there are shops even in this district that would gladly purchase these to sell onto their clients. Watch this."

Adi looked horrified as I pulled out the Platz Church watercolour and rushed into the café. A couple of minutes later I returned with a fist full of money in the palm of my hand, which I handed back to Adi triumphantly.

"I do not understand?" He stared confused at the pile of coins before him.

"Cafes like this are all too eager to look for items to sell to their clientele and don't forget how many foreign visitors a place such as this serves on a daily basis, and all of them looking for a meaningful souvenir to remind them of their stay in this great city. And what better than one of your paintings? Better than a tiny postcard, don't you think? And besides, the owner is a , and we Jews stick together. Come on."

I tossed the money for our food onto the table, picked up his folder and raced across the street toward the next café where, to his astonishment, I performed the same trick. Then there were the tobacconists and the sellers of fine confectionary, all eager to take two, even three pieces in some cases. By the time we had finished, even on that one busy square, Adi's folder was emptied by almost half and his pocket full of tinkling change.

We collapsed laughing onto a small square of grass where I lit us both a cigarette, a small treat for our triumphant work. He took it and inhaled gratefully and we both sat there watching the elegant Fiacre as it stopped to unload its equally elegant passengers.

"I have always wanted to travel in one of those—I think their huge horses draped in white make an imposing sight pulling those hooded carriages around the streets. I think one must be of some import to be pulled by such a thing."

I slapped my hand against his back gently.

"And so you will, my friend, so you will. We shall keep selling your paintings, and who knows?"

We laughed again, the sound so innocent against the afternoon sun, our breaths crisp and biliously white in the air.

"You have helped me at a time of great despair, my new friend and I am most grateful to you. You have shown me the way, so I may begin to find a means to feed myself rather than relying on the handouts of others. Mind, I shall miss the sights at Meidling, prettier girls have I seldom seen."

"Why, Adi, you letch. Surely those are Nuns."

Adi blushed then and turned his head away bashfully.

"Not all are Nuns."

I shot up off the floor with a brilliant idea.

"Then you shall show me the delights of Meidling and we shall take a Fiacre and be driven there in style."

The journey was short but the look on Adi's face as he saw others looking at him so enviously, pulled around in such style made the exorbitant fee worthwhile. God bless Adi, he tried very hard to force some of his newfound money into my pockets, but I was having none of it.

I have been to soup kitchens before, as a volunteer, but I didn't tell Adi that. So the conditions of its patrons and the conditions of the hall itself did not surprise me. Soup kitchens and squalor seem to go hand-in-hand. It was fast approaching late afternoon and the Nuns were busily preparing themselves for the evening rush, so the hall was not as busy as it might have been. Adi noticed me looking around at the dirty walls.

"Places such as these should not be necessary. If there were work for the people, then there would be no need for the people to resort to such things. Moreover, if there is no work in the private sector, then it is the government's duty to put such souls to work constructing roads and bridges, and then it would be the government's responsibility to feed those mouths. Handouts are for dogs."

"You are an idealist."

"No, I am a realist. Put the youth of this country to work, and use the experience and the knowledge of the old to better the German way, it is simple mechanics."

"Are you causing trouble again, Adi? I have told you before about spouting your political stuff in here."

The voice tinkled across the hall toward us as though an angel had spoken the words, such was the humour and the sweetness that caressed our ears. Adi reddened visibly as a pretty – actually, a very pretty – young woman came skipping toward us, black hair flying wildly around her shoulders. A fine dusting of flour covered the vision from head to foot. She scooted Adi further along the bench and sat opposite me, her hands, also covered in flour, spread flat on the surface of the bench. She had lovely long fingers, but I could not help notice her painfully short fingernails.

"I hate the dough getting under my fingernails," she said

noticing my interest. "Who are you, then?" Adi did not indicate he was going to make an introduction, and I noticed how cowed he had suddenly become. He made a concerted effort that no part of his body touched that exquisite creature sitting next to him.

"Isaiah Nathan Silberman – and you might be?"

"Eva, Eva Steinberg." She extended a floured hand toward me and I took it enthusiastically, my heart beating inside my chest. She was so perfect, cheeks flushed red, eyes green as the grass, her lips so pouty and alluring, I found myself wanting to kiss her there and then.

"So what brings you here, Isaiah? You don't look as though you are in need of our services."

Before I knew it, I had told her all about my meeting Adi, our chase through the streets and our little commercial venture. The words poured out of my mouth breathlessly while Adi simply sat there quietly looking into his lap. However, I kept looking into her face, into her glorious eyes, my gaze unwavering. I did not wish to waste a single moment looking at anything else in the room. Her warm smile radiated kindness, and she lit up when I explained how Adi could now sell his work.

"Why that is wonderful, Adi, you must be so pleased?" Adi didn't look up but simply shrugged. "Well it is a wonderful thing, and I think it very generous of you Mr. Silberman..."

"Oh, call me Isaiah, please. Mr. Silberman is my father." She blushed. Eva actually blushed.

"Yes, well, Isaiah, it's a very generous thing you have done for Adi here. There are not many who would extend such a hand of friendship to those less fortunate than themselves."

"It could quite easily be any one of us. I don't think anyone is more than a day away from being on the breadline. Yet you too work here as a volunteer, which easily makes you more generous than I, one would think."

Her laughter transformed her face into a thing of joy and I saw so much humanity in that laughing face, so much sincerity, so much caring. This girl could not have been much younger than I, yet, here she was, baking bread for the poor when all I did, in *reality, was paint pretty pictures day in day out. That made me think, I can tell you. Someone called out her name, and much to my disappointment, Eva got up to leave.*

"Please do excuse me — my bread is ready to come out of the oven. And well done, Adi, I'm proud of you."

With that, she was gone, leaving nothing but the sound of her laughter in her wake.

"What's wrong with you, Adi? Lost your voice?"

"Girls, I cannot speak to girls, so much giggling, and I don't know what to say to them."

I threw back my head and laughed wildly. This enigmatic young man was full of surprises.

"They are girls, Adi, who knows what you are supposed to say to girls. That is one of life's greatest mysteries."

"You did not seem to have any problem." *He looked at me then with such an intense stare a chill ran down my spine. It had not occurred to me that maybe Adi liked her. The silence between us grew awkward, but I wasn't about to let anything spoil what had been a most eventful and exhilarating day.*

"You never told me why you go to the Hapsburg every day. What's in that display case that fascinates you so?"

A look flashed across his face, and I saw then a glimpse of a different person. The intensity that oozed out of his very pores darkened his aura, and his eyes filled with a steely passion I have never seen before in any man. He sat upright in his seat, shoulders square, back ramrod straight, and he gazed at me, through me and it suddenly struck me what a powerful face he had, a face that demanded attention, a commanding face.

"What lies in that case, my friend, is destiny," *he whispered.* "I just don't know whose."

"I don't understand."

"Meet me in the treasury area tomorrow afternoon at four and I will explain."

He extended his hand toward me then, which I took as a sign it was time for me to go. The palm of his hand was cold and clammy, but he gripped my fingers tightly and shook my hand most enthusiastically. Then he turned his back on me and walked into a growing crowd of beggars queuing up for their food.

As I left the building, I turned around once to see a rather stern looking Nun slop food onto his plate. Adi had his head bowed again, unable to look the woman in the face. But there, in the background was Eva, watching me as I hesitated in the doorway. Her hand shot into the air and she waved to me, her face beaming. My heart filled to the point of bursting and I left the building with a spring in my step powerful enough to leap tall buildings.

Tonight I shall sleep the sleep of the contented. As I finish this rather long and extraordinary entry, I know that when my head hits my pillow, I will be thinking of Eva Steinberg.

March 5th 1909 Vienna

If it were not for the lectures I had to attend this evening then I don't think I could have brought myself to leave Adi's side today. He has told me a story that has so captured my imagination that my brain can hardly contain its thoughts. Even now as I pour through my notes, hastily scribbled during today's encounter, I can barely restrain myself.

I met him as agreed at the museum by the cabinet that transfixed him so, though I noticed and it did make me smirk I must admit, that he had procured another chair, which sat empty next to him.

"You came?" He seemed surprised I would keep our appointment.

"We are friends, are we not?" Adi smiled then, and the smile looked uncomfortable on his face, as though it were not used to pulling such a shape. There is much sadness and loneliness about my new friend, which I am determined to disperse. He indicated for me to sit and I did. His attention fell back onto the cabinet and I noticed, for the first time, what lay inside, nestling on a white velvet cushion. It was a spear, a beautifully crafted artefact forged from steel. A wide base with metal flanges, which the writing next to it informs, depicts the wings of a dove and supports the long *tapering point. Within the central aperture is a hammer-headed nail secured by a cuff threaded with metal wire. According to the inscription, the spear is rumoured to be the one that pierced the side of Christ at the crucifixion.*

A cold shiver trickled down my spine and I looked at Adi. His eyes were huge, as though the thing had mesmerised him, and his voice sounded so strange, so far away.

"I have long sat here quietly gazing upon it, quite oblivious to the scene around me. It seems to carry some hidden inner meaning. But that meaning evades me, a meaning I feel inwardly, burning inside of me, and yet I cannot bring it into consciousness. Sometimes, when I look at it, it feels as though I myself had held it before in some earlier century of history. That I myself had once claimed it as my talisman of power and held the destiny of the world in my hands." The conviction in his voice held me in his grip and I could almost believe that history itself lay before us in that cabinet.

"But it is only a metal spear, a piece of archaeology that has had some fantastical story entwined around it." As I spoke, I saw fury in his eyes, a flicker of outrage that froze the words in my throat. It vanished just as quickly as it had appeared, but it left me slightly nervous and very apprehensive.

"Wars have been fought and kingdoms have been lost over such things, my friend. Do you know the story of Gaius Cassius Longinus?" I shook my head, indicating I did not, and Adi continued, barely stopping for breath, such was his passion and his belief.

"Gaius Cassius Longinus was a Roman Centurion at the time of the crucifixion. Roman soldiers were a proud breed, a strong breed, and did not tolerate imperfection within their ranks, but Longinus had long been suffering with his eyes and by that point was almost blind. Being a proud and stubborn young man, Longinus continued in his duties rather than face the shame of dismissal from the Legion. And so Jesus hung on the cross in Golgotha, but the Jews did not want a body hanging there the next day, which was their Sabbath, so they asked Pilate to hasten the

deaths of the crucified, whereby Pilate commanded that their legs be broken to accelerate their deaths and thus the bodies removed in time. But when they came to Jesus, they saw that he was dead already, so they left his legs untouched. One of the soldiers, Gaius Cassius Longinus, pierced his side with a spear whereby blood and water flowed out of the wound, splashing onto Longinus's upturned face. Even in death, the blood of Jesus continued to perform its miracle, and the blindness that had so cruelly afflicted Longinus cured itself instantly.

"The story does not end there, though. Legend tells us that Longinus, cured of all earthly ailments by the blood of Jesus, became something more than human, but so terrified were the Romans of this supernatural being that they banished him to a cave on the outskirts of the city. There, the story claims, he was attacked and badly mauled by a lion every night until dawn, whereby he would then climb back into his cave and his wounds would heal miraculously and completely. He kept the spear with him at all times.

"Afraid that Longinus would emerge from the cave to become some new Messiah, the Emperor dispatched a Legion of men to the mountaintop to destroy Longinus by dismemberment. But with Christianity spreading through the ranks like wild fire, the men refused to raise a hand against a being so blessed by Jesus. Furious, their Commander ordered decimation and chose ten men to face the sword – their bodies run through and disposed of in an unmarked grave. The next day, according to legend, the grave had been disturbed and the bodies removed, lost in the sands of history.

"Still refusing to move, the ritual of decimation again invoked, twenty men went to the slaughter and this time their bodies burned on a funeral pyre of white ash. But that night a terrible plague swept through the camp, the bloodcurdling cries of men reaching as far as the gates of Rome itself. Two hundred men slaughtered in the dark, nothing remaining, but empty tents and pools of blood. Fearing that Longinus had ventured from his cave by night to seek revenge, the Commander climbed the rock face to the mouth of the cave and, sword in hand he ventured into its

depths. There lay the bodies of his two hundred men, lying as though asleep in each other's arms, but of Longinus and the Spear there was no trace. The Commander picked up one of the nearest bodies and carried it into the light, perhaps with the intention of shaming his soldiers in the camp below, but no sooner had the body hit the sun than it burst into flames in his arms, dissolving into dust. Proclaiming the abomination as the work of the devil, the Commander sealed the entrance to the cave for all eternity, striking its location from every map in Rome. The disobedient Legion and its Commander were subsequently put to death by their Emperor for fear that word of such events would spread through the empire and encourage dissidence amongst the ranks."

I wrote down his words furiously, not wishing to miss a moment of his fantastical story. It felt as though the room grew darker suddenly, and I got the distinct impression that someone was watching me. I glanced around but saw no one, but even so, the feeling persisted.

"Surely you do not think this to be the actual spear?"

"How does one prove the existence or the validity of the Spear of Destiny? If I were to reach into this case now and hold it in my hand, would I raise the biggest and most powerful army this world has ever seen? Would I become immortal? Would it give me the power to bend this planet to my will?"

My heart stopped as he reached out a hand toward the glass case. He showed no fear, and yet I was suddenly terrified. Adi's fingers moved so slowly, so inexorably toward the case and I feared that he would take the spear from its cushion, regardless of the consequences. I couldn't stand it — I kept looking from his fingers to his face, a face filled with purpose, darkness, determination. I reached out suddenly and snatched his fingers away from the glass.

"No. Don't."

"Do not touch me!" He leaped out of his chair, fury bubbling from his lips in a shower of spittle. "How dare you touch me? To own the spear is to own the world. Who are you to say otherwise?"

"Adi? I'm sorry, I didn't mean to upset you... I just thought, you know, it's bound to be alarmed, you would be banned..."

He sat back down, suddenly calm, calculating, composed, and he glared at me with those piercing blue eyes of his, the ones that tore at my very soul.

"Never, never stop me from doing what I must... from what I want... that is something you must learn if you are to be my friend, Isaiah Nathan Silberman. And it is a lesson you must learn quickly. You will leave me now."

I stood shocked and not a little upset by my abrupt dismissal.

"May I meet you here again tomorrow? Maybe you could share more of your stories about the relic, maybe you could help me understand?"

"If you must."

I stood looking at him for what seemed an age, but he neither spoke to me nor looked at me, he just stared straight ahead at the spear. So I left. But as Adi was about to leave my sights, I spotted the elegantly dressed stranger walking toward him from the opposite side of the room. I don't know why I felt so shocked when the tall man sat next to him where I had sat only a few moments before. It was an unwarranted, irrational fear, but I felt it just the same. It... disturbed me. I felt like I was witnessing a new chapter of his life, an intimate moment that no one should have been privy to, a moment that would change everything. I wanted to run over to this man with his wild shadows and immaculate suit and rip him from the chair, though why I felt Adi needed protection from him, I do not know. Instead, I turned my back and headed determinedly into the day, relieved to feel the sunshine upon my face once again.

The early part of the evening was a torment. I could focus on neither my drawing nor the torrent of words pouring from my lecturers mouth, such was my mind preoccupied by the events of the afternoon. As luck would have it, our evening lecture ended early, cut short by a fortuitous case of food poisoning. I, however, ran straight to the library before it shut and began to pour through books and bibles, desperate for information, any reference to Longinus and the Spear of Destiny that would justify Adi's fantastical claims.

I sat there for hours, pouring through various books and texts, filling up my own notebooks with a steady stream of information. Three times the caretaker asked me to leave, and three times I begged him with all my considerable charm to let me stay. To find so much documented evidence, so much history relating to Longinus and in particular, the spear, filled me with a growing sense of excitement. Here was a mystery as old as history itself. The legends surrounding the spear made for fascinating reading. Some of the greatest minds and most feared dictators in history were rumoured to have possessed the spear at some point, Theodosius Alaric, responsible for the sacking of Rome. Charles Martel, who defeated the Muslim hordes in 733 AD, Frederick Barbarossa, even Charlemagne, all claimed to have held the spear and risen to power as a direct result. The history books went on and on, and my mind exploded with information.

Could it be real? Could the Spear that nestled on a velvet cushion in this very city be real? Many fakes had surfaced through the ages, according to the texts, but how would you know? And how did I know that the Spear that had Adi so obsessed was not the actual Spear that pierced the side of Christ?

I finish writing now, for my hands throb and my fingers have taken on the shape of the pencil by which I write. Tomorrow I will see Adi and I will show him what I have found, the history of which I have barely scratched the surface. There is provenance in this story, and maybe in this spear as well. Maybe my enthusiasm will show Adi I am indeed his friend. And who knows, maybe I too will become a believer.

March 6th 1909 Vienna

What an extraordinary day. Not at all the day I had expected, but one I shall hold dear in my heart for always.

Once my morning lectures had concluded, I rushed to the museum, my satchel laden with the information I had gleaned and my lips desperate to impart said knowledge. But when I got to the museum, Adi was not there. I must admit I was surprised, but also taken aback by how disappointed I felt. I had learned so much and I so wanted – no, needed to talk to him about it, to someone who felt the spear as much as I was now beginning to. His absence made me feel uneasy, a strange feeling, and I could not explain why.

Call me a fool, and maybe I am, but I searched for Adi, relentlessly. In a city the size of Vienna, I actually searched for him, like the proverbial needle in a haystack. I went to the Hostel in Brigittenau, the public rooms at Warmestuben – I even checked the café where we ate chocolate cake. The only other place where I thought I might find him was the soup kitchen at Meidling and it was with a heavy heart I found myself on its doorstep, my last best hope.

I wandered through the empty faces of the poor and the destitute, and their agony filled my heart with sorrow. So many people in need of the essentials of life, so many displaced souls with nowhere to go, nowhere to belong, and it hurt. I could not help but think that no man deserved such a fate, deprived of such human basic rights that seemed unbefitting for a supposedly civilised society.

And then that heavenly voice reached me through the crowds.

"Isaiah?"

She floated effortlessly through the disenchanted, her smile illuminating the path before her, and suddenly my mood felt lighter.

"Hello, Eva." That was all I could think of to say. What I should have said was how pretty she looked in her pale blue gingham apron, how lovely her dark hair was as the beams of the sun glistened on each strand, how wonderful and glorious was her smile that warmed the coldest hearts. But no, I just said hello. Sheesh.

Then she stood before me looking up into my face, and I could smell her lilac perfume, the jasmine oil she used in her hair, I could smell her very womanliness. I could feel my cheeks burning, I could hear my heart thumping away in my chest and I was lost in her.

"What brings you here?"

You bring me here was what I wanted to say, I came here for your smile and to gaze into those green eyes of yours, but no, oh no.

"Have you seen Adi?" I'm afraid that my lips and my heart do not always work in tandem.

"Why, yes. I saw him during this morning's shift, but he left early with a gentleman, a rather finely dressed gentleman, I must say, and so very tall."

There it was, that sudden plummeting of my stomach into my boots. A cold prickling sweat burst across my forehead, my arms tingled with nervous electricity and I felt nauseous. She said a tall well-dressed man, the same strange man that I have seen three times now with his impossibly monstrous and twisted shadow.

"Isaiah, are you okay?" Without even realising it, Eva had taken me gently by the arm and led me to a bench where she sat me down, looking at me with such worry and concern. "You look as though you have seen a ghost. You went so very grey suddenly."

"No, no, I'm fine, honestly, I just felt a bit queer momentarily, must be the heat," I lied. I blushed yet again at the touch of her hand against my skin.

"Well, the colour seems to be returning to your face once more." She said this with a smirk and I couldn't help but smile. This girl is an astute creature, sharp, intelligent, beautiful. Every second spent in her company tightens her grip around my swelling heart.

"I should go – I am keeping you from your work." I didn't want to go, every part of my being wanted to stay by her side, to bathe in her brilliance.

"Have you ever baked bread?"

"You know, I can't say that I have." With that, she grabbed me by the hand and pulled me helplessly through the crowd and into the kitchen area where she unceremoniously dumped a great lump of soggy dough in front of me and poured flour over the entire gloopy mess. She plopped another amorphous blob in front of herself and began to demonstrate the kneading process.

"Like this, with the palms of your hands." She began to pound the sticky blob of dough with unbridled glee, pushing the thing out

with the hard pads of her palms then pulling it back into a ball, repeating the process endlessly.

I attacked the sticky wet thing before me and my hands immediately became encased in what looked like cement. It clung to my fingers, my nails, my wrists and it was thoroughly unpleasant. Eva burst out laughing and I laughed too. I threw a lump of dough at her playfully but my flour-encrusted hands sprayed a fine coating of white powder over her face. Eva gasped through a mask of powdery shock. Then a chilling look of utter mischief spread across her white features and she pursed her lips in grim determination. She grabbed a hand full of flour and threw it into my face. I coughed as the fine white substance shot down my gapping mouth and up my nose. She stood there and laughed at me, laughed! Well I was having none of it. I scooped up two handfuls of flour and threw it at her so that she resembled a blinking, sneezing snowman. I watched in horror as she picked up a jug of water and she was about to throw it over me when a Nun suddenly appeared at our table. Now if looks could kill I would be a dead man. She didn't say a word, and she didn't need to. We both dusted ourselves down and began to attend to the dough once more, trying to convey as much innocence as we possibly could. The Nun tutted and shook her head as she walked away from the table.

"I feel thoroughly chastised."

"And so you should, attacking an innocent young woman like that."

"Something tells me that you are not as innocent or defenceless as you proclaim, young lady."

"I don't know what you could possibly mean."

I laughed. This girl has an unnerving knack for making me laugh, a rare gift indeed. We continued to knead the dough in silence with just the occasional shy glance at each other that sent my heart racing. Her dough was beginning to come together nicely but my own effort defeated me. I held up my hands in supplication.

"Let me show you." She took my hands and placed them onto the dough. We were so close together that my lips nearly brushed *her slender neck. Every impulse was telling me to kiss that neck, to brush that exquisite flesh with my lips, but propriety prevented me from such action. She pushed the palms of my hands into the dough, I marvelled at how strong she was and before I knew it, I was kneading the dough like an old pro. Very soon, the dough began to take on a springy texture and form a less sticky ball beneath my fingers. I looked at the vile sticky bits trapped beneath my nails and grimaced.*

"Now you know why I cut my nails so short. Here now, put it in this tin and we shall let it rise before baking."

We soon had a little production line going as lumps of wet dough transformed into springy balls, resplendent in their tins for rising.

As we waited for the first batch to bake, she pointed out certain clients – not vagrants, as I had called them – and she told me their stories. Shopkeepers, bankers, even teachers, fallen on hard times by misfortune, bad luck and betrayal. Each story was a tragedy in its own right and, not for the first time, I found myself thankful for all I had.

I walked home this evening cradling my very own loaf of bread in my arms as though it were a baby. Eva had presented it to me hot from the oven, and as I sit in my room writing this up in my journal, I eat great lumps of the loaf slathered with butter, enjoying every little morsel. Today has been a good day, and while I feel a little reluctant to admit this on paper, if I record it in writing then it may feel more real, for I cannot believe it myself. I am falling for Eva Steinberg.

March 8th 1909 Vienna

It has been a few days since my last entry and three days since I have seen Adi. Each day I have been to all his old haunts and each day they informed me that he left early with a tall, well-dressed gentleman. I cannot help but worry about him and I desperately want to know who this man is that seems to have such a grip on Adi. Maybe it is none of my business and maybe I should forget about the fiery little man, but something is not right, something is telling me there is more to this, I sense it, I smell it.

I have spent a lot more time with Eva, and not just within the confines of the kitchen. Today we ventured into the drab, drizzle-soaked streets of Vienna in our search for Adi, and I told her everything, including what I saw when I first glimpsed the tall man. I told her about the spear and Adi's obsession and my growing fascination with the subject. I saw the light bulb go off above her head and she gripped my hand with alarming force and rushed me to the Vienna Public Library, where she placed in front of me a huge, ancient bible.

"You need to read this," she said excitedly as she began to leaf through hundreds of yellowed pages. Excitedly she found what she wanted and pointed to the page with a glorious smile of triumph plastered across her pretty face. I began to read the passages with a growing sense of anxiety, and as I did so, my heart quickened to deafening proportions within my chest. The one section made me gasp.

The Gospel According to Saint John
Chapter 199
19:31 The Jews therefore, because it was the preparation, that the bodies should not remain upon the cross on the Sabbath day, (for that Sabbath day was an high day,) besought Pilate that their legs might be broken and that they might be taken away.

19:32 Then came the soldiers and brake the legs of the first and of the other, which was crucified with him.

19:33 But when they came to Jesus and saw that he was dead already, they brake not his legs: 19:34 But one of the soldiers with a spear pierced his side and forthwith came there out blood and water.

19:35 And he that saw it bare record and his record is true: and he knoweth that he saith true, that ye might believe.

19:36 For these things were done, that the scripture should be fulfilled, A bone of him shall not be broken.

19:37 And again another scripture saith, They shall look on him whom they pierced.

Yet more evidence, yet more mystery. The more I delve into this enigma, the more I am convinced there is some truth to it. Is the spear a weapon? Does the power of God imbue the spear? And if so, what does it do? Tomorrow I will get up very early and I will find Adi, despite his new friend.

March 9th 1909 Vienna

Today I have stared into the face of the devil, and I have never been so frightened in all my short life. I don't know what he is, but I know now, without doubt, that he is not human. My god, I have involved myself in something terrible. I have involved Eva in something terrible.

As I sit in my room committing this feverish nightmare to paper, I watch every shadow, every dark corner for fear that thing, that tall devil masquerading as a man, may step out of those shadows to consume my soul. Such is the terror that has gripped my heart. Tomorrow, Eva and I will leave this place, we will leave Vienna for good, but I fear the horrors that we have witnessed here today are only the beginning of something, something of a much greater magnitude, and that these flames of terror will lash out to consume this world. Nevertheless, we have to leave, even if the notion of safety is just an illusion.

Safety, are these words really on the same pages as love and laughter and happiness? My world is upside down, my eyes are open to a new world, one of darkness, one of supernatural horrors, one that I must learn to oppose at every given opportunity. My path is clear, and there is much to learn. But learn I will in order to face those demonic forces, those devils.

As planned, I arrived at Meidling early, greeted with much enthusiasm by the effervescent Eva. She guided me to a quiet corner and brought me a hot sweet mug of strong coffee that instantly woke me from my sleepy stupor. I am not a morning person, and getting up at five AM to be sitting in that cold draughty hall at six AM was a shock to my system. Eva sat next to me, and much to my surprise and delight, she placed her hand on my own as she talked, and the gesture felt like the most natural thing in the world. That was where her hand belonged, in mine. I looked into the depths of her eyes, the words forming on my lips but I was afraid to give them voice. If I spoke those words there would be no turning back.

"You do realise I am falling for you, my sweet little baker extraordinaire."

Even as I see those words written in black and white before my eyes, written by my own unsteady hand, I cannot believe my courage allowed me to utter them to her face. Then her hand tightened around my own and her eyes sparkled as though lit by some internal light.

"And I should think so too, Isaiah Nathan Silberman, otherwise I should feel the fool for loving you so."

My god those words. My skin tingled from head to foot and my head spun like a child's toy. She said that she loved me, me! I could not believe my ears.

"What did you just say?"

Eva tossed her head back and giggled then she leaned in toward me and her lips touched mine. They were so soft and so gentle, so wonderfully feminine, and for a second I was too afraid to reciprocate, but then her tongue found my lips and there was no stopping my passion. The fingers of my free hand wound themselves through her hair that felt so soft and luxurious and I became lost in her embrace. My heart, my body, my soul, all now belonged to Eva.

We became aware of a figure standing over us and I thought it was one of the Nuns coming to prise us apart, but when we tore ourselves away from each other and looked up, it was Adi. He glared at us, his face a mask of barely disguised rage.

"Adi. Adi I'm so glad to see you." I leaped to my feet and extended my hand to my friend, but he did not take it. His eyes burned with a terrifying ferocity, a gaze that fixed unswervingly upon my Eva.

"You have cut your hair short." The disdain in his voice was unmistakable. Eva instinctively brought her hand up to her hair, fingers twirling through the locks. I had failed to notice any change and quite why Adi brought it up I failed to understand.

"Just a little, so little I am surprised you noticed."

"I do not approve." Adi was bristling with emotion, and his entire body seemed to tremble.

"And quite what business that is of yours I fail to see. Now if you will excuse me, I shall leave you two gentlemen to it – some of us have work to do." With a sly wink in my direction, Eva flounced away toward the kitchen. I could barely conceal my smirk.

Adi sat on the bench opposite me. His demeanour seemed changed somehow – he held himself more erect, effecting an aura of confidence, of authority.

"I do not approve of girls with short hair. It is not the German way – it is non-Aryan, and borders on the edge of deviancy."

"Steady on old boy, don't you think you are being a bit melodramatic?"

"Not when it concerns the purity of the Aryan race. You are either pure German, or you are not."

Adi had changed, something within him had turned into stone, and I did not like it. It made me feel... uncomfortable. I had quickly come to realise during our short relationship that Adi was prone to extreme highs and lows when it came to his emotions, but this was the first time I had seen any hint of bigotry.

"Surely as an individual we are free to make our own choices, Adi?"

"Freedom is a luxury ill afforded. It is our duty, my duty... my destiny... to guide the German people to purity, to becoming the true Aryan race that we were always destined to be, to be the true leaders of man. There will be difficult choices to make on this path to glory – do you have the stomach for such glory, Isaiah?"

"Adi, what has happened to you? I haven't seen you for days, I was worried about you."

His eyes looked not at me, but through me, piercing, as sharply as the Spear he revered so very much.

"I have seen the truth, Isaiah, and I have embraced it. I have come to accept certain... revelations, my eyes and my heart opened to wondrous possibilities – such revelations, Isaiah, you could not possibly imagine. You would do well to listen to my words, my Jewish friend, for there is something coming, a great revolution that will make Germany the centre of the world."

He seemed so distant and remote, so insular. His face bore the expression of the enraptured, his voice the tone of the fanatic. It disturbed me. I decided to change tactics and speak to him of the spear in the hope that it would shake him from these unhealthy dramatics.

"You will never guess what information I have found about the spear, Adi. So much documentation, legends, rumours. And just the other day Eva showed me a passage from the Gospels that seem to affirm the legend of Longinus."

The smirk that crept across his face seemed cruel, cold, and he regarded me with callous eyes.

"What does a mere woman know of such things? Nothing, I tell you! And you, taken in by her pretty face and her feminine ways."

I felt my anger swell inside me and it tainted my voice more than I had intended.

"Do not speak of Eva in such a way. I always got the impression you were rather fond of her yourself – how could you speak of her so unkindly?" I forced the words from between my clenched teeth, and I could see that my little outburst had amused him. Adi sat back in his chair with a self-satisfied grin that split his face unkindly.

"And yet you kiss the one you presume I have affection for. What does that make you, Isaiah?"

His words cut me to the bone. It was true that I suspected he *had feelings of some sort for Eva, and yet I had barely seen him say two words to her. What was happening between Eva and me was neither planned nor deliberate, and nothing on this earth could prevent it. I would not let it.*

"*Your silence is confession enough, Jew, the Jewess no longer mean anything to me, you may use her as you see fit.*"

Before I could utter my protestations, of which there were very many, a third party joined our table, and the sight of him made me start.

He oozed onto the bench opposite me, his long limbs creeping over the wood, moving like a spider. Long hands with very long fingers rested palms down on the table in front of me like two tarantulas waiting to pounce. The face looked human, but it had none of the characteristic lines or creases that make us individual. It reminded me of a sculpture, the crude beginnings of a more detailed work—the basics were there, but the character was missing. And those eyes, dead eyes glistening from within deep-set sockets, shark's eyes. They moved and they blinked, but there was no feeling in them, no life, with no spark of recognisable humanity. He had hair, but it was short and stubbly and a black top hat sat rather uncomfortably on his oversized crown. The man was immaculately dressed in a tightly fitted black morning coat and grey stripped trousers with a high-collared white shirt and sky blue tie, just as I remembered from the museum. Was that really only six days ago?

The sight of that strange proto-human shocked me so much I could not take my eyes off him. My brain was telling me he was just another man, a very tall, very well-dressed man, but my heart was screaming something different, that there sat something unknown, something that had no right to walk the face of God's good earth.

"*May I present to you a friend of mine? His name is Klingsor.*"

The creature extended a long arm toward me, the movement slow and deliberate, brittle looking fingers unfurling from a plate-sized hand, and it reminded me of a praying mantis I once saw in a glass case in school as a child. The touch of his flesh repulsed me. I cannot explain it – there are no words to describe how it felt other than it felt unreal somehow fake, not like human flesh at all.

"I have heard a great deal about you, and I understand you share our friend's enthralment for the Spear of Longinus."

His voice was as dry as a dead leaf. I felt each spoken word in the marrow of my bones like a tremor, and my own voice dried up in my rapidly tightening throat.

"Does this Jew speak?"

"This Jew does nothing but speak. And he is forever finding new ways to use his tongue," quipped Adi caustically. "Perhaps you should explain to our silent friend here a little about yourself and the group you represent."

"Well, Jew with no tongue, have you ever heard of the Vril Society?"

By the pricking of my thumbs, something wicked this way comes. Shakespeare was a perceptive fellow.

"Only recently, while I was researching the Spear of Longinus. The Vril Society is a group of occultists obsessed with holy relics, is it not?"

"So the Jew has a tongue after all. Yes, young Jew, the Vril Society is interested in holy relics and the legends that surround them, but we are much more than that. We are the great bankers of the world. Money is power, and money gives us the resources to further our educational system of beliefs throughout the German Empire and beyond. It is our belief the Aryan race is the sole inheritor of Mother earth, and it is our duty to further the cause of the Aryan race. This we will achieve through our educational programmes, indoctrination of our youth and the control of all major political parties. As for occultists? Other less educated people call us occultists because of our search for relics that pertain to have power, but as for calling up the devil to do our bidding? Ludicrous! I would like to see anyone try to make him do their bidding. I don't see anybody calling Alexander Graham Bell, Benjamin Franklin, or Faraday occultists, and they changed the world forever, did they not? We are in favour of progress, my Jewish friend, progress attained through strong leadership and *power. Money is a means to that end."*

"Those are the words of a dictator, my friend, and my name is Isaiah Nathan Silberman. The word Jew denotes my ethnicity, not my name. Adi, surely you do not subscribe to such things?"

"Years of lethargy have made the German people weak — we need a new direction, a strong defined route to Aryan supremacy. The Vril Society can offer us, offer me that."

"I heard you speak of your research into the Spear of Longinus," said the man-thing, Klingsor, but I did not take my gaze away from Adi. I found his sudden hostility disquieting, and to be entirely truthful, it devastated me.

"May I?" Klingsor indicated the thick folder that rested on the table, and I flicked the file half-heartedly toward him. Fingers crawled across the wood and it made me shudder as those long digits wrapped around the folder and dragged it away from me. He used the long nail of his index finger to flick through the pages, his dead eyes scanning my hasty writing. We sat in silence, the three of us, the only sound the rustling of paper as Klingsor devoured my notes.

"Why?" said Adi at length. The question took me by surprise.

"Why? I do not understand, why what?"

"Your research? What possible use can you have for the Spear of Destiny?"

For some reason the question upset me. During our short-lived friendship, I felt that Adi and I had found a connection, and his interest in the spear had infected me — Adi had infected me. Obviously, I was naïve enough to think that my time and effort researching the spear would further cement our growing friendship. How could I have been so wrong?

"You told me about the spear, Adi, remember that. But why are you so interested in it? What do you want with the spear?"

"The spear is power. Whoever shall possess the spear will hold the word of God in their hand and all shall bow down to them."

"Is that what you want? You think the spear will bring you power? Do you want me to bow down to you, Adi?"

He sat there and smirked, a supercilious grin I wanted to smack *away from his face. I am not a violent man, but he was really pushing me. I noticed Eva was watching from the door of the kitchen and I gave her a reassuring wink. Adi saw this and his grin turned into a scowl that curdled my blood.*

"*I am impressed, young Isaiah, you seem to have found a great deal of information in a very short space of time. Of course this is nothing that the Vril have not known all along, and we know so much more still, but impressive none the less.*"

"*And what, may I ask, are your interests in the spear? Do you crave power as well?*" *I did not bother to mask the sarcasm that laced my words, but to that creature, it was like water off a duck's back.*

"*Power is not something we are short of... Mr. Silberman. Relics of this kind interest us, and the spear is the ultimate relic, do you not think? To have pierced the side of Christ, to have been drenched in his blood, if this is truly the Spear of Longinus, touched by the blood of God, then surely to use the spear would be to coax God himself from the heavens.*"

"*You wish to see the face of God?*"

"*Oh please, that boat sailed a long time ago. Let's just say it would be nice to pique his interest.*"

"*It's a legend, a story, fantasy, nothing more.*"

"*You think so, little, Jew?*" *He delved into a pocket inside his beautifully tailored jacket and pulled out a clear glass test tube with a golden stopper. He passed it to me, held like a vice between two repulsive fingers. I took it from him and looked through the glass at a tiny fragment of wood, a splinter no more than an inch in length. I looked at Klingsor questioningly and he smiled through his bloodless lips.*

"*Open it and hold it in the palm of your hand.*"

Gently I pulled out the golden stopper and tipped the shard of wood into my open hand.

The sensation hit me with such intense power I nearly tumbled backward off my bench. Images flashed through my head, terrible images of pain and of blood, of a wrist pierced with a nail, each painful blow pounding through my soul, and I felt the heat of the sun on my face, I felt the agony of understanding, the agony of the inevitable death. I felt power.

With a gasp, I dropped the wooden shard onto the table, afraid to touch it. With inhuman speed, Klingsor reached across the table and scooped up the shard, snatching the glass tube from my hand and with a gentleness unbefitting his terrible persona he placed the shard into the tube and re-sealed it. In a flash, it disappeared into his inner jacket pocket. He sat forward with fingers entwined, his face seemingly alive for the first time, and I swear I saw tears in his eyes.

"That is but a mere fraction, a splinter of the true cross. You felt its power. You saw the travesty that it once witnessed two thousand years ago. If a mere splinter of wood can do that, imagine what the spear could do."

I was in shock. I could not believe the images I had seen, what my body had felt, and the intensity of that experience still tingles through me even now, as I write this.

"Who are you? What are you?"

Klingsor threw back his head and laughed loudly, a chilling sound that no human ears should experience.

"I am many things, little man, and I have had many names. But I am a man — make no mistake of that, the first man, you might say. Tell me, little Jew, the spear. How would you validate the one held in the Hapsburg museum? You are obviously a man of keen intellect, how would you know if it were the real deal?"

"Surely, if a piece of the true cross can instil such images in one's mind, then the spear would instil the same reaction. Just to hold it in your hand would be proof enough."

"Your logic is sound, my friend, but the spear that resides inside the museum is but one of many throughout the world claiming to be the true Spear of Longinus, and time has seen much alteration to that particular spear. Within the central aperture of the blade resides a hammer-headed nail, supposedly used during the crucifixion of Christ. How would we know if it was the nail or the spear that were the genuine article?"

"There are more spears?"

"Oh yes, and some of them can show you images that would burn your soul. But as for which one is real, no one can know for sure."

"Then surely research is your only recourse, to examine its provenance and trace it back to its origin as far as possible."

"I see from your notes you have a natural ability for such things."

"I like a good mystery."

Klingsor stood and smiled down at me from an impossible height. He looked as though he was trying to make up his mind about something and I did not like the way he looked at me, not one little bit.

"Come, my friend." He indicated for Adi to rise. "The others await our return."

Others? I desperately wanted to know, but at the same time, I could not bear to be in his company any longer. I needed to be free from his cold gaze and from the suffocating aura that infused the air around us with such blackness. I needed to breathe.

"Adi? Will I see you again?" His eyes fell on me with such a look of disdain I felt crushed.

"Maybe." He turned his back on me and walked away. Just as Klingsor was about to leave, he hesitated and glanced back, his head rotating almost a hundred and eighty degrees. I shrivelled away from him as he snatched up my notes.

"I will keep you in mind, little Jew, always be assured of that."

No sooner had the figure left the table than Eva was back at my side, one arm gently draped around my neck as she whispered in my ear. Thank god for the touch of a good woman.

"Who was that?"

I was out of my seat and heading toward the door before my brain had made the decision to do so. Eva scurried after me, her face full of worry.

"Isaiah, what is wrong? Where are you going? Who was he?"

I spun around in the doorway and held her by the shoulders, my eyes bulging from my head like some deranged animal. What a testament to her mettle that she did not flinch from me, despite the *horror so obvious in my eyes.*

"I don't know who or what he is, Eva, but something is happening to Adi, and I know that fiend is responsible for it. Listen to me and listen to me carefully. I do not understand what is happening here and I do not like it. The way he spoke to you, no one should speak to you in that manner, no one. You must promise me you will stay away from him, never be alone with him or his strange friend. Promise me, Eva."

"Adi? For the love of God tell me what's wrong, let me help you."

"You can help, Eva, by staying here, by being safe, by being here for me when I return. Please, you must promise me that?"

"I do, Isaiah, I promise."

I pulled her to my chest and bent my head to kiss her soft lips and she accepted my advance without hesitation, her arms wrapped tightly around my back. It was with great reluctance I wrenched her from my grasp and pushed her away from me into the building. I just prayed I would be able to get back to her, because I was about to do something very stupid.

As I raced through the streets of Vienna, I tried to convince myself I was doing the right thing. I could just walk away — turn my back on Adi and his power hungry friend, to remain in the arms of Eva forever. Walk away, Isaiah — I kept telling myself to walk away, to forget what I had seen, what I had felt, but I had touched the power of God and how does one turn away from that? As this battle of conscience raged inside my mind, I kept my focus very firmly planted on the two I pursued. They gave no indication they were aware of me as they weaved skilfully through the streets of Vienna unnoticed by the multitude of innocent souls surrounding them, and I had no idea where they were leading me.

The twin spires of the Maximillion Church loomed skyward ahead of me, and Adi and Klingsor headed straight for it. I found the location curious, that a church should be their place of meeting, but I was determined to follow, no matter where it led me.

I held back as they entered through the huge wooden doors and then I crept forward, sliding through the door before it had the chance to close. The gloom inside caught me off balance and it took me a couple of seconds to adjust, just in time to see the two enter a side door in the east side of the building. I wandered innocently down the aisle amid the few worshipers clutching their bibles, beads dangling from penitent fingers and sparkling defiantly in the weak light. No one seemed to take the blindest bit of notice of my presence, so I darted to the east door and the terror awaiting me.

Beyond the door lay a staircase plunging into the dark bowels of the church. I descended through darkness down a narrow passage so steep I had to grip the rough walls either side of me to prevent my stumbling head first into the blackness below.

When I reached the bottom, which seemed to take forever, the space suddenly opened up into a vast square chamber lit by hundreds of candles and flaming wall sconces, and I hunkered down on all fours and edged around the wall until I reached a huge square stone set into the floor. Flames spewed fiercely from a carved urn perched on the stone altar, and I peeked around its corner warily.

At the far end of the chamber stood two enormous thrones, their ornate gilt finish twinkling in the candlelight. Klingsor sat in one throne and another being, female, sat in the other. Like Klingsor, she was a strange looking creature with long elongated limbs and naïve, incomplete features. Her hair trickled down over her shoulders in long flowing curly locks of gold, and she wore a beautiful black bodice enriched with beads and crystals with a skirt that consisted of multiple layers of fabric arranged around her long legs. Her feet were bare, and to my horror, I saw that her toes looked as long as her fingers.

My hair stood on end and a cold chill rippled down my spine at the sight of the thing behind them. I nearly screamed, the figure frightened me so. It stood behind the thrones, draped in a shroud of gold and green brocade with just two holes from which its yellow eyes blazed across the scene. The thing rippled and twitched. That, more than anything I had seen thus far, frightened me the most, it was so bizarre and yet deeply disturbing. A large glittering cauldron, fashioned from what could only be pure gold, glistened at the feet of the shrouded thing.

A row of kneeling figures flanked the thrones either side, each covered in a long black cowl that obscured their faces. Each row of six figures clenched their hands before them, but instead of their fingers pointing skyward in the traditional form of prayer, they pointed down toward the ground. Suddenly, the back of the nearest figure to me shifted and I had to stifle a cry of horror as I realised that each figure had something on its back, some indistinguishable hump perched on their shoulder blades, something alive that squirmed beneath the robes.

In the centre of the room, lying on his back with his arms outstretched, lay Adi. He stared skyward at a ceiling decorated with esoteric symbols that I could not begin to understand or decipher, symbols that continued down the walls and onto the floor, culminating in a strange kind of star shape in the middle of the cavern upon which Adi lay. The shape consisted of four arms radiating out from a central point, and each straight arm had a smaller arm branching off at a ninety-degree angle.

Klingsor rose slowly from his chair and opened his arms to the expectant crowd.

"Children, our beloved Vril, we have summoned you here today so you may witness the birth of that which we have sought for so very long. We deliver before you our Black Messiah, he who will deliver us from this hell on earth so that we may once more take our rightful place in paradise. For far too long we have been denied the voice of our Father, denied his love, denied his respect. He created us out of love, as you too... our dearest... we also created out of love. But that love was taken away from us, without question and without remorse, and now the one promised to us so very long ago has been delivered, and we will endure, my children, we will reclaim paradise and dispel those imposters who assumed our rightful position."

Klingsor oozed toward the prone figure on the floor, his movements fluid and unnatural until he stood directly over Adi's head.

"Do you understand what it is that is required of you?"

"I do."

"Once you have become our Black Messiah, once you have accepted the gifts that we offer, you will be one of us, above all others, superior to all humans that walk this earth, you will become a God – do you understand what that entails? Do you give yourself over to the Vril, selflessly, unquestioningly and with utter devotion?"

"I do!"

"Then you will drink from The Mother so you may accept the gift of her child. You will become Thule, the highest of all Vril."

Klingsor walked back to his throne and the extraordinary woman sitting next to him stood. Klingsor looked at her as I always found myself looking at Eva, with wonder and with love, with heartfelt devotion that transcended all else. She knelt over him, her lips touching his and even from my vantage point, I could see their long tongues flicking in and out of each other's mouths. It made me feel sick.

She moved down toward Adi, and as she did so, she ripped the skirts away from her waist to reveal the nakedness beneath. I had to clamp my hands across my mouth to prevent the gasp of terror that nearly escaped through my clenched lips. Her long legs ended with a hairless vagina that rippled softly as though alive, its numerous layers of flesh pulsing with a life of their own. Blood dribbled from the lips and run down her legs in thick black-red clots. She looked back at Klingsor as he sat forward on his throne in eager anticipation, his face a portrait of utter ecstasy. She blew him a kiss.

"See my beloved, see how I give him my kiss," she crooned. With that, she positioned herself over Adi's head and hunkered down so that her wriggling vagina covered Adi's lips. He didn't move and he didn't struggle. She began to writhe on his face, pushing her bloody womanhood deeper into his mouth as thick rivulets of black-red gore began to pour over Adi's face, down his chin and across his cheeks in glutinous chunks.

"Drink deeply from my cunt, let me lead you into temptation, for this will be your kingdom, forever eternal."

Bile filled my mouth and I had to swallow it. It took all my concentration to stop the vomit from gushing up my throat, for never have I witnessed anything so repulsive.

Klingsor's empoisoned voiced boomed through the chamber triumphantly. "See how the Black Messiah drinks from the Garden of Eden. Now he shall be with child and we will welcome him into our fold with the corruption of innocence and imbue unto him the drink of the fallen."

The woman, Maria, disengaged her vagina from Adi's mouth, and as she stood, long stringy bands of clotted blood snapped from her womanly parts into Adi's open mouth, now completely engorged with blood. She slid over his body and knelt over his waist, spidery fingers working at Adi's trousers until his manhood stood erect before her. With her back to Klingsor, she lowered herself onto Adi's penis and began to move up and down. As she gyrated relentlessly, she bent at the waist backward, the top of her head almost touching Adi's knees, and I felt faint.

"See, husband, how our Messiah ploughs our garden, how he seeds new life!"

She sat up suddenly and screamed, a bloodcurdling sound that reverberated off the cavern walls and seeped into my bones. Adi gasped, then Maria detached herself from his penis and tucked it back into Adi's trousers. Ever so gently, she took Adi by the hand and pulled him into a sitting position facing the thrones.

"Watch, watch as I give birth to my child, to your child."

As Maria walked, her stomach began to distend, ballooning right before my horrified eyes. I could hear her bones cracking as her stomach bulged obscenely, skin rippling as though something moved within, desperate to get out. She managed to reach her throne and with a scream, she opened her legs wide.

From her vagina poured a mixture of blood and mucus that splashed down the dais toward Adi, soaking his trousers. I could not bear the sight of her writhing in pain, of the filth that gushed from her body, but I could not look away. I wanted to cover my eyes, to block out the sound from my head, to run screaming from that building, from those demons atop their golden thrones. I wanted to wake up in my bed, safe in the knowledge this was all a bad dream, the result of some poorly digested food poisoning my system. How could this be happening, how could God allow this to happen? My mommy always said there were no monsters — no real ones — but there are. They surrounded me.

Something grey and wet squirmed between her legs, heaving its flaccid bulk out from her vaginal walls. Tentacles wriggled and slapped against her thighs and something shapeless began to crown, the head of some obscene baby. Suddenly a thing, bulbous and rancid, slapped onto the floor in a writhing nest of grey tentacles that squirmed across its body and slapped against the ground. I could see a single eye tearing its lid open from amongst the morass of snake-like appendages. And that eye, that single red eye peeping out from its centre, burned with a voracious intelligence and malevolence beyond that of any earthly creature.

Klingsor scooped up the monstrous form and brought it to his lips, kissing its wet flesh.

"Mother has given us a new child, the most important child of all, a child for our Black Messiah."

With the creature clutched to his chest, Klingsor approached Adi, who immediately stripped to the waist. Klingsor placed the foul thing onto Adi's back and the tentacles wrapped themselves around his body and his neck. Adi did not move or utter a sound as the monster settled onto his body, its singular eye looking over his right shoulder. Then, to my astonishment, it began to fade, to become the same colour as Adi's flesh until I could barely conceive of it except for a suggestion out of the corner of my eye.

"You can come out now, Isaiah." I froze, unable to move, my limbs and my nerves stiff with fear as Klingsor called my name. "I have known you were there all the time, little Jew, I can smell your distinct brand of humanity. All cut foreskin and falafel."

I stood silently and felt the weight of their gaze upon me. Adi smirked as he covered his torso with his shirt, and I saw the lump beneath the cloth squirm. The female thing, Maria, flew from her throne and drifted toward me with her arms and fingers dancing grotesquely in the air before her like some surreal puppet. Blood clung thickly to her legs and clotted lumps of gore fell to the floor in her wake. She extended a long arm toward me, her fingers wrapped around my trembling hand, and before I realised I had even moved, I was standing before the thrones, her lips caressing my cheek, making me shudder with disgust. A long pale tongue flickered from between her bloodless lips and brushed across my face, and I thought I would pass out from the terror of it, from the terror of her touch.

"He tastes of innocence, my husband, such unblemished virtue. He has not known the warmth of a woman's cunt around his cut cock."

Maria slid to her husband, her tongue darted into his mouth and Klingsor sucked on it as though it were some delicious iced confectionary.

"Mmmm, indeed, my beloved, he does taste quite delectable, does he not. But we have another sweet morsel for our Messiah to taste this day."

"Isaiah!"

I spun around, horrified at the sound of that scream, that voice which I had come to cherish so very much. Two men dressed in black military styled uniforms dragged Eva into the cavern. Upon seeing me, she wrenched herself free from their grasp and ran into my arms, her entire body trembling, face soaked with tears.

"I'm sorry, Isaiah, I followed you, I had to know you would be safe, your words frightened me so. Then these thugs in uniform grabbed me upstairs as I was about to follow you down. What is this place, Isaiah?"

Her eyes settled on Adi and the bloody mess around his lips, then suddenly, her eyes widened in abject terror, her voice a strangled cry from between her ruby lips.

"There is something on his back!"

Anger once again fuelled my response and I swung around to face our triumphant captors.

"Why have you brought her here? What do you intend to do with her? Tell me!"

Klingsor leaned forward and smelled the air before him, his

nostrils flaring as he inhaled deeply.

"Ahh, the smell of sweet innocence, so intoxicating yes? And here we are, blessed with two such creatures, how opportune. There is nothing more abhorrent to the eyes of God than the corruption of such innocence."

Adi smirked slyly as the meaning of Klingsor's words begun to sink in.

"No. Over my dead body. You will have to kill me first if you think I am going to stand by and let you do that."

"Oh, come now, dear boy, let's not be dramatic. You are of interest to me, I told you that, what a great shame it would be to allow such a talent to go to waste. I'm sure we can come to some sort of... arrangement?"

"Anything, I will do anything... to spare her, please, what must I do?"

"Two things actually, but the second one will not be asked of you for a while, but rest assured I will come for you, Isaiah, you will be of use to me, but for now you will remove your clothing and get on your hands and knees before the Black Messiah."

Eva pulled away from me, her face full of pleading, full of dread.

"Isaiah no, please, you cannot do this, let them have me, for the sake of your own sanity let them do to me as they will." She rushed once more into my arms and sobbed into my chest, her voice a barely audible whisper. "I wanted it to be you, Isaiah, my beloved, but if I have to do this to save you, then I will do it. Just promise me, promise me you will still love me afterward."

Her big green eyes looked at me with such intensity, such desperation that I could barely hold back the sob that escaped my own throat. I held her tightly and I kissed her forehead. No one was going to touch her, not while I still breathed. I looked across at Klingsor and gave him an almost imperceptible nod at which point a black uniformed guard came forward and wrestled Eva from my grasp.

"No, Isaiah, you mustn't, let me be the one, for the love of God let me do this!" The guard dragged her away from me as I slipped off my shoes and began to strip. "Isaiah no! No!"

I slipped off my undergarments and hunkered down on all fours facing Klingsor, who sat back in his throne with a smug expression plastered across his inhuman face. Maria perched on his knee, her hand between his legs, stroking his manhood that bulged through his trousers. And that thing, the shrouded thing behind them, twitched with excitement, piercing yellow eyes blazing with anticipation. I felt Adi move behind me. It was all a dream, nothing but a terrible dream. I bowed my head in shame.

"Look at me, little Jew," demanded Klingsor. "Do not take your gaze away from me."

I gritted my teeth and looked up to see Maria had freed his penis from his trousers and was beginning to pleasure him with her hands.

I cannot write the words, such is my shame. The pain, the humiliation, the degradation of the human spirit inflicted upon my person in that chamber is too much for me to commit to paper. Even as I suffered, even as my masculinity lay broken inside me, they laughed, enjoying my agony as Eva wept at my suffering.

Would I be able to father a child after such torture? The pain, the burning, the tearing searing agony told me otherwise. In that moment of absolute horror, that was all I could think about, that I would not be able to have a child with the woman I loved. And I wept. Maria began to move her hands faster and faster and Klingsor began to twitch on his throne, a low guttural moan issuing from his wide mouth. Suddenly, Klingsor let out a loud cry as thick black ejaculate shot from his penis into her open mouth. She lapped it up greedily.

When it was over, I stood up quickly, desperate to cover myself, but the pain that blossomed inside my body almost made me concede to the darkness that threatened to blanket my existence. Adi knelt in a pool of his own blood, himself ruined. "Look what you did to me, you tight Jew."

I fell backward, my legs shaking so much they were unable to support my weight. Eva rushed to my side, cradling my head in her arms, and I grabbed my discarded clothes in an attempt to cover myself from her eyes.

"Ssshh, my love, it's over, it's over, let me hold you in my loving arms and know that I love you more than I could possibly love any other man."

I cried in her arms and buried my shame in the folds of her dress.

"Bravo, young Jew. That was a very fine show, and such selflessness. And don't worry, my friend – that particular service was a one-time job opportunity... unless you really want to try it again, of course. When I next call upon you, it will be for that extraordinary brain of yours. And now, just one more part to this little quartet, now Adi must drink from that which is fallen. Maria my dear, if you would be so kind as to do the honours?"

Maria picked up a jewelled dagger and swayed toward the terrifying figure behind the throne. An immaculate hand, pale and perfectly formed appeared from beneath the cloth and exposed its wrist, on which Maria made a quick slicing motion. Thick black blood dripped into the golden cauldron at its feet and the hand disappeared back beneath the shroud.

"What is that?" I asked. Klingsor chuckled as Maria passed the cauldron to him.

"The beginning and the end."

One after the other, Maria and Klingsor opened their veins and poured their black blood into the cauldron. Klingsor held the cauldron out to Adi's outstretched hands.

"Drink. Become that which you are destined. You are now Thule, the greatest of the Vril, our Black Messiah."

Adi lifted the cauldron to his lips and begun to drink, gulping down mouthfuls of viscous black liquid.

"Drink long and drink deep. Our blood, the blood of Menarche will make you strong, but the blood of the fallen will make you a god eternal! You will be the ultimate man, the ultimate leader, the Black Messiah who will rise and consume all in your path!"

The cauldron tumbled from Adi's grip and clattered onto the floor in a glittering clamour of gold. But there was nothing left to spill from its interior.

"I see him," said Adi and the look on his face was of utter astonishment. "I see the spear — it is true — it is all true!" His body convulsed and he held his arms out to the side. The blood that smeared his face and dripped from his loins melted into his skin and I watched dumfounded as his penis began to heal, absorbing the blood that crawled across the floor and up his legs.

"The spear is power — the spear is life and death, the beginning and the end! I will be the beginning and I will be the end!" He screamed suddenly, blinding white light issuing from his eyes, and I had to shield myself from the terrible glare. The space filled with a howling wind that whipped at the candles and our clothes. Adi began to lift, arms outstretched, then his feet left the ground as he spun above our heads, twin beams from his eyes spinning in a cascade of white light. The wind seemed to coalesce around his body in a broiling maelstrom until suddenly there was an intense rush of energy that made my ears pop.

Then the storm was gone.

Adi slowly descended to the floor and touched down with perfect poise and composure. He looked at his hands, felt his skin, felt his face and his chest. He looked different, invigorated, and his eyes burned white with an intense, hypnotic, unwavering intelligence.

"I have been reborn. The Black Messiah has come." He spoke with such clarity, such conviction, every word spoken with a passion bordering on the edge of hysteria. "Hail your new Messiah!"

Maria, Klingsor and everyone gathered in the space rose to their feet and raised their hands in a one armed salute and their cry was deafening to behold.

"Heil!"

"Today marks the beginning of a new era for the Aryan race! We will sweep across this land and purge the people of their impurities, we will build a Germany that is fit to rule, fit to rule not just this land, but all lands, and Heaven itself shall bow down before me!"

"Heil!"

I struggled back into my clothes and Eva helped me to my feet. Pain shot through my bowels but I gritted my teeth against it, feeling my torn insides rip further. I was ruined, my parts shattered within, I could feel it. Funny how in that moment that I should think of such a thing — could I still be a man? Could I still produce children? Would Eva still want me?

A long bony hand touched my shoulder, fingers dripping down my upper chest.

"You may go now, little Jew, you and your woman are free to leave. But remember, I will be watching you, and I will be calling upon you to perform a service from time to time, such is the bond of our agreement. Failure to comply will see those you love pay dearly for your disobedience. Remember."

"Please, do not harm her, anything else... just not her." *The words caught in the back of my throat, devoured by my pain.*

"Then when I call, you will come."

Klingsor glared at me with his cold dead eyes and I nodded my understanding. Eva began to lead me toward the staircase and the church above, but I had to try once more, try to appeal to the last vestiges of decency that may still be lurking in his heart.

"Adi, don't do this, leave this place, it is not too late."

It was clear by the look on his face that he was long past saving and that it was, in fact, very late indeed. As Eva helped me to mount the first steep stair, Adi's voice echoed toward me loudly, and it was no longer the voice of my friend, of the shy, meek individual I met once in a museum, but the voice of a megalomaniacal tyrant.

"Little Jew, do not ever call me by that name again. Adi is dead. I am the Black Messiah. I am the beginning and I am the end. I am the name that will strike terror into the hearts of men. I am the name that will flatten cities. My name is Adolf Hitler."

Chapter Fourteen: A Short Conversation with the Devil Part Two

My God, I was suffering from information overload. For once Malachi was speechless, and I knew how he felt. What could I say after that? But Daniyyel, the angel, bowed his head in shame, and I stared at him, willing him, daring him to say something. So much horror, so much suffering and he allowed all that shit to happen. Heaven stood by as a monster was born. Daniyyel was an angel, the right hand of God, and if he had wanted, he could have stopped Hitler from being born or destroyed him at birth. It was all within his power.

Fuck the bloody Covenant.

Could I do that? If I knew a child would grow to become the greatest tyrant the world had ever known, could I kill him? To hold a life between the tips of my fingers, to know I could extinguish the germ of evil held within the palm of my hand. Would I do it?

Too fucking right, I would do it.

But not Daniyyel, not the angel, he wouldn't get his lily-white hands dirty. And fuck the lot of us.

But Ethan, he looked devastated. He closed the book and turned away, his shoulders slumped, the weight of his pain crushing him. He looked so tiny suddenly, not the strapping young man, but a child desperate for his parents. A howl of agony burst from his trembling lips. He stifled it with a fist, holding back the flood of emotions that threatened to engulf him. I could not begin to imagine what was going through his mind. To find that his father was involved with the greatest evil of the modern world was one thing, but to know he was regularly in the employ of Hitler's dark collaborators was another.

Dark collaborators that I knew, that I had fought, that terrified me.

"I'm sorry, Ethan. I don't know what to say." My words sounded pathetic as they spilled from my lips, but I needed him to talk. I needed him to tell me what he was feeling.

"Who am I?"

I was not expecting that. It took me by surprise. His tear-filled eyes pleaded for an answer, but I had nothing to offer, even though I had asked myself that very same question so many times. How could I know who he was, who anyone was, if I did not know myself? It made me feel thoroughly inadequate. Every fibre of my body wanted to scoop him into my arms and hold him close, to brush the tears from his soft cheeks with my fingers and comfort him. I wanted to lay my heart bare before him and offer him my soul. That man, that complete stranger, he asked me who he was and I wanted to tell him he was mine.

"Am I even his son?" Desperate emotion coloured each trembling word. "Was she even my mama? You read it too, he said it, that he was damaged, broken inside, so what does that make me?" His eyes widened, filling with a horror that was dreadful to behold.

"Ethan, no, of course they are your parents, you are here, so he was wrong, of course he was wrong."

"You think so? All those times he went away for *work* – and he did work, didn't he, for them, for those things, for fucking Hitler. All those years and I still do not know the man who raised me." Anger tainted his words, corrupted his memories. "He never told me. He never told me. So what else didn't he tell me? What else was he hiding from me?"

"Do not start down this path, Ethan. He *is* your father and he loves you, your mother loved you. What they did, they did out of love – he had no choice."

"Papa has been obsessed with religious relics all his life – he has travelled all around the world for his *work,* and now I know why, it was all for *him,* for Hitler, for this Vril Society. My papa the Jew, working for Hitler, helping Hitler, tell me how I can reconcile that with everything that monster has done, with the millions he has slaughtered in his fucking war! Tell me where my papa's love is in that!"

He was distraught. Horror had stolen his rationality, his brain running on shock, fuelled by anger, his body burning with adrenalin. He was a time bomb about to explode, and it was up to me to defuse him.

So I spoke those immortal words.

"It's not as simple as that." Hush my stupid fucking mouth.

Boom! The bomb went off. Ethan exploded out of his chair, the blast directed toward me.

"Have you any idea of what is going on out there? Of what that man has done? There is a death camp right in your front garden, just there on the other side of your front door, where he kills hundreds, thousands, all in *his* name, the great and powerful Hitler. And here you sit feeling sorry for yourself and doing nothing while he slaughters innocent people right under your fucking nose. And do you know what the worst of it is? Do you? *My* papa is in that camp, and I don't know if he is there as a prisoner or if he is there helping them. Is that simple enough for you?"

All eyes fell upon me and I withered under the crushing weight of their accusation. Fuck the lot of them.

But it was the look of bitter disappointment blistered across Ethan's face that crucified me the most. He was a stranger, but his words cut through me like a scythe and he was right—I could not bear the fact that he was right, or that the fucking angel was right. The world was crying out in pain and I ignored it, safe in my ignorance, ignorant in my selfishness.

I was a coward.

I felt hemmed in, trapped. So I did the only thing any self-respecting homosexual could do – I walked out.

The icy wind felt so good against my skin after the suffocating atmosphere of Alte. I raised my face to the heavens and basked in the chill that encrusted my face, the moon making my skin luminescent, and I sucked in a lung full of icy particles just to feel the cold sting my chest. It felt so bloody good.

With one elegant leap through the air, I stood at the rim of the surrounding forest and with another graceful leap—I fucking loved my body—I knelt by the stream that cut the valley in two. The water flowed blackly below as I hovered over its rippling surface and I glared defiantly into the glassy surface demanding my image to appear, but there was no reflection, nothing to tell the water I was there. Even the elements had abandoned me. So I flew to a nearby rock on the frozen riverbank and did what every petulant child has done throughout eternity, threw pebbles angrily across the surface of the water.

"Still avoiding the world, I see."

That was all I fucking needed, the devil on my shoulder.

"Melek."

"I just love the way you manage to make my name sound like you have just stepped in shit. Is that a natural gift you have, or something you have honed to perfection over the centuries?"

"Piss off, Melek, there's enough shit at my door without you adding to it."

"Oh I know dear heart... .I *so* know... why do you think I am here?"

"Surprise me, why don't you."

"I might just do that, watch this space."

I forced myself to look at him, the devil incarnate in his black figure-hugging suit and white shirt. He clenched his hands before him and considered me with some amusement. Fair play, he cut a fine figure of a man and was handsome, devilishly handsome, but I would not let him burn me with those yellow eyes.

Yellow eyes.

"It was you, in that crypt — it was your blood they gave to Hitler."

"You might well think that, but I..."

"Oh shut the fuck up, Melek, I know it was you. They are your thugs, after all. Maria and Klingsor now, is it, that's what they are calling themselves?"

"Oh that. How they do so love all the dramatics."

"Why, Melek? Why Ethan's father? What is your interest in him? What did you call Ethan — Redivivus?"

Melek clapped his hands together with delight and beamed at me. His mouth filled his face. I shivered.

"Ha! Now that would be telling. Spoilers, dear heart, spoilers."

"You're just as bad as that fucking angel." His face darkened. Take that, bitch.

"I see you have lost none of your bile, vampire."

"And I see you are still playing your games, *devil*."

"Ha!" he cried, his mood shifting as quickly as the ripples on the river. "The great game, yes. It's always about the spear, my friend — there is nothing ever further from my mind."

"And what about Hitler, is he part of your game as well?" I felt tired suddenly, lost. "Melek, please, don't do this to me again. London was hell, and I just want it to end, I need it to end, I can't fight you anymore. I'm so tired of it all."

"Moi?"

"Don't give me that shit. Everything that has ever happened to me is because of you and those two freaks of yours. They took everything away from me in London. Gideon is gone because of you." As I said the name, as I heard the word, I was surprised by the searing pain I felt rip through my empty heart. It was still there, the agony of loss, always lurking just beneath the surface.

"I think you will find that Gideon left you long before I arrived on the scene, dear heart. Such a secretive one, more of a taker than a giver wouldn't you say?"

I flew at him, my talons distended and my teeth bared. He simply gripped me by the neck with one hand and threw me to the ground, as though I was nothing more than a speck of lint on his black suit.

"Don't blame me for your marital problems, dear heart. So what, he wouldn't let you feed from him, get over it, move on, get a life, get a death." He bent down and breathed into my face, his breath hot against my cold flesh, his lips barely an inch from my ear. Then he whispered those words that made me tremble. "But Gideon isn't the only one with secrets is he?"

I squirmed on the ground, feeling so minute under his gaze. Did everybody know? My great shame, my great disgrace, a festering wound for all to see, my guilt laid bare, and I could not hide it.

"Don't worry, dear heart." He chuckled, standing straight. "Who you chew on is of no concern to me. Your conscience is yours to torment as you see fit. I just enjoy watching."

He began to pace around me, his long fingers clenched into a fist behind his back. I hated him. I really fucking hated him.

"You have an angel under your roof."

"And your point is?"

"Has he asked you the question?"

I scrambled backward against a large boulder and buried my head in my hands. The angel would never ask me the question. I wasn't willing to pay the price. Was that my punishment, that never-ending torture of existence with no end? I was living in purgatory, an infinite coil of torment and anguish, destined to be alone for all of time because I had closed my heart to the world. If I didn't care, then I could not be hurt, and no one would hurt me ever again.

But I was beginning to care and I was beginning to hurt.

"I see by your silence he has not. Funny. Obviously, your brand of selfishness does not appeal. Afraid of being alone again, are we?"

It was pointless my protesting, for every word that ushered from his lips was true. I wanted to rot in a heap of my own steaming piss and shit.

"Leave me alone, Melek, fuck off, I have nothing left to give."

"Well that's not entirely true is it? What if I were to ask you the question?"

He might as well have stuck his cock in my mouth, I was so shocked. My mouth fell open. So Heaven didn't want me but Hell did? What did that say about me?

"You have got to be fucking kidding me."

"On the contrary, dear heart, if the angel won't take you, I will. You could be my right hand man, sit at my side. Be my second in command. And trust me, that would really piss God off."

"That's why you want me, to piss God off?" The idea seemed to amuse him to no end.

"Don't misunderstand me, the fact that God would be

outraged is just a happy coincidence, but to have you at my side, raging the good fight with me, well, the value of that is incalculable. Come over to the dark side, Eli. Let me show you how real power works."

Jesus fucking H. Christ. The devil was offering me a job. My day could just not get any worse.

"And what would I be then?"

"Sorry? I don't get you."

"Would I still be a vampire? Or would I become human? A ghost? What would I be?"

Melek paced back and forth. I could almost hear the cogs spinning around in his head. He chose his words very carefully.

"This is awkward, I know — you still don't know who you are, do you? So let me say this. When I choose someone to join me, when I offer them the choice of coming home with me to Hell and they say yes, they cease to be what they once were. Regardless of who or what they were. They become demon, subservient to my will. There are certain rules even I cannot change. In Heaven, you have fluffy clouds, pearly gates, angels, and heaven forbid, God as your king, oh and some harp playing. In Hell, you have fire and brimstone, and real quantifiable power, as much sex as you like, regardless of your persuasion. And me as your glorious king. Now doesn't that sound like fun to you? If you were to accept my offer, Eli, you would no longer be vampire. You would become more than just a demon, you would become my equal."

I felt sick. He was trying to tell me something, something important, something about me, who I was and I could almost see it, just there, out of the corner of my eye, tantalisingly close. My skin rippled with goose bumps as my brain desperately tried to grasp the elusive threads he dangled before my eyes. But as always, I failed. I thought about his words, so carefully chosen and so deliberately spoken. They ran around and around in my head until my vision swam before me and my temples hurt.

"Why would God be so outraged if I said yes to you?"

Melek's smile turned my stomach. His mouth became so wide as to almost cut his head in half. There stood the creature I hated above all else and yet, he was offering me everything. He was offering me release.

"I have said too much already."

"No," I implored jumping to my feet, "you have not said enough. I asked you before, in London, and now I'm asking you again. Who am I?"

Melek held up his hands and backed away, but I could see by his face he was itching to tell me. So I pushed.

"Why would God be so pissed off, what do I matter to him? Why would I, above all others, be your equal if I said yes? Why do you want me so bad? Who the fuck am I?"

"Eli, Eli, calm yourself, you will give yourself an aneurism."

"Why now, hmm? You could have asked me in London, I might even have said yes — I would have said yes, at the end. So why wait until now? Tell me."

The devil stood before me in a blur, too quick for even my eyes to perceive. He cupped my face in his hands and brought his face level with mine, his mouth so close I thought for one moment he was going to kiss me. His bright yellow eyes looked upon my face with something akin to affection and it frightened me, because I liked it.

"The game is moving forward swiftly, young vampire. I was not ready for you before, in that cesspit of a city, but now the end approaches, and God *will* leave the heavens and face me. So now I gather my pieces, the final pawns upon my board."

I could have said yes. It would have liberated me from

that existence as a bloodsucker, liberation I so desperately desired. I could see in his eyes I was important to him and that for some reason he wanted *me,* and it was that wanting that made his offer so enticing, peace at last.

His lips touched mine. I felt his tongue press into my mouth, hot and burning, his passion flooding my mouth, setting my body on fire.

"You are a convict trapped in a prison that is not of your making, let me set you free."

I jerked away suddenly, pulling myself free of his embrace and his tempting tongue.

"Convict? Prison? Why do you use those words?"

"And there I was thinking we were about to get it on. And I changed my underwear especially for the occasion, how disappointing."

"Is this what you did to them? To Maria and Klingsor, did you tempt them? Did you corrupt them with your words and your tongue?"

"It didn't take much, trust me. Well, the offer still stands, and unlike the angel's, mine does not expire. Choices, Eli, it's all about choices, it always has been. So make sure you make the right one."

"And if I don't?"

"There will be nothing left for you to go home to."

A plume of smoke erupted from the ground around Melek and flames began to lick at his suit. He slowly descended into the earth, the gaze of his smiling eyes never leaving my face. With a crack of thunder and a shower of sparks, he disappeared and the ground sealed closed behind him. The man was nothing if not a walking cliché. He always was a showy bastard.

I was in a daze. The devil had just asked me to join him, to be his equal, to free me from my *prison.* I had never thought of it in those terms before, and it made my brain explode. Was I a prisoner? Was this existence, this purgatory, my prison? And why would my defection to the devil anger God so much?

Was I the straw destined to break the camel's back?

All those thoughts raged through my mind as I flew back to Alte, and the more I thought about it, the more I felt I was onto something—for the first time ever I was onto something. My brain could not grasp what that was, it was beyond my perception, frustratingly just out of my reach. I hated Melek, but he had just brought me closer to the truth, my own personal truth, than I had ever thought possible.

Chapter Fifteen: Battle Plans

My stomach emptied into my shoes as I approached Alte. I was shitting myself. My petulant outburst was about to bite me on the ass, and I do not eat humble pie. The very thought made me wince. All of those accusing eyes boring into me. And I did so like a good boring.

Alte rose from the ground before me in all her grand magnificence. She had been a home to me for so long, my shelter, my hideaway. I would have to leave her because of what I was considering—not even her solid walls could protect me from the demons that would soon be snapping at my heels. She had lain empty for so long before I came along, and if they forced me to run again, if they forced me to leave my sanctuary, she would be empty again, a lonely tower of abandoned brick and mortar.

I knew how she felt.

The door opened and Ethan stepped out into the evening sunshine. A little bit of shit ran down my leg. Brave heart Eli.

"Can we talk?" we both said together. It was becoming a habit. We laughed, but it was a forced and uncomfortable sound.

I had an idea. We needed to get away from Alte, away from judgemental eyes and prying ears. We needed privacy. No pressure, no arguing, no angel. No Mal to huff and puff because he didn't understand what was going on.

But would he want to be alone with me?

"Okay, so look, I know this place, some thirty miles from

here where *we can talk without anyone listening in!*" I deliberately raised my voice so Mal, who undoubtedly had his ear pressed against the doors, could hear me. Ethan chuckled gently and I felt relieved by the genuine tone of the sound.

"That's if you don't mind being alone with me."

"And why should I?" he said quietly as he stepped toward me, his fierce eyes unwavering in their sincerity. The greenness of them made me shiver. He made me shiver.

"Just saying, me being a vampire and all, just thought..."

"That you might fancy a quick suck?" He said it with such deadpan seriousness that for a moment I didn't know if he was serious or not. Did he realise what he had just said? But then I saw the smile curl wickedly at the sides of his mouth, and his eyes sparkled with mischief.

Cheeky bastard.

"So, this place, thirty miles away you say? That's a long walk." And still he stepped closer.

"I wasn't intending to walk," I said as I closed the small distance between us and scooped him up effortlessly into my arms. I heard him gasp as he flung a muscular limb around my neck, and my skin tingled at his touch. He felt so good in my arms, as though he had always belonged there. The smell of him filled my nostrils. The feel of him thrilled my senses and yet again, the overwhelming familiarity of him coursed through my very being.

"Is this how you brought me here?" His face was so close to mine, my lips almost touching his. I could have eaten him on the spot, in every way.

"You were barely alive."

"And now I am more alive than I have ever been."

I felt dizzy, I wanted to spin him around and smash my lips against his, I wanted him to feel the beat of my long dead heart banging against my chest, to feel the warmth that filled my veins with burning ferocity, the flame of a passion, of a feeling long extinguished.

"Hold onto me."

"I intend to."

I felt the tingle and pulling sensation tugging at my shoulder blades and we lifted effortlessly into the air, rising vertically into the sky until we were high over the canopy of trees, breaking through the clouds into glorious blue sky. His body tensed in my arms and I could sense his fear tightening his bulging muscles, but I could also sense his wonder.

"Don't panic, I won't let you fall."

"I believe you."

I carried him through the air at tremendous speed, the landscape around us nothing but a blur of glittering blue light. Ethan's fear dissipated and he relaxed in my grasp, his muscles melting into my body, fitting my body. His eyes opened wide, full of amazement as he looked around at the endless space surrounding us, the infinite sky that belonged to us and us alone. It was so beautiful—the air above the clouds so clear, the striating bands of piercing blue that extended in ever darkening gradients toward the infinity of space. And Ethan could see it all, wrapped in the arms of a vampire, wrapped in my arms. It was quite the experience, for us both.

I changed my course slightly and we began to sink toward the canopy of clouds beneath so my lower legs ploughed through the broiling vapours, creating a curling contrail that billowed insubstantially behind us. Ethan reached out a hand and his fingers brushed the fluffy sea beneath. He laughed with delight as the cumulous pillows enveloped his fingers.

"It's cold. Look at the ice on my fingers." He lifted his hand for me to see the tiny particles of ice glittering in the sunshine and he laughed as they melted away just as quickly. I laughed with him. I simply couldn't help it.

The cloud cover began to thin considerably, the sun burning away its flimsy existence in gentle wisps of steam that evaporated into the ether. I was glad, because what he was about to see would blow his mind. As I began to descend, the sky remained pure and clear with the promise of a brilliant sunset to enrich the experience.

"My god! Look! What is that?"

Looming magnificently before us, jutting out of the earth like a row of gargantuan stone fingers, stood Externsteine. The edifice lay there as though placed by some monstrous giant, a tor of extraordinarily shaped freestanding rock rising from the rim of Teutoburg Forest to tumble into the nearby lake. The tallest of the fingers stood over a hundred feet high and the formation ran some several hundred metres in length, with the last finger just dipping its toes in the water. It was an awe-inspiring sight, a place filled with a tangible magic and a testament to the power of Mother Nature.

I brought us down to the foot of the last finger and Ethan disengaged from my neck and ran his hands over the weirdly shaped sandstone.

"This place is incredible. What is it?"

"It's called Externsteine. It was once a site of ancient pagan worship and sacrifice. There is much legend and mystery surrounding this place. Can you see those weird carvings covering the stone? No one knows who made them, something your father may appreciate, I think?"

Ethan's bright eyes scanned the formation eagerly. I wondered how much of his father had rubbed off on him, the burning curiosity, the insatiable lust for knowledge and understanding so apparent in the diaries. Looking at his face then, I imagined him to be a younger version of Isaiah.

"Yes. Yes, I can see them. But what are those weird tree things?" Ethan was pointing to a frieze that depicted a group of people removing a crucified figure from a large cross, and just to the middle right of the relief was a strange bent tree like object, expertly carved in sandstone by ancient hands.

"The tree is called an Irminsul, Old Saxon for *All-Pillar that holds up the Universe.* Very Germanic, very pagan, something to do with the Pillars of Hercules and the old Germanic gods, blah, blah."

Ethan turned and regarded me with curious eyes.

"How old are you... really?"

"Hey! Fucking cheek. I'm not that old. I just like to know things. Keeps my brain alive."

"Hmmm."

"Right. Take my hand." Without waiting for him to proffer said limb, I snatched up his hand and we shot upward with a loud whoosh, and to my utter satisfaction, Ethan yelped with sudden alarm. That would teach the cheeky fucker.

A pagan temple perched stoically atop the central tor—a monument to the winter solstice. The temple consisted of a large hollowed out arch flanked by two weird, esoteric symbols that baffled me. In the middle of the arch sat a stone altar and above that, in the middle of the wall, a circular hole, a window out onto the vast expanse beyond. It was to that temple at the top of the world I deposited a breathless Ethan and he sat, grateful to have his feet back on solid ground, on one side of the stone altar while I sat on the other, staring out onto the magnificent vista before us.

My eyes devoured the breath-taking view, trees, lake, river, mountains—it was a truly inspiring, sight where one could really believe nothing evil could exist on God's great canvas. How could the dark shadow of man threaten to eclipse such vistas and tarnish such purity? And how could I yearn so badly to be a man, for surely as a man, I would run the risk of such darkness tainting me.

We both started to talk at the same time and we both stopped and looked down at our feet. He was blushing.

"You first." How unselfish of me.

"I should not have said those things, I had no right. You owe me nothing, and I owe you my life. You did not have to pull me from that ditch, and I am grateful, truly, but I am feeling much stronger now and tomorrow I will leave."

"And where will you go?" Anxiety banged away mercilessly within my chest.

"Welwelsburg Village, or what is left of it, then onto the castle. Papa is in there somewhere, and I need to find some way of getting him out."

"You still want to find him, then?"

"He is my papa, and I love him. And I need answers, lots of answers."

"What happened to him, Ethan?"

"The night of broken glass. The ninth of November nineteen thirty-eight started as any normal day. Papa had not long returned home, and he worked in his room as usual, pouring over his books, locking me out. He had been to Vienna. When Hitler's forces annexed Austria in March of that year, Papa received a telegram, and he left for Vienna and did not return until the end of October. He came back looking like a ghost, haunted, disturbed.

"It began during the night of November ninth. With no warning, German citizens and soldiers alike took to the streets. Jewish homes, Jewish businesses, were ransacked and destroyed, people I knew, at least those who remained, dragged into the streets and beaten, some loaded into the back of trucks, some left for dead where they lay. Papa's beloved Fasanenstrasse Synagogue burned to the ground. I stood with him and watched it burn. He didn't say a word, but the tears poured down his face, and as the magnificent copulas of the roof begun to collapse, he turned and walked away, a man broken as much as the building he had loved so much.

"It struck me odd then, though after reading his diary I now understand, but we were not touched by the German thugs that rampaged through the streets. One group did approach us with batons raised ready to strike, but two SS soldiers ordered them to stop and to my amazement, they escorted us home. Our house, unlike all the others around it, remained untouched.

"A black SS Jaguar sat parked in front of our house and the sight of it stopped Papa dead in his tracks. Two figures got out of the car, and I recognised the one immediately. Reichsfuhrer Heinrich Himmler stood with his hands clamped behind his back and stared at us. That man, in his black uniform and swastika armbands, struck terror into everyone, us Jews in particular, his image and his name burned into our psyche. I was petrified. Papa looked resigned. There followed a brief exchange of words between the Nazi and the Jew, then Papa dragged me into the house.

"I tried to question him, I begged him to tell me what was happening, but he would not speak. He threw his belongings, mainly books and his diaries, into battered carpetbags. I sat at the table watching him, but I might as well have been on the other side of the planet, for all the notice he took of me. Only when his precious books lay secure in his bags did he deem to look at me. He didn't say a word. The look on his face said desperation and hopelessness. Then he bent down, kissing the top of my head before walking out of the door. I heard the doors of the car slam and the engine roar. When the sound of the car had faded from my ears, I laid my head on the table and cried. The last remnants of my heart broke at that dining table, and

I haven't seen Papa since.

"The next morning the streets were covered with shards of glass as though it had fallen from the heavens like snow. Every window, every window belonging to a Jewish home or a Jewish business lay shattered. I knew at that instant my life in Berlin was over. I packed what little I had and left my house for the last time. I have been looking for him ever since. Finding those diaries is the first solid lead I have found. It's all I have left."

"Have you considered that he left them there for you?" I prompted gently. The look on his face confirmed that it had not even crossed his mind. "Think about it, no one knows you better than your father, no one. You have been looking for him for years and who, do you suppose, left that trail of breadcrumbs for you? Subtly, yes, he dare not risk exposing you, or his duplicity, especially if he has been under such constant supervision. But Isaiah knew you would be looking for him, he knew his son would not give up on him, and so his trail of breadcrumbs have brought you here, and it is here, for some reason known only to him, that he wants you to learn the truth. So he left those books in the room for you to find them."

The look on his face said he wanted to believe, that more than anything he wanted to believe his father had been reaching out to him through the Nazi darkness. More than anything, he wanted to believe his father was still the man he had loved so dearly as a child.

"It's a bit of a stretch."

"So are vampires, ghosts, angels and demons. What would you rather believe?"

"You have a point."

"I usually do. Good job I found you in a puddle of your own shit and piss then, isn't it, or you would still be none the wiser."

"Nice turn of phrase you have there."

"Thank you, it's a gift I have. And you think that I want you to leave?"

He sighed deeply. "I get the impression the world is something you would rather leave behind. I can't do that. And that is not an accusation or a judgement. I don't know what was done to you to make you so... distant. But I have to fight, I have to try and save my people, save Papa, wherever that may lead."

Distant, a good word, an accurate word, I was distant.

The sun was beginning to set, and rays of red and gold poured through the circular window above our heads, bathing Ethan in a warm halo. He was beautiful, so very beautiful, and I was beginning to see that his beauty went way beyond the skin.

If I told him, would he understand? Would he hate me? Would I scare him off?

"I loved Gideon." There, I said it aloud. The words almost made me choke. "He was my life and my reason for existing. We were together for so long I could not imagine an existence without him. I think that a part of me still loves him, and maybe that will never go away. But *he* went away, he went away and he took my heart with him. He broke me. I never, ever want to go through that again. So yes, maybe I have become dispassionate, distant. But at least then it cannot hurt me."

"What happened?"

I winced. The pain must have shown on my face, because suddenly his hand was on mine, the warmth of his flesh comforting against my own cold skin.

"I'm sorry. You don't have to tell me, it's none of my business."

"A million things happened. And maybe, one day, I will tell you the whole, pathetic story. But I do miss him still, even now, even after all the lies and the secrets." It came over me in a wave of crippling emotion, unexpected and unwelcome. "He ruined me, Ethan, he destroyed me. He left me with nothing, I am nothing." My voice broke.

My hands flew to my eyes in a vain attempt to stem the flow of tears that suddenly spilled unexpectedly down my face, fingers clawing at my lids, palms covering my face in shame.

"I did terrible things... I am not proud... of what I did, anything to be touched, anything to feel wanted." The words and the pain poured out of my mouth as easily as the tears poured down my face, and I could not stop them.

"I think time is a relentless killer, and it breeds apathy. I just wanted him—I just wanted to feel his touch, for him to want me. The more he pushed me away the worse I got, the more desperate I became, the more I craved... needed... just to be touched." The world swam around my eyes in a blur of self-loathing. To my surprise, I felt Ethan's arms slip around my shoulders as he pulled me to his chest.

No, he couldn't, he shouldn't, there was more, my confession was not yet over.

I pushed him away reluctantly. "No, Ethan, no, there is more, there is something that you have to know." I wiped my eyes, looking into his concerned face, and I realised I could tell him anything, and more importantly, I wanted to tell him everything.

"I thought moving to London would change things, you know, new place, new life. I was wrong. London was a nightmare, another story for another time, but the creatures your father mentioned, Klingsor and Maria, they were there, though I knew them by a different name, and their son, Morbius. He was a monster, a creature more vicious and evil than even the demons that spawned him. They were looking for the spear even then. You have to know, Ethan, they are like me, that the creatures now calling themselves Klingsor and Maria are Menarche, not vampires, but Menarche of a different sort, the original beings you might say. I caught Morbius feeding from Gideon. I walked in on them. I saw their naked bodies writhing together with his teeth and mouth fixed firmly to Gideon's neck, sucking him dry. Nothing could have hurt me more than catching him in the act so denied to me by my own lover. Before I could react, before I could rip that monster from the body of my partner, Morbius produced a knife, a spear and ripped Gideon's throat out.

"Gideon needed blood, a lot of blood in order to heal and I gave it to him, from my own veins. I would leave him and feed myself, without killing, you understand, then return to his side and feed him again, filling his veins with fresh life. I did this a number of times that night until he was strong enough to stand on his own two feet. But it left him unhinged, darkness filled his soul, and the wound across his throat refused to heal. Gideon needed more blood than I could give, he needed to drink the life from some poor soul. I couldn't stop him. Gideon was Menarche, and he was much stronger than I was. He left me then, he told me to find my own path, to leave him alone, never to look for him. The trouble is, I ignored his warning and I did look for him and what I found will live with me for the rest of eternity."

That was all I could bring myself to say. I felt drained, exhausted by the rush of emotion and words that had gushed from my body. But at least he knew. At least he had some inkling of the creatures that haunted his life as they had haunted me.

Ethan stared at the ground and I wondered if I had said too much. I had just spilled my guts out to a vampire Hunter. What was I doing? I had never talked to anyone about those things, ever.

"Say something. Please."

"I think I would have killed him," he said finally.

"Which one?"

"Both of them!"

"A Menarche is almost impossible to kill."

"Almost?"

I smiled then, despite myself. "Oh, I killed Morbius. Trust me. With a splinter."

"Pardon?"

I laughed. "Your father's diary, he spoke of a splinter, one that showed him a vision of the crucifixion? I shoved that splinter into that fucker's heart and I watched him shrivel up before my eyes."

"Fuck."

"He is gone, just mummy and daddy to deal with now. I just don't know if I'm the one to do it."

"I understand."

"I can't get close to anyone. I will not get close to anyone. I do not want to feel, I do not want to depend on anyone, I do not want to love and I do not want to be hurt."

"You've got it all ass about tit. You cannot possibly hurt so much without feeling so deeply and you are still *feeling* deeply, you are still *capable* of feeling deeply—otherwise, you would not be so frightened of being hurt again."

I thought about that long and hard and I didn't know whether to be angry at his annoyingly accurate observation or touched by his heart-wrenching sensitivity. One thing was certain though. I had finally made up my mind. I stood up and held out my hand.

"Come on. Let's go get your father."

I was about to get into the fight of my life.

The imposing doors to Alte stood before us as I slowly, and with some reluctance, lowered Ethan to the floor. The moon shone full and glowed in the clear night sky, a glowing orb of such intense purity, bathing us both with its chastened radiance. For once, we both looked the same, a pale ghostly white, and it made me smirk.

"What's so funny?"

"You, you look like me, pale, like a vampire. It looks like I've sucked you dry."

"I can but wish," he murmured under his breath as he turned away from me and walked toward Alte. He knew I could hear him. I had impeccable hearing. Blood surged through my body, most of it into my cock, and I had to force the rush of desire back into the shattered remnants of my heart where it belonged. It was just one little emotion, slipping through a crack to flutter free around my chest in a desperate bid for liberation. But I could not allow it. I swallowed it down, hard.

"You don't have to do this, you know," he said, fixing me once more with his blazing eyes, so colourless in the moonlight. It made him look all the more magnificent, if that was at all possible.

"Yes, I do. This was my fight before you were born. It has dug me out of my grave and spat in my face. I bloody well intend to finish it. It's about time I got involved with the world again, if the world will have me."

"It would be a fool not to."

We stared at each other for what seemed like an eternity. Why did his words always touch me? Why were his words capable of reaching my heart when I had worked so hard to bury it? If I reached out, I could brush his smooth cheek, or kiss his perfectly formed lips. Would he stop me? Did I want to? My body said yes but my brain said no. I was nothing but a bundle of confliction.

His eyes said *kiss me*.

I stepped forward and reached out with a trembling hand.

I brushed his smooth cheek with the side of my finger, the sensation electric and erotically intimate. I felt my cock engorge, solid in my pants, then my face was next to his, his breath hard and fast against my flesh and I could see his anticipation rising.

The doors of Alte flew open with a loud crack and I leaped away from Ethan. Malachi stood framed in the doorway with his hands on his hips, glaring at us both.

"And where on earth have you two been? I was getting worried. You have been gone for hours."

"I've been out reacquainting myself with the world. Is that okay by you or would you like me to write you a letter?" I said curtly, walking straight through the stunned ghost. He shivered and made an exaggerated show of brushing himself down.

"Do you mind?"" Mal squealed. "I hate it when you do that, it goes right through me."

A light went on above my head.

I spun around and beamed at Mal. "You are a fucking genius!"

Mal glared at me as though I had lost my marbles. "One of these days you are going to make sense, do you know that? Speak plain English, man." Mal slammed the doors shut behind us as if to give emphasis to his indignation.

I had an idea. I had a dangerous idea. But then all my ideas invariably turned out to be dangerous. But this one was a humdinger.

"That's how we find your father," I said excitedly but I could see Ethan didn't have a clue as to my meaning either. "Where's the angel? Ah, there you are. Sit down, all of you, Mal, you just... erm... float over there, there's a good ghost. Give me space to think this through."

They obeyed without question, but I could feel their expectant eyes boring into my brain as I paced around agitated. The plan was forming in my head and I needed to work it out, to understand exactly what I was about to do.

"How many were taken from Welwelsburg Village?"

"I don't know, a hundred, more maybe."

"One hundred and thirty-eight souls currently reside in Welwelsburg Concentration Camp and new prisoners arrive weekly," chipped in Daniyyel innocently. I was dying to know how he knew that, but my mind was racing.

"And we are going to get them out, all of them!"

"Excuse me?" Mal spluttered.

"We are going to save them, all of them! And your father, Ethan. We are going to get him out too. And by *we*, I mean Mal and I."

"Now just you wait a cotton picking minute! He's my papa, and I am going in with you!"

"How? How are you going to get in there? You are a Jew. They will lock you up with the others as soon as they clap eyes on you."

"I'm not sitting around here while you risk everything trying to get *my* papa out of there."

"Be reasonable. This is going to be hard enough as it is, I can't be worried about you as well. Let me go in and let me get your father out." He made to protest further, but I silenced him with one of my famous looks. I could halt an elephant at fifty feet just by raising my eyebrows. I had very animated eyebrows, very expressive. "You need to be here, safe, waiting for your father — god knows what condition he will be in when I get him out."

"He's my papa." He slumped down into his chair, his arms folded defiantly.

"Yes, he is, but this is not going to be pretty and there are going to be a lot of very frightened people pouring out of that hellhole when this is over, not to mention a swarm of mightily pissed off Nazis. When I bring your father back,

Ethan, we are going to have to leave this place, all of us. You need to be ready for that, we all do." I surveyed their faces as the realisation of my words began to sink in. Daniyyel looked pleased and I winked at him slyly. His lips turned up ever so slightly, a subtle flicker that no human eyes could see, but I saw it, and I appreciated it.

Mal floated down and perched himself on the edge of the table and crossed one leg over the other, hands outstretched to clasp hold of his knee. Fuck me sideways, he was so camp. Could we really get away with my absurd plan?

"So where exactly do I figure in this little escapade, may I ask?"

Daniyyel's face darkened. Did he guess what was coming next, I wondered? They were not going to like it. I didn't fucking like it. But it was all I had.

"You, my dear friend are my secret weapon. While I'm freeing the prisoners and dealing with the guards on the grounds, you will be looking for Ethan's father."

"And prey, do tell how I am to do that?"

"Easy, you will have a disguise." It took a moment or two for the meaning of my words to sink in, then he rose into the air, spinning in a frenzy of panic.

"Are you out of your mind? You yourself said how dangerous that is!"

"It won't be for long, it will work, trust me. You brought the German here, now you can put him to use, it's perfect. He will know the castle, its layout, he will know where to look. Better still, with you inside him, he will be able to escort Isaiah out of the camp without being stopped."

"Out of the question!" The angel's booming voice filled Alte with his disapproval. I knew that was coming.

"Then you get him out." Like that would ever happen.

"Possession leads to corruption, Eli. I cannot condone this course of action, as noble as the intentions may be."

"Oh come on, Dan, Mal is already as corrupt as they come, the dirty little fucker."

"That is very true," said Mal grinning.

"This is no laughing matter!" The angel was pissed. "The corruption of a soul is a serious and heinous thing. If he is lost, if he becomes demon, he will be something that goes against all that I stand for, all that my Father stands for. He will belong to someone else and I will no longer be able to ask him the question. Would you deny him his chance in Heaven? Do you really want that on your conscience as well?"

"Then offer me another way, Daniyyel, help us."

He glared at me. He opened his mouth but no words came out. The angel stood impotent with silence.

"I thought so. Why are you here, Daniyyel? What good are you if you will not help? What sort of angel are you?"

His eyes burned white, and for a moment I feared the release of his inner warrior, but I continued regardless, aware he could probably smite me with one flick of his angelic finger.

"I'm doing what I can, I'm getting involved. Isn't that what you wanted? Isn't that what you were counting on, hmm? That's it, isn't it, that's why you lot stand by watching as the world goes to shit around you, because you turn *us* into your weapons, you turn *us* into your army, you manipulate *us* into doing *your* dirty work."

I winced as his angelic fury intensified and I could see he was trembling with the exertion of keeping his anger back. I had hit a nerve, and the angel did not like it. Suddenly he shot upward in a tremendous whoosh of air. I got the brief impression of huge silver wings filling the space above our heads, then he was gone.

Ethan and Malachi looked at me astonished.

"Well he had it coming, fucking hypocrite."

"There is just one little chink in this wonderful plan of yours as far as I can see. I do not know what Isaiah looks like. What am I supposed to do, mince around until I see a man that looks remotely Jewish, in a camp full of Jews, then ask him if he is Isaiah Silberman? Do you not think that may be just a tad suspicious?"

"Oh come off it, Mal, it's not a hotel you know, surely if he is in the castle he will be the one *not* wearing an SS uniform."

"I can help with that."

"Well I am just saying, I do not know what the man looks like, so it is not as if I can go *oh look, Isaiah, let us get out of here*, now is it?"

"I can help with that."

"For fuck's sake, Mal, how many Jewish professors do you think they have stuffed into that castle of theirs? Please."

"I can help you with that."

"Well I was just saying... sheesh... no need to get all uppity now is there just because someone has discovered the tiniest flaw in your marvellous plan."

"I... can... help... with... that!" Our heads turned to Ethan, shocked by his sudden outburst. "I can help you with that, let me do that much at least. I can show Malachi what Papa looks like."

"Oooo, family lithographs. I love lithographs."

"No, Mal, I don't think that's what he has in mind. Are you sure, Ethan? It won't be pleasant."

"I know. Do it."

"What? Oh," said Malachi as the penny finally dropped.

"Be quick, Mal, just a quick look around then out okay?" Malachi was appraising Ethan's magnificent body and I could almost see the drool dripping from his lips at the thought of being inside the stunning man. "Mal!"

"Okay, okay, just a quick one, I understand. Girder your loins, lovely boy, here I come."

Ethan barely had time to breathe before Mal shot across the table and dived down his throat. Ethan jerked stiffly in his chair, a look of shocked bewilderment written across his handsome features. As my best friend insinuated himself into every muscle and fibre of my future husband's body, I became more and more uncomfortable, especially when a sly grin began to creep across Ethan's face.

"Mal? Ethan?"

Malthan stretched out his arms in front of himself then began to grope his own body, hands moving across his muscular torso, cupping his own impressive pecks, hands moving inexorably down his perfectly sculptured abdomen and his face lit up with wonderment and awe. Before I could say anything, his hands shot between his legs and he gasped with incredulous delight.

"My god, Eli, you should feel this! It's like a whole new other person down here, he's built like a..."

"Mal! Don't you bloody dare! Put your hands on the table where I can see them."

"But he's so..."

"Mal! Now!"

Malthan's hands slammed onto the table and his face twisted into a massive sulky pout, Malachi's default expression when he didn't get his own way. I was trying desperately not to smile because it really was so fucking funny.

"In and out, remember?"

"Fine. Spoilsport."

"Mal!"

"Okay, okay I'm looking already!" *Malthan's* face glistened with perspiration as he concentrated, beads of perspiration trickling down his impressive brow. I think I was a little bit jealous of Mal at that moment, the fact he was *inside* Ethan and all the while, I had been thinking about Ethan being inside me.

"It's very dark in here, poor bastard, the things he's seen." Horror twisted his face and his eyes widened with terror. "So much pain, so much hurt, so much loneliness. My god his loneliness is overwhelming, he doesn't belong, Eli, he doesn't belong anywhere anymore."

"Concentrate, Mal, look for Isaiah. Let Ethan show you."

"Yes... I see him... sitting at a table and there is a woman, such a lovely woman standing by his side, her apron covered with flour and she is looking at me... she is smiling at me." Tears began to pour down Ethan's cheek and I felt dreadfully guilty for allowing that thing to happen, for making that man witness the sorrow of his life for a second time.

"Papa is calling to me, his big hands are open, pulling me to him. He kisses my cheeks, kisses my neck, making me giggle, his big hand ruffling my hair. Mama is laughing too." His voice suddenly deepened and grew darker, barely a hissed whisper emanating from his throat. "But there is something behind her, it thinks I cannot see it, but I can."

Dread flowed over me like a black cloud and a chill raised the skin of my flesh. Chips of painted wood flew from my fingernails.

"What is it, Mal, what can you see?"

"Don't make me look, it doesn't want me to look, he doesn't want me to see him, but he is there, standing over her shoulder, he has always been there, this shadow man, ever since the beginning, watching, waiting."

"Waiting for what, Mal, can you tell me what it wants?"

"It wants her, it has always wanted her. Oh god, Eli, it's looking at me, it's moving around her, coming closer to me and I can see its eyes burning, burning white, reaching into my soul."

"Get out, Mal, get out now!"

"She belongs to him, he has splintered his soul so he can always be with her, always know where she is and he wants her dead, he wants Isaiah to suffer, for taking her away from him. Help me, Eli. It hurts, my god it hurts."

I knew then who it was and I felt sick. She never stood a chance. Ethan's mother had been marked from that moment in Vienna, destined to die a terrible death even as she gave birth to the man sitting opposite me.

Ethan's entire body shook violently and I gripped his hands, so cold and clammy. *Come back to me, Ethan. Come back. I will never let you go again.*

"Follow my voice, Mal, listen to my voice. Turn away from the shadow, close your eyes and block him from your mind, come back to me, come back to us, come back to safety." I was trying to be calm but my innards twisted with fear. I tried to make every word a comfort but feared the tremor in my voice gave away my anxiety.

Ethan's features began to shimmer and blur and I knew Mal was nearly out. My body went cold with relief. Two faces occupied the same body, then Mal slipped away with a loud scream that issued from both mouths simultaneously. I gripped Ethan's hands tighter as he fought to break free.

"Stay with me, Ethan, it's nearly over, come on, Mal, one last effort, follow my voice."

With a violent snapping noise, the two bodies disengaged from each other and Ethan slumped onto the table, his breath howling from his lips in long laboured gasps. Mal slid into the chair next to him and for a moment, just for a split second, I thought his eyes glowed yellow, demon yellow.

"I saw it. I saw it through your eyes, Malachi... that thing... at Mama's shoulder..." He was gasping, barely able to speak. "He had white eyes. It was him, wasn't it?"

"Yes, it was Adi, Hitler. The Black Messiah. Whatever they made him drink changed him, made him more than human, and somehow he managed to fracture a part of himself and attach it to your mother. He must have been with her all that time, watching her and Isaiah."

"But why?" Tears poured down his face and his pain broke my heart. I reached out and held his hand, which he took without hesitation.

"He did not want to let her go. I think perhaps he loved her."

"And yet he allowed her to die!"

"Yes, it was his revenge against Isaiah, if Hitler could not have her then no one could. I'm sorry, Ethan, I'm sorry you had to see that."

He stiffened and pulled his hand away from me, his features hardening.

"Get my papa, Eli, bring him back to me. And then I'm going to kill Hitler. That German cunt will not have both of them."

About the Author

I think that as I approach that milestone that is fifty, I must be one of the oldest gamers on the face of this earth. Many a day you will find me lashed to my PS4 enjoying a good session of Skyrim. Who doesn't love a good session of Skyrim?

I love writing—I have done it since I was a child when I would happily write about the latest episode of Doctor Who (Tom Baker in those days) in my schoolbooks. Growing up and becoming a business owner with my friend Jayne left little time to pursue my dream of publication, but of late the desire and the compulsion to put words onto paper have once again dominated my life so that now, my laptop has become surgically fused to my fingertips.

There is something desperately satisfying about telling a story. My fascination with History, Religion and Conspiracy theories have, in this instance, gone hand-in-hand with my love of all things vampire, fantasy, sci-fi and horror. I drove my parents nuts when I was young because that was all I would read about in books, all I would watch on television, but they have held me in good stead, and long may my obsession with the subjects continue, at least, that is, until the day they put me in my own wooden box. And imagination is such a wonderful thing. I once had a rather vivid dream about David Tennant and the Tardis console, but I could not possibly go into details about that here. Let's just say that my polarity was well and truly reversed.

Dead Camp is just the beginning. I have to check my

knickers every day at the thought that this book is now in the public domain. My first book, and I hope the first of many. And to those out there who love to write, who love to transport us to new worlds, or old worlds with a twisted perspective, I say to you keep going. I never thought I would ever see my work available to download, and thanks to eXtasy Books, the dream that I always thought unobtainable has finally come true. So thank you all at eXtasy, I am one happy homosexual thanks to you, and thank you the reader for taking the time to read this strange tale and allowing Eli and the incomparable Malachi into your lives.

And now I really need Skyrim.

Printed in Great Britain
by Amazon